How Greek Is Your Love?

Sequel to A Saint For The Summer

By **MARJORY McGINN**

@@@@@@
Pelagos Press

How Greek Is Your Love?

Published by Pelagos Press, 2020.

ISBN: 978-1999995737.

Copyright ©Marjory McGinn, 2020.

Front cover illustration by Tony Hannaford (www.anthony hannaford.co.uk)

Editing, formatting and author photograph by Jim Bruce (www.ebooklover.co.uk)

Dedication

In memory of my parents, John and Mary

About the author

Marjory McGinn is a Scottish-born author and journalist, brought up in Australia and now based in England. Her journalism has appeared in leading newspapers in Australia and Britain, including *The Sydney Morning Herald*, *The Sun-Herald*, *The Daily Mail*, *The Times* and Scotland's *The Herald*.

A youthful work/travel year in Athens inspired a lifelong fascination for Greece. In 2010, together with her husband Jim and their Jack Russell dog, Wallace, she set off from Britain on an adventure to the southern Peloponnese that lasted four years and was the basis for her four travel memoirs and inspired her debut novel, *A Saint For The Summer*.

Marjory also writes a blog with a Greek theme on the website www.bigfatgreekodyssey.com and she can be followed on Twitter www.twitter.com/@fatgreekodyssey and on Facebook www.facebook.com/MarjoryMcGinnAuthor

Other books by the author

Things Can Only Get Feta
Homer's Where The Heart Is
A Scorpion In The Lemon Tree
A Donkey On The Catwalk
A Saint For The Summer

Author's note

How Greek Is Your Love? is the sequel to the novel *A Saint For The Summer*. With the same characters reappearing and a few new ones too, it can be read as a stand-alone novel, but if you are keen to learn the full story of the World War Two family mystery that first brought Bronte McKnight to Greece, and how it was solved, you will probably want to read the first novel too.

The mystery surrounds the disappearance of Bronte's grandfather Kieran McKnight during the infamous Battle of Kalamata in southern Greece, often described as "the Greek Dunkirk".

The names of the main village Marathousa and the mountain settlement of Platanos were inspired by real villages in the Mani, though their names have been changed, and the characters in this book are fictitious. The right-wing political party Ellines Patriotes Enomeni mentioned in this story is a fictitious party, however it is based on at least one similar extreme party operating in Greece during the economic crisis.

Language: Any Greek used in the text appears in Roman script and written much as it would be pronounced in Greek. Differences in some endings result from nouns, for example, being written in the feminine or masculine forms such as *xenos* for foreigner (male) and *xeni* for a female.

There are a few Scots words also in the text which are generally obvious from the context. But in case you are still confused, two of the most used words are the popular Scots word for fed-up, *skunnered*, and for messy/dirty, *clarty*.

Map of the area

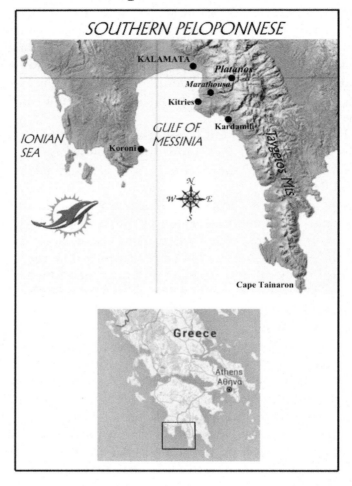

Contents

Take my hand
I'm a stranger in paradise
All lost in a wonderland
A stranger in paradise
*

But open your angel's arms
To the stranger in paradise
And tell me that I may be
A stranger no more.

– Lyrics from A Stranger in Paradise, 1953
Broadway production of Kismet

1

The oracle of Marathousa

On the road from Marathousa nothing stirred, apart from the Ionian wind gently toying with the heads of olive trees. No people, no passing traffic and the small farmhouses in the orchards were shuttered for the afternoon siesta. Etched on a deep blue sky above the gulf was a single line of small spherical clouds like the throw of dice. A perfect day!

I tramped along the ragged verge of the road with the warm spring sun on my bare arms, lost in my thoughts, excited about the evening ahead, about seeing Leonidas for the first time that week. I was still in the sweet giddy days of new love and content enough with my tentative place on this foreign shore, trying to navigate its complex culture. I couldn't say it was always easy but most days brought modest triumphs. Just as well! This day wouldn't be one of them.

Some 20 minutes from home, the serenity of early afternoon was scuppered by a rasping noise, faint to start with and far behind me, at the edge of the village. It steadily grew louder, becoming a stroppy buzz, like a bee plugged into an amplifier. That's when the day began to spool away from me. The perfect line of clouds breaking up.

It was an old blue scooter with a decrepit engine, like many you hear in rural Greece. As the buzz intensified, a stray dog came crashing through an olive grove onto the road, ragged and dirty, taking up its sentry position by an industrial-sized bin overflowing with rubbish, the only blight on this glorious stretch of road.

I glanced behind me. The scooter was close now, the rider leaning it slightly to the right to counter the heavy weight of a bulging plastic bag hooked over the handlebar. I was on the right-hand side of the road and as the scooter passed me, I felt something shove at my left arm, hard enough for me to lose my balance. I stumbled, knees and palms landing painfully on the stony verge. The rider stopped just ahead.

"What the hell!" I crouched in the dirt, watching him. He wasn't coming to help but swivelled round on his scooter, staring hard. It was the dog that rushed towards me, unwelcome, yapping. A creep and a feral dog. The happiness of five minutes ago had given way to quiet terror. I never saw it coming – but Elpida had.

An hour earlier I was sitting in Elpida's *kafeneio*, the Zefiros, checking emails, enjoying the specialties of the day, which was always honey cake with a side order of gossip. Elpida, the owner, was short, sturdy and just on the right side of curvaceous. When she smiled, her small white teeth gave her the appearance of a feisty terrier. She knew everyone who lived within a few miles of this Mani hillside. She knew most of what went on as well, and she liked to impart her findings. She had a gift for it and something else more valuable. Elpida had robust intuitions.

"My stomach is twitching," she would say, "And when my stomach twitches, for sure something's not right."

Elpida's stomach twitched at regular intervals in her *kafeneio*. She occasionally shared the reasons for it, trifling though they seemed: a snippet of conversation overheard, a certain facial expression on one of her clients, even the way a villager might walk across the *plateia*, the square where the Zefiros was its beating heart. The twitch could be inspired by anything, but generally it was something she could plunder for intimations of havoc, and future gossip. But whatever the superior gifts were of this homely Greek oracle, her stomach was usually right.

It was quiet in the village as people made their way home for an afternoon sleep. Elpida sat beside me at one of the metal tables under the huge plane tree that dominated the square, chatting and watching the road. She jerked her head towards a small lay-by on the roadside, presumably to draw my attention to a couple of men on old scooters who were chatting, their heads leaning together. There was a blue metal installation nearby with locked, numbered boxes. Most people in Marathousa collected their mail here but it was also a place where villagers gathered, where the hawkers stopped their vans, and the bus from the coast disgorged passengers onto the dusty roadside.

"Who are they?" I asked her, glancing towards the two dark-haired characters, who were similar to so many other rural men in Greece.

"*Xenoi,*" she said, flicking her eyebrows up and grimacing lightly at the same time, a Greek gesture of cynicism. I laughed. *Xenoi,* I had learnt, was the Greek word for foreigners, for non-Greeks, I assumed.

"They don't look like foreigners."

"They're from down the Mani somewhere, I think. I can tell from the way they talk, but I don't think I've seen them much before."

So, the word covered other villagers as well and I wondered how far outside Marathousa you had to be to earn the title of a 'foreigner'.

"I don't like the look of them," she said. Her big brown eyes, with their heavy lids, were full of distrust.

"Why not?"

"I can't say yet, Bronte, but they look like they're plotting."

"Plotting what?"

She shrugged manfully. "Don't know, but I will watch out for them, don't worry." Twitch, twitch. I could almost feel it myself.

When I finally paid up and set off for home, she stood on the edge of the paved *plateia*, hands on hips, her eyes strafing the road. She shouted in her usual way, "*Sto kalo*," or 'Go to the good'. A warm but curious Greek farewell that carried, I always thought, the insinuation you might be leaning the other way, towards a little strife, but implored you to reconsider the righteous road. In the spring of 2013, in one of the worst years of the country's economic crisis so far, there was no need to seek out trouble, it had a way of finding you, at times when you least saw it coming. Even when a day presented itself as perfect.

The way back to the house from Marathousa was part of the route that connected the coast with the main road further inland, which led one way to Kalamata and the other way further down the peninsula. Marathousa was the only village in this area, built up the side of a hill like a small citadel. The *plateia* was its natural centre, with a taverna at the back, the *kafeneio* on the right, and on the left flank was the main church of the Anastasi, or Resurrection. The road traversed a dramatic stretch of rural Greece, wedged between the broad Messinian gulf below, with Kalamata at its head, and the Taygetos mountains, which run the length of the Mani peninsula in the southern Peloponnese, one of the wildest regions of Greece. On either side of the village road were miles of lush olive groves.

Just outside the village, I passed the church of the Ayia Triada (Holy Trinity) and its small graveyard nearby, enclosed in a high stone wall. From the road, a couple of farm tracks on the right wound up through the orchards towards the foothills of the Taygetos. I'd been in no hurry, enjoying the walk, the warm spring weather, the solitude of the early afternoon, lost in contented thoughts.

But now I was on my hands and knees on the edge of the road with a strange man and a filthy stray mutt.

The man kept to his scooter, a short distance in front of me. His head swivelled round, eyes staring hard.

"Bastard!" I said loudly, rocking back onto my haunches, wiping gravel from my hands. One palm bled from a small cut. Still the creep stared; dark soulless eyes, a long bony nose, long oily hair. Had he done it on purpose? I felt nervous suddenly with no-one around, no passing cars.

The dog rushed towards me in a fizz of dark grey matted fur, yapping, agitated, then backed off, instinctively wary, watching me and the creep, by turns. Trouble on his patch of canine misery. I was on my feet now, gathering up my bag. Some of the contents had spilled onto the side of the road, like the small box of honey biscuits Elpida had given me for Angus because she knew my father loved them. The dog lifted its nose in the air and sniffed but kept its distance. The creep kept up the stare and then finally spoke.

"Very sorry. Just accident," he said in a thick, clumsy accent, with a sneer that made him look anything but sorry. It only ramped up my anger even more, but I felt the frustration of not having enough Greek to parry with. I was still an apprentice with this difficult language.

"*Poli kako*," I said forcefully. Telling the creep his behaviour was 'very bad' was banal but I thought he'd at least scarper now. Instead, he glowered at me, got off the scooter and pushed it towards the wire fence bordering the road, letting the machine sag against it. He started walking towards me and I began to fret, regretting my Greek outburst.

Whatever the creep had in mind, the dog didn't like it and began barking, big wild gusts of noise, strangely energetic for a skinny, starved mutt. It ran at the man, retreated, and then ran again, almost comically, barking all the while. I mentally urged it on, relieved the dog had turned into a scrappy defender. The creep stopped and faced off angrily with the dog, shouting a stream of oaths, or so it seemed. Then he raked about on the edge of the road until he found a stone, the size of a tennis ball, and threw it, hitting the animal just above one eye. It yelped loudly and backed off.

"Hey, don't do that!" I shouted.

No apology this time, but a laugh like a door with rusty hinges. The dog started up again, barking fiercely despite the blow to its head, until the creep gave up. He spat vibrantly on the roadside before grabbing his scooter. Before he buzzed off he gave me one final toxic stare that made me think, perhaps illogically, that I hadn't seen the last of him. Elpida's twitching stomach had been dead right.

The dog went mental and tore up the road after the scooter, galloping like the north wind, its filthy fur flying out in all directions. After it ran out of puff, it hung about the roadside, as if waiting for me to catch up. Then it rushed at me, eyes alert, tail wagging lustily, and I caught the sweaty aroma of its wild, homeless life. It was a curious, slightly comical-looking dog: dark grey fur with a large patch of dirty white over the left side of its face and just above the eye, like a small *Phantom of the Opera* mask, and one tuft of white on the top of its head, standing up like a cockatoo's crest feathers. There was a large patch of white on its chest as well, now the colour of a café latte. It looked like no breed in particular, the size of a collie dog with long legs but with some of the features and keenness of a Jack Russell terrier. Close up I could see it was a male dog. The blood from the head wound was trickling over his brow, about to trace a dramatic red line down the Phantom mask.

"Poor old mutt," I said, warming to my solitary crusader. He had probably saved me, but from what exactly? Surely it wasn't an accident. I had the vague recollection that when the creep buzzed past me, he'd stuck his hand out, deliberately catching at my arm. It wasn't normal for village Greeks to behave like that, not in my limited experience. If he had mischief in mind, why hadn't he snatched my bag instead? At least he'd have scored the wonderful honey biscuits, if nothing else. I smiled. That would be a first in Greece: mugging a woman for her confectionary!

I trudged on, wishing someone would come by and give me a lift to the house. I'd have clambered onto Myrto's donkey if she'd been passing by with it. But if our neighbour Myrto had been here, the creep would have been no match for a shrewd, tough Maniot farm woman like her.

The dog was still following me, but I couldn't shoo him away now, not with a head wound. I bit on my lower lip. The day had turned fiendish. 'Go to the good?' Perhaps, but this was a side trip I hadn't seen coming.

By the time we got to Villa Anemos, the dog was panting. Starving, no doubt. Up close he had nice eyes: big, pale chestnut coloured. His teeth looked strong and white for a stray.

"Come on, boy. I'll clean you up somehow, but then you have to go." Go where? Back to garbage bin cuisine, kicks and stones, or maybe finally the *foles* I'd heard about: bits of poisoned meat often left on rural roads, next to the bins, to kill stray dogs or foxes. Up until this afternoon, I'd never had to think about these things too clearly. Now I did.

I led the dog down the side of the house to the wooden gate into the backyard.

"You stay in here for now and don't make any trouble."

In the house, Angus was sitting at the dining table, with a sheath of papers in front of him and some on the floor, which he was reading and correcting. Angus was writing a book and it had occupied him all over winter. It was the story of the Battle of Kalamata, the heroic last-ditch attempt by the Allies in 1941 to repel the Germans as they invaded southern Greece. It was a battle that had occupied us both in many ways after I'd arrived in Greece from Scotland the previous September. It was a subject close to Angus's heart and one that had been rarely written about, despite the devastating consequences for this region. It was a book that involved us personally too, with a family mystery attached to it.

The house was a bit of a mess. There were bread crumbs on the floor around the table and on the kitchen floor.

"Are you leaving a trail of crumbs so I know where to find you when the papers pile up around your chair?" I said, in the bantering fashion that Angus and I often used with each other.

He looked over at me, his hazel eyes sensing something was wrong, the way a father would. I told him the whole story of the creep on the scooter, and about the dog.

"I don't like the sound of that. Despite his feeble apology, it looks like this creep meant to knock you over. Did you get a good look at him?"

"Well, yes and no. He looked like dozens of other men you see in villages. But this one's mean-looking. Don't think I've seen him in Marathousa before. I was in the *kafeneio* when I first saw him, and Elpida did too, out on the road with his blue scooter. She thinks he comes from further down the Mani."

Angus pulled a face. "Did you get a reg number for the scooter?"

"No. It's a crap old thing. Don't think it had number plates."

"If you see him again, get a good description. Take a photo with your mobile. We'll report it to the police. God only knows what he might have done if that dog hadn't barked, eh?" Angus dragged his teeth over his bottom lip. "I've been hearing things around the village, reports of followers of the far-right party that's gaining a foothold here because of the crisis, and there's a few of those thugs down the Mani. Seems to be a favourite haunt in this part of Greece. Well, it's always been a wild region, that's its charm, but it's also a place where cowboys can find easy refuge."

"You're trying to frighten me now. You and Elpida. I bet he was just a bored thug, looking to cause some trouble."

"The fact that you're an expat would wind him up. Watch your step. I don't need to remind you these are difficult times."

"No, you don't."

It was just my luck to decide to settle here during this era of Greek history, when the country was enmeshed in an economic crisis, with spiralling debts, crippling austerity measures and heading into a social upheaval, the progress of which no-one could quite predict.

I took a plate of leftovers from the fridge, the meatballs I'd made the night before. I tipped half into a bowl.

Angus glanced at me. "Lunchtime already?" he said, corralling his papers briskly into a rough pile on the table.

"Not quite. I forgot to mention that the thug threw a rock at that dog and his head's bleeding. He's also starving. He's in the back garden."

Angus moaned. "Oh, no, you've not brought that mangy critter here. I just hope it's not the grey one with the clarty fur always hanging about the bins."

I nodded. "That's the one, but I have to feed him at least. The poor guy helped me and I think he might need stitches."

Angus sighed. "Whatever! Just don't bring him into the house. Leonidas won't care for that."

I imagined he wouldn't. Leonidas was very clean and particular about things, as you'd expect a doctor to be, and his own house next door, Villa Ambelia, was immaculate. Angus had not lost the sense that he was still the landlord of our villa, which is how I'd met Leonidas Papachristou when I first came to Greece the previous year and stayed with Angus – and never left, to be precise. But Leonidas had never acted like any kind of archetypical landlord and was generous and mostly easy-going. Stray dogs might be pushing it, however.

I went out the back door into the garden and set the bowl down before the dog. He gulped the food. I'd never seen a pile of meatballs disappear that quickly, not mine anyway. I bent down and looked at the head wound. It was still raw and a bit deep. On the other side of his head above the brow I saw the greenish bloated body of a tick. I winced in disgust, wondering how many other ticks and critters he was hosting. It would have been easier to let him out the front gate and leave him to his fate. These street dogs were tough. He'd survive. Then I heard Myrto next door in her yard, raking about, shouting at goats. She had 15 or so going manic in their pens, kicking over buckets, their bells chiming out sweet nonsense. It gave me an idea.

I set off, with the dog following me. The gate to Myrto's farm compound was unlocked, the open padlock hooked over a spar in the metal gate. She was still shouting at the goats until she saw me arrive with the dog. I knew that Myrto, with her kind heart and rural acumen, would know exactly what to do with a stray.

"Shoot it, Bronte!" she said vibrantly after I told her about the incident on the road. Myrto was forthright, that's why I liked her. She'd spent some years in Australia, where she moved to with her Greek husband before returning to her farm in Marathousa alone after Fotis died in a car crash in Sydney. It had been a difficult marriage, and the second one for Fotis, who had been cunning and profligate, and his son Hector even more so. All this had given her a different spin on life. She was a battler, but was chilled in her outlook, and amusing too.

"Yep, Bronte, shoot the bugger, and I am the one that does it. We live near the bush in Aussieland and I shoot pesky kangaroos. I can shoot a filthy *skilos*, no worries," she said with her charming take on the Aussie 'dialect'. I had always loved the way she mostly spoke in the present tense, as if everything that had happened, or could, was taking place that minute. It gave life a cracking immediacy.

"You're joking, I know. You love animals."

"Best thing for this boy, Bronte," she said, having given the mutt a cursory inspection. I told her a bit more about the guy on the scooter, thinking that would make her more sympathetic.

"Yep, shooting is good and if I see that *malakas* who pushes you over, I shoot him as well." She descended into a long diatribe in Greek, with plenty of colourful oaths. That much of Greek I recognised, at least.

"Seriously, Myrto, I think I need to take the dog to a vet to get his head wound looked at."

Her eyes widened. "Look, he's okay, my girl. He's tough. No need for some doctor who charges you rip-off money. The dog goes off on his own a few days and in no time he's better, back on the roads again."

"I'd still like to get him looked at. He's riddled with ticks, and God knows what else. But I need to wash him at least."

She palm-slapped her forehead, hard. "Wash him, *panayia mou!*" *Holy mother!* She poked the toe of her welly boot at his flank and pulled a face. "He stinks, that's true."

"We can do it here, with the hose and some soap. Just clean him up a bit so I can get him into Angus's car and take him to a vet. There's one just down on the seafront."

The dog was looking at us with huge, unbelieving eyes. The kind of look we all have when the day we end up with isn't exactly what the rosy sunrise promised us. And that was pretty much my day as well now.

Myrto gave me a strange, sad look. "Okay, Bronte, the dog's a bit cute but if you're gagging for a dog companion, I can get you a nice puppy. I know people with pups for sale, not this *vromiko*, filthy thing. You might as well waltz with a poxy goanna than take this one."

I laughed, as I often did at her bizarre Aussie expressions.

"I can't have a puppy right now. And I can't keep this one either, but I've heard the local vet works together with an animal rescue centre in Kalamata. Maybe they can rehome him."

She pulled a face. Despite her Aussie years, like most rural Greeks she still saw dogs as working creatures, not things to be pampered or rehomed. Myrto would just say that in the crisis people were struggling to keep their homes, never mind dogs looking for new ones.

"Look, Myrto, let's get started with the washing. Maybe one bucket of warm water to begin with and then I can hose him."

She sighed and finally gave in, picking up a length of rope from a nearby midden heap of disparate objects, the kind you often see on rural farms in Greece. She tied one end of the rope about his neck and the other to an olive tree, but not the same tree her donkey Zeus was tethered to. That would never do because to Myrto there was nothing so precious in the world as Zeus, a proper working donkey with a stout wooden saddle.

Myrto disappeared into her house and returned with a bucket of warm water, a bar of soap, a big sponge and disposable gloves for me, showing that some of her rural edges at least were bevelled slightly. While I lathered away at the dog, he was compliant, good natured for a stray, or was it just that the meatballs had becalmed him as well as the promise of more?

His matted hair would have benefitted from a good clip but he looked better already, the fur fluffing out, and he smelt better as well. I washed out the head wound and it started to bleed again, but not too much. The tick had survived though and Myrto eyed it up. She was wearing a casual jacket with lots of pockets that I was sure were full of rural salves and unknown implements. She whipped out a small plastic hook and twisted the tick out of the dog's head in one deft movement, then dropped the tick on the ground, swivelling her welly foot over it, hard.

"Thanks, Myrto."

"Don' thank me, Bronte. This boy will have dozens more, for sure."

With that in mind, I was sure she'd refuse when I pleaded for her to keep the dog in her compound just for the night. The vet would now be shut for the afternoon. Angus wouldn't want the dog and Leonidas wouldn't either. I was seeing Leonidas in the early evening. He was at his villa for the weekend before returning to Kalamata for his first surgery on Monday morning. All week I had been dreaming of this evening and nothing, not even the scrappy crusader, was going to spoil it.

Myrto put her hands on her hips and pursed her lips at the dog. "Okay, I keep him, but only because I like you, Bronte. I put him under the house where Zeus sleeps at night but he better not annoy my donkey or there will be *megalo*, big, trouble."

"Thanks. I do appreciate it," I said, touched by her offer and the fact that letting a stray dog share the same hallowed space as her beloved donkey, named after a Greek god, was no small thing. And neither was our friendship, possibly one of the most unusual in my new Greek life.

Myrto lived on the first floor of her old stone house, accessed by the front steps. Underneath was an enclosed area, like a ramshackle stable, with a stout metal door with a window in the upper half shielded by a row of metal bars, so that animals could have some air at night in summer. She had a stall for the donkey at one end. The dog would sleep, I imagined, at the other. I planned to come back later with more meatballs, and that would be him sorted for the night. For a scrappy waster, he would be on his best behaviour – I hoped.

I didn't have time to mull over this a minute longer and legged it out of Myrto's farm compound without a backward glance. I needed to shower and get ready for my night out with Leonidas. That was the only kind of hot animal attraction fizzing in my mind at that precise moment!

2

The heart of the Spartan

"I've missed you this week, Bronte," said Leonidas, leaning closer into the table, an errant lock of his curly black hair flopping down over his brow, as it often did. It was one of the things that always made me feel crazy with desire when I was with him.

We were having dinner at our favourite taverna in the small sheltered cove of Kitries, down the coast. The table was right by the water's edge with a view across the gulf. I felt happy, as I always did when Leonidas was back in the village for the weekend. I was doing most of the talking, about my week in the village, but I didn't mention the guy on the scooter or the stray dog. That would have spoilt an otherwise perfect night. Leonidas was indulging my chatter, gracious as always.

"You always have such interesting things to tell me about your time in Marathousa. You make me see village life from a more entertaining angle," he said smiling, his dark eyes crinkling lightly at the corners. He reached over the table and stroked the back of my hand. I stealthily glanced at my watch. We'd barely ordered our meal and yet already I was calculating how long it would be until we were back in his villa for the night. I'd have been happy to skip dinner and have Leonidas instead. But I was also content to let him talk for a while about his working week in Kalamata, in his slightly formal English, which was one of the things I also found endearing about him.

The old cliché about absence quickening the heart was true in my experience. Leonidas had a busy surgery in the centre of Kalamata and an apartment nearby, where he stayed during the week. On weekends he habitually came back to Villa Ambelia, his village house. His grandfather had built Villa Anemos first when the family moved down from the mountain village of Platanos, on a nearby peak of the Taygetos, seeking an easier life. He later built the second house next to it, Villa Ambelia, for his elder son Grigoris, Leonidas's father, when he got married. Ambelia means vineyards and it had been the grandfather's ambitious plan to have small vineyards behind both houses to produce his own wine. Although olive trees were eventually planted instead, the name had stuck, to honour an old man's fantasy perhaps.

Decades later, when Grigoris moved to Kalamata to live and Leonidas started his medical practice there, he took over Villa Ambelia, renovated it and used it as a weekend retreat.

Angus was renting Villa Anemos when I first came to Greece. When I decided to stay on it was natural for me to live there with him, even though it was an old place by now and earned its name. Anemos is the Greek word for 'wind' and during the winter, the raw easterlies from the snow-capped Taygetos peaks would claw through the old terracotta pantiles. During the past winter, Leonidas had the place renovated and it was now a comfortable house, if a little small, but at least I could keep an eye on Angus after his health problems the year before when a heart attack had narrowly been averted by hospital treatment in Athens. It was because of his ill health that he'd first summoned me from Scotland on a few weeks' leave from my job as a feature writer on The Alba newspaper in Edinburgh. Then a few weeks had grown into a few more.

Angus had surprised all the McKnight family when he announced at 60 he was taking redundancy from his teaching post to spend a year in Greece. It seemed to my mother

Marcella and my sister Shona that he'd lost his mind, going off on a crazy mid-life odyssey, and that he'd return when the money ran out. But he didn't. He stayed for 10 years and later he and Marcella separated. For that decade, while Angus led his dream life in Greece, I had a thorny relationship with him, and negotiating a long leave from work to help him with his problems had ramped up hostilities. The timing was also bad, with The Alba perishing after a harsh takeover, but there was no-one else to help Angus. Shona had two young kids and a full-time job. But once in Greece, Angus and I had become reconciled.

The most compelling reason, however, for throwing in my job and settling in Greece was Leonidas.

"You're looking suddenly thoughtful, *agapi mou*," he said, tapping the back of my hand lightly. I liked the Greek for 'my love'. It sounded robust when he said it. "I fear, Bronte, I am talking too much."

"Not at all. And anyway, I've done plenty of talking myself. But I've got some news I forgot to mention. I have a new commission. I've been asked by a Scottish newspaper to write a weekly column about life in Greece. I've even written the first one, to be published quite soon."

"That is fantastic, Bronte. I'm proud of you."

The column had come out of the blue when a rival paper to The Alba had contacted me to ask if I'd write the weekly piece for its Saturday magazine.

"So, I assume your first column will be about the crisis," Leonidas said, finishing the last of a plate of calamari and sipping his wine.

"Hard to avoid it, really," I replied. "Sadly, it's what most people associate with Greece these days."

Greece had been in crisis since 2010, with debts of around 300 billion euros. The EU had offered a bailout package of 110 billion euros, but in return, it had forced on the Greek government a raft of stringent austerity measures.

"I believe you will never run out of things to write about in Greece, especially now," Leonidas said. "Things are getting worse. There are many new taxes that working people are struggling with. A property tax put on the electricity bill so people cannot avoid paying it. Those who don't pay have their electricity cut and go into debt to the company. People are becoming angry. Just the other day I heard ..." He stopped abruptly and looked at me, pressing his lips together.

"What did you hear?"

"Oh, nothing, my love. I won't talk about it now."

"Something serious then?" I said, becoming more intrigued.

He nodded, twisting his wine glass by the stem. "I will tell you another time. And you may want to write about it one day."

"Perhaps," I said. But I wasn't planning to focus only on gloomy subjects for the column. I would also chart the frustrations of a foreigner's life here, the cultural differences, and the funny and banal, weaving in a few village characters. But I imagined that, like most Greeks, Leonidas wouldn't see the funny side of life here at the moment, the way a foreigner might.

Leonidas asked for the bill and when it arrived the waiter brought a complementary plate of new-season strawberries with a pyramid of thick yoghurt in the middle drizzled with honey. We ate them, watching the sun shimmying lower behind the opposite peninsula, leaving a golden trail over the water.

"Did I tell you that my aunt Thekla is moving back to Marathousa, to her village house? She is tired of Athens and the upheaval of the crisis. She thinks it's not safe there any more."

He bit into a strawberry with his perfect white teeth, a trickle of juice staining his lower lip. He licked it off with a flick of his tongue and suddenly I wasn't interested in his

25

aunt and looked sheepishly at my watch again, but he seemed to have a mind to tell me more.

"She and her husband Kostas have retired. They had a clothing shop in the city. Very successful and now they are comfortable. He likes the city lifestyle and does not want to leave. Not yet. He fears he will be bored in Marathousa, as they have only ever come back for holidays."

"She wants to live there on her own?"

"She has many friends in Marathousa and some cousins and in-laws and so forth," he said, waving his arm around to encompass the archetypical extended Greek family that I was beginning to understand the importance of.

"What will she do?"

He shrugged. "Whatever women of her age like to do: gossip, embroider, make cheese pies, go to church."

I gave him a mocking look. "You don't have much opinion of older women and the breadth of their interests, I see."

"Oh, I respect them, believe me. They are indestructible, like the Parthenon itself, but their lives are run on certain lines. There are rules. You will find out in time." It sounded like a good-natured warning.

While Leonidas's father Grigoris and the family had originated many generations back in Sparta, hence Leonidas's name, inspired by a great Spartan warrior king, Thekla was from his mother Eleni's side. I well remembered that this branch of the family was more clannish and tough and came from the area further south called the Deep Mani, where feuds were rife. I wondered if the aunt would be equally troublesome. Surely not, but for some reason the breeze that was starting to funnel its way across the gulf had a colder undertone to it with all this talk of Thekla.

"Is her house near to yours?" I asked, with certain dread.

"Not far, on the other side of the road, the stone house with the tower. They had this added about 10 years ago. You know how we Maniots like our towers," he smirked.

I knew the house well. I had passed it almost every day not knowing who it belonged to. It looked pretentious with the flat-topped tower stuck on the side. Many Greeks and expats too were building houses with these additions, a nod to the old fortified dwellings of the Deep Mani, a region that had once been like Scotland crossed with Sicily for its level of clan feuds.

"Don't worry, Thekla is okay. She will like you." He winked.

"I don't embroider."

"That's all right, neither does she."

"You've been winding me up, haven't you?"

"Yes," he said, laughing. I had always liked the way Leonidas could seem serious on the surface but there was a gremlin of mischief in his soul that I knew too well now.

"Thekla does like to gossip, and she's *very* religious," he said with a comical grimace. "But enough talking, Bronte. Let's go home."

At those words I was like a horse at the starters' gate and sprang to my feet, accidentally bumping a carafe of water, sending it gurgling over the table top.

"I hope that's not a bad omen," I said to Leonidas as I dabbed at the mess until the waiter arrived to clear the table.

"We Maniots tend to think that spilt water signifies a future baptism," he said with a slip of a smile.

"Really?" I said, unconsciously hurrying him along towards his car.

As long as it wasn't a baptism by fire instead, I thought, as Leonidas gunned the car out of the car park.

3

Barking mad

At midnight Leonidas and I were in bed, wrapped in each other's arms. It was a tender moment, our passion spent, as we enjoyed the intimacy of a close, loving embrace. This had been worth waiting all week for. We were almost asleep when a loud aggravating howl started up from the direction of Myrto's farm.

"What on earth is that?" Leonidas said, wide awake, leaning up on one elbow, his hair damp and tussled. The howling went on.

"A stray, Leo. They're everywhere now," I said, pulling him towards me and kissing him to distract him from the sound of the grey mutt at Myrto's. It couldn't have been anything else. Damn bloody dog! Ten minutes earlier and it would have been damnably distracting. Worthy of Myrto's shotgun. I remembered then that I hadn't gone back later with the rest of the meatballs as planned. The dog was still starving and Myrto probably hadn't fed him.

The howling went down a notch to loud barking. Leonidas got out of bed and pushed the window open, leaning out, his hair a wild outline against a full moon.

"Come back to bed, don't worry. It will quieten down soon."

"Bronte, you don't know these village dogs. They can bark all night when they are hungry or a fox is nearby. It sounds like it's coming from Myrto's house. Does she have a dog now?"

"No, not that I know of," I said in a high thin voice, rubbing my hands over my forehead. Would I have to get dressed and slip out later to feed it? The dog went on barking and then there was a wave of obscenities that went crashing through the still night air, and the jarring sound of a door being wrenched open. Myrto at the animal enclosure giving the mutt hell. I even managed to smile at that. Leonidas shut the window and came back to bed with a sigh.

"I am sorry. This is not the way I hoped the evening to end."

"Oh, don't be sorry, It's not your fault."

"How can you ever forget in Marathousa that you're in a rural location: goats, donkeys, mad dogs, and the sound always carries. Remind me to see Myrto tomorrow to find out if this barking dog is hers. It will keep you and Angus awake every night."

I panicked. "Oh, don't bother yourself. I'll talk to her. I see her most days."

"Okay, whatever you wish, *agapi mou*."

He pulled up the top bed sheet. He held me tight under it and kissed me softly on the face and the mouth. I wanted him again and yet, within minutes of laying his head on the pillow, I heard his breathing grow heavy and I knew he was asleep. I lay on my side watching him, the errant black curl hanging over his brow as usual. I reached out and felt it, smooth and silky to my touch, and moved it off his forehead but it sprang back fitfully. I loved this man more than anyone I'd ever met, but there was so much I still didn't know. A depth of foreignness amid all the warmth and attraction that sometimes made our relationship seem fragile, as if it could easily be unpicked by an incoming force. Even something as insignificant as an aunt. How illogical that seemed. Or perhaps not.

It was warm enough the next morning to sit outside in the garden in the sun. Leonidas had set out breakfast on the patio table while I showered. Yoghurt, fresh fruit, honey, a pot of coffee and a crusty loaf.

"You've been to the bakery already," I said, admiring the healthy spread.

"I woke up early and felt refreshed, despite that damned dog." He uttered a short tirade in Greek, then gave a warm smile. The Greek temperament is like the local weather: rain can patter down, then dry completely before the umbrella's up.

He looked relaxed, his skin glowing, the dark hair slightly more tamed. He was wearing jeans and a light cotton jumper. Everything about Leonidas always seemed easy to me, and fresh.

"Why don't you move into my villa now, Bronte? There would be much more space for you in this house instead of you and Angus squeezed into Villa Anemos."

"I don't know, Leo. I'm used to living there now. It's company during the week and I can make sure Angus is taking all his heart medication, and not drinking too much. I love this house, but it's big. I'd just rattle around here on my own."

He smiled at my description. "Like a stone in a bottle?"

"Something like that."

"You could convert one of the bedrooms and make a proper study for yourself."

Now he was tempting me. At the moment, my study was the front corner of the sitting room in Villa Anemos with a window overlooking the road but with the mountains careering up in the distance at least. It made sense to have a bigger work space now that I was securing regular freelance features for several publications back in the UK, and the newspaper column as well. But I had a better idea.

"Why don't you spend more time here? You don't need to stay over in Kalamata all week, do you? The drive from here is easy, 30 minutes."

"There and back every day would be fine, Bronte, but you forget that because of the siesta time I would drive back and forth at least four times. And then there are the call-outs, sometimes in the night, usually Kalamatans."

"Yes, of course, you're right. It wouldn't make any sense." But so early in our relationship, I wondered if perhaps he liked to keep his own space in Kalamata. And while he didn't seem to care what the villagers might say if I moved in here, I already knew enough about rural Greek life to realise there were still expectations, rules, gossip, that applied to women above all. And foreign women especially, I imagined. In Greek society, doctors were gods, almost above priests, and Leonidas was well respected here. For him to be seen living with a foreigner would be beyond the pale for some. But then again, if people bitched at me, I wouldn't understand them anyway. It would take years to get my Greek up to speed.

"At least come here if you want some quiet to do your work. You have a key. Do as you wish, Bronte. Treat the place like your own, my love," he said, quietly scrolling through messages on his work mobile phone. "I have a couple of patients to see this morning in the Mani, so I will be out for a few hours. What are you doing?"

"Oh, some work, and I'll call in on Myrto. Remember?"

"Ah, that. Please do. I don't want the dog waking us all up every night." He said something under his breath in Greek.

"You don't like dogs then?"

"I don't like those big ugly things that roam around the streets, though it's not their fault. The council is to blame for not controlling things. It's cruel actually. Anyway, I think I like small dogs, easy ones."

"What, like poodles?"

"Yes, things you can put in a bag, or under your arm."

I snorted with laughter. The idea of Leonidas with a poodle under his arm was too funny.

"You're winding me up again, aren't you?"

"Yes, I am," he said, his eyes sparkling with mirth. "Anyway, you know we Greeks are not so obsessed about dogs as you are in Britain."

"Yes, I've noticed. And I've seen all the poor dogs chained up in farmyards and used as security guards." Until someone got tired of feeding them, or ran out of money and set them loose on the streets.

He put his phone in his pocket and kissed me. "See you in the afternoon, *agapi mou*."

When I walked into Myrto's compound a bit later, I could see the dog and the donkey both tied to the same tree. The evening must have cemented a friendship at least. The donkey looked calm, as did the dog, until he saw me and strained at his rope, fizzing with excitement. Myrto walked towards me, her big hands on her hips.

"Well, Bronte. Bladdy load of howling going on last night. You heard?"

I nodded. "Everyone heard. I'm sorry."

She rolled her eyes. "I give him a bit of barking myself and wave a stick at him. Then I have to give him some tucker. He was hungry."

I'd brought more food from Villa Anemos and tipped it into a metal bowl by the tree. It was the last of the meatballs. In the blink of an eye, they were gone.

"I got my shotgun handy if you want to shoot him now." She laughed heartily.

I shook my head. "You know I don't want that. But look, I'm taking him to the vet this morning, like I said, to get that head wound looked at."

"What you do if the doctor fellow can't help with finding a new home. You bring him back here?" she said, pursing her lips.

"I'll sort something out, don't worry."

"I don' say any more now. You got a fixed mind on this. Might as well comb a cloud," she said, with what I took to be a folksy saying, the kind of thing Angus would come out with.

I took the dog down to the vet's surgery in Angus's car, parking outside on the road opposite a small shingle beach just south of Kalamata, a place where a few British expats lived, but mostly Greeks, slightly more well-heeled. The kind of people who did keep animals as pets.

The vet had a fabulous name, Dr Mavrofidi, Dr Black-snake. It was written in Greek and English on a nameplate outside the surgery. I smiled and expected to see a man who was old and wily-looking, but the vet was perhaps 40 and good-looking, with dark, spiky hair. The only snake-like attributes were his round and vibrant green eyes. I gave him a short version of what had happened with the dog. No point in rolling out the whole tale, and he didn't look like he had the time for it. Dr Blacksnake set to work, looking him over. He parted some of the fur on the dog's neck and uncovered another fat green tick.

"That must come out," he said, "and there will be more, I'm sure of it. I will give him some drops on the skin for those. They will all die off soon enough. The cut on the head doesn't need stitches. Just try to keep it clean."

The vet spoke very good English, telling me he'd done post-graduate studies in England.

"This dog, I would say, is not especially wild. He has had an owner some time, I think. He's quite well-behaved and his teeth are in good condition. He is perhaps around two years old."

Somehow that didn't surprise me. He wasn't like the other strays lurking at the rubbish bins. He was also comfortable with people, apart from the creep.

"He was probably left on the streets by someone who couldn't afford to look after him any more. He will need some vaccinations and treatments now. Are you happy for me to do all that?"

"Of course."

"And what do you plan to do with this dog?"

"I've heard you work with the local dog rehoming group, Animal Angels. Would they be able to take him? He's quite a nice sort really."

"I could contact them for you but it will take a few days before they can collect. They have a lot of work now. They have a facility on the other side of the city. They are sending dogs to Germany, Austria, sometimes to Britain. Is that what you want?"

I nodded. "Better than chucking him back on the street."

He smiled. "You foreigners are very kind to animals. We Greeks are getting better but we still need to do more."

It was as if the dog had understood. He put his paw on the vet's arm and whined softly.

Dr Blacksnake laughed. "Okay, my canine friend, you might have a good life after all. We shall see."

That was easy, I thought, as I walked back to the car with the dog on a lead, with a new collar, bought from the surgery. The dog had a jauntier step, happier in his own fumigated skin. I was strangely glad that Animal Angels wouldn't be fetching him for a few days. I could have him a bit longer. Or Myrto could, I hoped!

On the way home I stopped at a small supermarket on the coast and bought some tins of dog food and a few treats, and something for Myrto too, a sweetener. A nice gift pack of her favourite chocolates with soft centres.

"Oh, not the mutt back!" she moaned when I strolled into the farmyard. I pressed the pack of chocolates into her hands before she could say any more. She cradled it as if it were a newborn, her eyes flickering with delight.

"You trying to fatten me up when I'm supposed to be on the Lenten fast now before Easter." She winked.

"Are you really fasting?"

She gave me a sly grin. "I don' eat no meat now, that's true, and each week we Greeks cut out other things bit by bit. Like a food torture, until all we eating in the end is the *horta*, the wild green veg, plain, with no olive oil. But nobody knows what Myrto eats here all alone in her *ktima*, farm," she said, caressing the chocolates.

Myrto was an outlaw at heart, and I smiled at the thought of her eating sweets alone while the rest of the village subsisted on the equivalent of grass clippings for the next few weeks. I explained the dog would only be here a few days until the Animal Angels turned up. She nodded, with resignation.

"The dog looks better now, don't you agree? And smells better too," I said.

"Yeah, sure, but he better not give me bladdy trouble in the nights."

"Don't worry, I've brought plenty of food for him. He should be quieter now," I said, handing her the bag of supplies.

She bent down and looked closely at the dog, puckering her eyes slightly. "The ticks all gone?"

"They will be soon enough. They've been zapped with special drops."

"Just a few days, right?"

"Yes, absolutely."

"Ha! You know in Greece there's no such thing as a few days. Have I told you that, Bronte? We have no idea of time. Could be he's here a few years."

Myrto walked towards her house, hugging her chocolates.

4
Running like the wind

When Leonidas returned to Kalamata early, on Sunday night, I felt at loose ends and realised I could never stay in his villa full-time without him there. It seemed to lack his presence in every way; seemed chilly and slightly diminished. That's when I happened to think about the dog. I went to Myrto's to see that everything was okay. She had her hands on her hips, watching me pat its head, checking on the wound. She had an uncanny way of sussing out how your mind was working.

"Why you don' keep him, Bronte? He likes you. I can tell. You got no cute animals to look after, only Angus." She rolled her eyes and I laughed, wondering if this was her being comical or getting her English wrong.

"I can't keep a dog there. Angus won't like that. Leonidas definitely wouldn't, I think."

"Oh no, the doctor much too neat and tidy for a big hairy *skilos*."

There had always been a little frisson of dislike between Leonidas and Myrto, which I'd discovered the previous year had something to do with their shared family history, or at least the fact their families, like many in Marathousa, came from the same village of Platanos, high in the Taygetos mountains behind us, where family feuds would have been the norm. Many of these families had come down to Marathousa in the past century seeking better grazing land and an easier life.

Despite any discord, Leonidas had done Myrto a good turn by suggesting his young nephew Angelos could come and help her to look after one of the olive groves she harvested, which had become too much for just one farmer. Myrto would teach Angelos the skills of pruning and harvesting and he would have a cut of the income from the resulting olive oil. It was a good solution for both of them, especially for Angelos, who had lost his job in Athens during the crisis and had returned to his rural roots.

On the Tuesday morning I took Myrto another treat – a box of honey cake – and told her to expect the Animal Angels late in the afternoon. Myrto was busy stacking up some of the olive branches she'd collected earlier in the morning, left over after the winter harvest. She had lugged them back from the adjacent field on the donkey.

"You want to repay me for the dog, Bronte? One day you can come with me down the field when I go to gather up all the other branches. Must be done before summer. It's nice work, out in the fresh air, with a mountain view," she said, twirling her hand towards the Taygetos peaks.

"Where's Angelos? Doesn't he help you to do that?"

"Oh, sure. He's done most of it, but he's been doing other chores too, like repairing my goat pen, building me a new shed for baby goats."

"Okay, I can spare you a few hours some time," I said, thinking that I'd probably be a hindrance rather than a help, as I was a novice at anything rural.

"I did you another favour too, Bronte," she said, her eyes flickering towards the olive tree where the dog was tied. He'd been so strangely quiet I'd forgotten to look at him. I turned quickly and saw a skinny, shivering mutt.

"What the hell's that?"

Myrto roared with laughter. "You don' recognise him?"

The dog had lost half its coat and a good year in age at least. He looked like a puppy with his fur sheared back to about an

37

inch. The hair was trimmed around his face so the white patch looked more visible, as well as the white crest on top, which was shorter now but spiked up again. Perhaps the dog had a touch of cockatoo in his veins as well as everything else.

"You did all that?"

"He was sore on my eyes, all that bladdy *vromiko* fur and the stink. I give him another bath too. See how clean he looks now."

"That was so kind, Myrto," I said, touched by the gesture, though I couldn't understand why she'd gone to all that trouble. "The cut's very good. You should start a dog-grooming business."

She guffawed, slapping her palms on her thighs. "I was taught to shear some sheep once in Aussieland – one of many jobs, Bronte. I was good with a big pair of special scissors. Now the dog gets a new home, no trouble. He's even a bit handsome, if you like dogs."

The dog was pleased with himself and jumped around when I went to feed him a few treats. I rubbed the fur on his head. No ticks, no smell. The white patch on his face and the crest were proper white and stood out, making him look more comical than ever and seeming to accentuate one brown eye over the other. The gash above his brow was starting to heal up nicely.

Myrto was watching me. "And in case the rehome people don' turn up today, maybe you can take him over your house, eh? And give Myrto a nice rest from dog-sitting."

So, the shearing had been part of a strategy to make sure the dog was either picked up or moved to Villa Anemos until it was. I didn't blame her, but it had an unintended consequence because when a young guy from Animal Angels finally arrived in a small white van in the late afternoon, I could hear all the refuge dogs inside yapping frantically, even from inside Villa Anemos. It was a mournful sound. Poor mutts! I managed to sprint out the door and round to Myrto's just as the dog was being untied from the olive tree. That's when I decided not to hand him over. I was keeping him.

Myrto slapped me on the shoulder as the van roared off. "I knew you do that. You are sucker for a cute critter. Okay, so now you're taking the dog to Villa Anemos, yes?"

"Of course."

She rubbed her hands together. It was a leathery crackle. As I led the dog out the front gate she shouted after me, "Chocolates all gone now, Bronte!"

"Already? Okay, I'll get you more."

I could hear her as I got to the road, talking loudly to the donkey, chastising him over something, filling his metal tin with water. I knew even if I'd not been able to take the dog, Myrto probably would have. Underneath the flinty carapace she was softer than the pack of chocolates she'd just devoured – and still weeks of Lent to go!

Angus raved for a while when I turned up with the dog.

"You can't keep that clarty thing here," he moaned. "Leonidas will go mad, unless, that is, you have the poor man wrapped round your pinkie now and he does all your bidding."

"No, he won't and no I don't," I said, in a snippy tone. But my mind was made up.

Angus frowned and gave the dog a visual inspection.

"The vet's given him all his shots and he's not clarty now. Myrto washed and trimmed him," I said.

"Myrto?"

I nodded.

"Well, well. Who knew she had so many gifts? I suppose the dog's not bad for a rural jakey," Angus said, using the Scottish word for a down-and-out. Angus took delight in using his old Scottish expressions, as Scots do when they're living overseas, as an emotional link back to the homeland. He tweaked the dog's cockatoo crest into a funny point, which was to become a regular occurrence.

"I suppose he'll play up somewhere along the line though and that will be it. He's not Greek if he doesn't bare his maverick soul," he said.

I laughed. "Like you, Angus?"

When I first came to Greece, I'd only seen Angus a few times in the preceding decade. It was like reconnecting with a stranger, certainly not the more conventional Scottish father I'd grown up with. When we met up, he was sporting a ponytail, but not the usual kind of scruffy grey version that many older men have. Angus's hair was one of his better features, thick and with only a streak of grey here and there, and yet I couldn't quite get to grips with it. Thankfully he was persuaded to have it cut into the healthy bob he now wore.

Those 10 years were something that I still learnt about as time passed, and marvelled at, as if the father I thought I knew really had two personalities: one a level-headed teacher and married man, the other a well-disguised maverick soul that finally broke out when he left the confines of his reserved Scottish upbringing. He and the dog would therefore understand each other well.

Ah, the stray dog, in our lives now and in the house. Perhaps not one of my smarter ideas in a country with low tolerance for pets, but the minute Myrto had clipped him I saw the possibilities, and that he was mine as much as he would be anyone's. The dog that saved me from the creep. Simple as that.

"He won't play up, Angus, and anyway, now there are weirdos about, like the scooter creep, I think it's a good idea to have a dog. Leonidas will see that. Well, he will in time."

"Okay, pet, you've won me over on that score. So, he might as well stay."

"Thanks, Dad," I said, kissing him on the cheek.

I didn't call him 'Dad' often. Since he left Scotland, I had called him Angus. Perhaps it had been my way of keeping him at a distance because of the hurt his odyssey had caused us all. Although we were close now, the name had stuck. But 'Dad' was always good when I was angling for special dispensation over something.

Angus tutted. It was that thing that Greeks do: saying nothing, but raising the eyebrows and shutting the eyes briefly. The gesture seemed to mean different things at different times, but often just conveyed a 'no comment'.

I decided to call the dog Zefiros, Zeffy for short, because I'd been in the Zefiros *kafeneio* the day he turned up on the road. And there was comical symmetry in a dog named after a zephyr wind, living in Windy Villa.

I'd tell Leonidas about the dog when I saw him the following weekend. I wouldn't be dissuaded from keeping him though. I had an instinct the dog was a good thing. He'd come along at the right time, on the road that day. Months from now I would understand that point a whole lot better.

Freelance work came in steadily, enough to support my independent life in Greece. It took the sting out of having left my job in Edinburgh as a feature writer at a time when I thought my career was at its peak, even with the sweetener of a redundancy payment. As far as freelancing in Greece went, Leonidas had been right: there were plenty of subjects to choose from in the crisis. And Greeks, I found, were refreshingly candid and generous people to interview, making me forget how petulant Brits could sometimes be, or at the very least how guarded – until a certain British actress turned best-selling author dropped onto my radar.

In April, I was emailed by the features editor at The Daily Messenger, a popular London tabloid with a huge circulation, for which I'd written a few small stories already about Greece. The editor had come across the curious fact that author Eve Peregrine had a holiday villa "near a place called

Santova beach, south of Kalamata". Would I like to contact her agent and see if Peregrine was currently in Greece? If so, all that was required was a straightforward piece about her part-time life in Greece, her thoughts on the economic crisis, her new book and so forth. It wasn't likely the features editor knew that Santova beach was just 10 minutes' drive from Marathousa and it was too remarkable a co-incidence to pass up.

I emailed the agent, Sylvia Rainford, who told me that, luckily, Peregrine was in Greece for a few weeks, and promised to set up an interview in the coming days.

"Eve's quite good about interviews but she tends not to like talking about the book she's currently working on, I'm afraid. She's superstitious, as most writers are. But you can try anyway. If she doesn't want to talk about anything, I assure you you'll definitely know about it," Rainford said in her email.

I went online and did some research on Peregrine. She'd started out in the 1980s as an actress with a few low-budget films under her belt, and then in the 1990s had picked up some leading roles on TV, particularly as a tough but sexy detective in a popular drama series, which became her best-known role, for which she was still remembered. While she was beautiful and certainly smart, with no shortage of men in her life it would seem, she'd never married and was currently without a partner. Despite her cop shop drama, she'd never been considered a great actress and other more illustrious roles weren't immediately forthcoming when the series ended.

This may have accounted for her switching careers and to everyone's surprise penning best-selling romance novels instead, with exotic settings, though not including Greece so far. I had only read one of her books, set in Mallorca. I gathered, however, that all her books were fairly similar, featuring strong, opinionated female professionals, often fractious, who seemed to find themselves engulfed in dramas often of their own making with generally dashing but foolhardy heroes, who tended to make things much worse before they got better, depending on how you looked at things. The books were oddly old-fashioned in style but witty too, kind of Vanity Fair meets Bridget Jones. Millions of women seemed to crave them. Her latest book was always hotly anticipated and she'd already made buckets of money.

I tracked down some of her previous interviews online that showed she was not unlike some of her heroines: flinty at times and given to spitting the dummy if she didn't get her way. Mostly it was a harmless performance but once she famously had a spirited strop with a reporter in the beer garden of a village pub before hurling his tape-recorder into a nearby water feature, which turned into a diverting fracas involving the landlord and other customers, and the ugly incident was reported in one of the red-top newspapers. There were fewer antics though in recent years. Her wealth and popularity as a writer had given her a certain cachet and confidence, no doubt. All the same, I would watch my step – and not bother with a tape-recorder.

5

From write to wrong

Eve Peregrine's house was called Villa Kaliopi, which seemed appropriate, as Kaliopi was one of the nine Greek muses. A nod to Peregrine's creative efforts, no doubt. The villa was predictably white with blue shutters and a stout blue door, but almost hidden behind a fringe of lemon trees and gardenia bushes. I had passed it many times in Angus's car but never really took much notice, being similar to many holiday homes in southern Greece. I arrived right on time at 5pm, an acceptable hour for meeting people after the siesta period.

At 51, Peregrine was still as attractive as she'd been in her acting heyday, with striking high cheekbones and full lips, her wavy, strawberry blonde hair pulled back into a ponytail. Her slightly husky voice had lost none of its appeal but without the hint of estuary English she'd assumed for her early TV cop role. She smiled when she ushered me in, though it had a hint of regal reserve about it that I'd expected. Perhaps this was the stance she assumed first up to cool any possible journalistic shenanigans. As if! From my trawl through the clippings, I'd already seen the shenanigans were all hers.

Inside the villa, the author had created a stylish space, with gleaming white walls and cool marble floors, all very expensively done. She led me through the sitting room to the front balcony, sheltered from the sun's glare by a striped awning. It had a similar view to Villa Anemos but at closer quarters to the gulf. You could see fishermen casting nets from the back of their blue caiques and small groups of bathers out in the gulf. Peregrine made tea and brought it on a tray with some cake.

"I have to say, I was surprised when my agent told me a local British journalist was coming from Marathousa, of all places. And you live there now?"

I nodded.

"What brought you here?" she asked.

I kept the explanation brief. It's always unsettling when the journalist is interviewed first, especially by a possibly thorny interviewee like Peregrine.

"What about you?" I countered, taking out my notebook and flicking to a fresh page.

She told me she'd come to one of the Greek islands for the first time at 20, had fallen in love with the place, and then a young local Greek. Nothing as clichéd as a waiter, but a singer in a local folk band. It had obviously rooted her youthful enthusiasm for the country, even when the relationship fizzled. Finally, she had bought her own Grecian hideaway seven years ago for summer breaks.

"I bought this villa because of all the places I'd seen in Greece, I thought this part of the mainland seemed more authentic. I thought of buying a place up in Marathousa originally, but I didn't want to get caught up in the faff of village life and there were the British expats. Quite a few of them, I think. I didn't want that either, you see," she said, wrinkling her nose in mild disdain.

I didn't bother to tell her she needn't have worried about the expats. They were quite benign. And they seemed to have no idea they had a celebrity in their midst. Not yet, anyway. I started to move her through my list of questions. She was more gracious than I'd expected from the cuttings. But perhaps it was an act. On the surface she seemed confident, but the more we spoke, the more her nervy mannerisms emerged. Her hands were restless and toyed around with the cup on its saucer at sporadic intervals. She also played with her ponytail of blonde hair a lot, twisting it about in her hand. I asked for her thoughts on the economic crisis and she had plenty to say on the subject.

She concluded by saying, "However, I'm no expert on economics, and the fine details of the Greek debt and the bailout often confuse me. It's certainly a scarier time to be in Greece and at the very least Greeks now seem quite depressed and that's not in the national character, as you know. But I have to admit the thing I love most about this part of Greece at least, it's a perfect place to relax and write, away from the distractions of London, where I have an apartment. No-one bothers you here. And the Greeks haven't a clue who I am, despite two of my books being translated into Greek."

"Maybe you need to actually set a book in Greece," I suggested.

"Yes, perhaps I should," she replied, with a sharp up-thrust of her neat chin. She fidgeted some more, twisting her cup on the saucer, and poured more tea from a seemingly endless pot, probably wondering how to move the subject off books, having stumbled onto it herself. But along with her millions of readers, I wanted to know what to expect from the hotly anticipated new book.

"Can you tell me anything about the plot of your new novel, at least where it's set?"

She didn't answer but abruptly got up from her chair with a sigh and leaned on the balcony railing as if someone had just called her from afar. She looked towards Kalamata at the head of the gulf, with its crystalline spread of white apartment blocks. She muttered something about an 'incomparable view, don't you think?' I've always hated it when interviewees, especially celebrities, make a nervy grab at walking round the room at a certain point in an interview as if they're about to leg it. But Peregrine was obviously not quite at that point because as quickly as she'd stood up, she sat down again, and I casually repeated the question.

"Well ... I'm still writing the new book, as it happens. It's set in Scotland this time, which you might appreciate, being Scottish ... but you know, I hate discussing a book I'm working on. It never seems right and I'm terribly superstitious," she said, her cheeks showing a pink bloom of irritation. The agent was right on the money with this work-in-progress phobia.

"I agree. It must be awkward," I offered. "And the industry's bitchy, I imagine. But your agent says the book's due out this summer, yes?"

"Well, it's nowhere near finished, so that looks unlikely. It's closer to an autumn release, I think." She gave me a kind of warning look, as if that was the end of that, but I decided to push on.

"Well, I do know what working to a deadline's like. It's okay with a feature, but a book, well that's another matter." I hadn't a clue what a book deadline would be like. Murder probably! But I had an instinct already that something wasn't quite right with this writer's anticipated opus, or with her state of mind probably. Her fingers were playing with her rings now, twisting them about. I was beginning to feel tired just watching her.

"Might we do the photos now," she said forcibly, as if to finally draw a line under the questioning. Or else!

"Yes, if you like," I said, thinking the interview would be good enough for a light feature but something more about the book would have been better and probably what the Daily Messenger would want.

I set up a few shots on the balcony with the gulf behind, which were perfect. And then in the sitting room, her seated on a white sofa with an array of Greek prints on the wall behind. It was very telling that she seemed to visibly relax once the interview was out of the way. Her shoulders dropped slightly and the rings were given a reprieve. She even offered me more tea but I declined.

"Might you prefer a glass of wine? I have a nice cold malagousia here."

I had to ask what malagousia was, as Angus and I usually preferred the local wine sold in village stores, which everyone drank, even one of the more pukka expats, who often referred to the wine as "eminently quaffable". I doubted Peregrine would agree.

"It's an excellent Greek wine, very peachy and nice," she said.

"Okay, one glass. I'm driving."

She shrugged sardonically. "Would that make a difference in rural Greece?"

"Probably not, but I'll try at least to be sensible," I said, offering a smile.

She returned with two crystal glasses of wine on a tray with a large dish of salted nuts. The wine was as peachy as she'd said and her change of mood was even peachier. Peregrine settled onto the sofa again and seemed to relish the wine, drinking it quickly as if to banish all bookish thoughts. I marvelled at how tense celebrities could be with journalists when they often do much scarier things in pursuit of fame than answering a few benign questions. It had hardly been a News Of The World type of interview.

I was beginning to understand what a curious and complex creature Peregrine was. The wine was nice, however, and as she relaxed, she became chatty. We passed some time talking about life in Greece. She refilled our glasses.

"By the way, have you looked at those wonderful photo-graphs on this wall?" She swivelled around towards the wall displaying three large black and white prints, which I was facing. "Aren't they divine? They're all shots of the Mesa

Mani, the Deep Mani, by a British photographer," she burbled.

The first one she pointed to was a starkly beautiful image of a stone ruin on a treeless promontory.

"It's a temple close to the mythical Cave of Hades near the Cape Tainaron lighthouse? Do you know about that?"

"A bit." I vaguely remembered Angus and Leonidas talking about the site, the doorway to the Underworld in ancient times, but I hadn't been there.

"Ah, you must go. It's so quiet down there, so beautiful. I adore that place," she said.

The second photo was of Porto Kayio, she told me, a small bay not far from the other location. Another remote kind of place, framed by low hills with a long promontory on one side. She then moved to the third picture. "But this place here is my absolute favourite." The photo showed a saddle of rock with a phalanx of tall towers, many derelict, ranged across it. The place looked severe, the image softened only by the olive trees straggling down the hillside. Another lonely outpost.

"Where's that?"

"It's the deserted village of Vathia, one of the real old Maniot strongholds. The tower houses were fortified in the days when clans fought each other for prominence. You must visit this village too. There are so many places like this in the Mesa Mani, places to escape the rat race."

She was on a roll now, her mood remarkably leavened from previously, and I jotted down the names of the places she gave me, more to be polite than anything.

"You tour quite a bit of this region when you're here, I take it," I said.

"I have in the past but not as much as I should. I come for a few months every year in early summer, mainly to work on my latest book. This year, the same. But I'll probably stay longer this time until I've ..." She didn't finish the sentence but I guessed what she was alluding to. A few rings were twisted again, then silence.

I should have let this thread go, but I must have had a gremlin on my shoulder, whispering in my lughole. I braved a return to the 'work in progress'. It seemed a shame not to.

"Perhaps when you've finished your novel, Eve, you might contact me and let me know. I could write a small piece about it for one of the British nationals." I raked about in my bag for my card and handed it to her.

She turned the card over in her hands a few times, frowning. "I really can't promise anything, you know."

"Okay, we can talk about it later," I said quickly, with an air of finality, glancing at my watch. Ready to bolt now.

Yet I could sense the gears in her brain thrumming away, working over a spiky response perhaps. I was about to get up when she sighed deeply.

"The thing is …. I can't promise an interview because … you see …" More twisting of the pony tail. "I have no idea when the book will be finished, actually."

"Oh, but you said it would now have an autumn launch, didn't you?"

"Well, that's what I'd hoped."

"But?" I said, trying to nudge her along.

Agonising silence and then, "Tell me, Bronte. Have you ever had writer's block?"

"Is that what's holding up this book?"

"Kind of," she said, "though I don't know why I'm telling you this. You must have an honest face, for a journalist, if you don't mind me saying that."

I laughed thinly. I don't think it was my face exactly. It wouldn't be the first time an interviewee had waited until the very last moment to reveal something significant. It was what I imagined a psychotherapy patient would do when they know their time's nearly up at a session. But when the confession came in an interview, in hindsight, it always felt as if the whole procedure had been leading to that final question.

"No, I've never suffered from writer's block. As a newspaper journalist I've never had that luxury. Deadlines and all that."

"It's not a luxury, I assure you," she said primly.

"I'm sorry to hear you're having problems with the book. I assume you don't want any of this to come out."

"No, please, it's strictly off the record. It would affect my reputation, not to mention rile my publisher."

"He doesn't know you're having this problem?"

"Not really. All he knows is that I'm a bit behind with things and that the book won't make the summer deadline, and that's bad enough."

"Ah, that's awkward," I said.

She nodded. "So, just to be clear, it's off the record and please abide by that because I can be a ferocious opponent when people cross me," she said with a flash of her eyes. I didn't doubt it. "I don't know that it's writer's *block* exactly. I find that a bit extreme. Sometimes words just don't flow as they should ... they get ... you know ... waylaid." She flapped her hands around.

A luvvie's euphemism, no doubt, for words stacking up in a U-bend. It was a block all right, the iconic undoing of many a scribe, but rarely admitted to.

"I'm sure it's just a temporary blip. After all, you've penned so many best-sellers already."

"It doesn't feel like a blip. I thought that spending more time in Greece would offer a solution but ...," she trailed off, shrugging her shoulders mournfully. "I don't mind telling you, and again it's off the record, this has really brought me a bit low at times. And I've probably said far too much and I apologise for moaning about my writing career. It's not what I intended."

If I'd expected her to give me more insights into her literary heartbreak, I was wrong. The drawbridge was cranked up and there was a slight return to chilliness. All the same I felt a bit sorry for her if she was telling the truth. I picked up my bag.

"Thanks for the interview and the refreshments," I said, smiling, but I was keen to be on my way. "If you want to talk again about the subject, do call me. Perhaps I can help in some way." Though I couldn't really see how.

She quickly rose from the sofa, rubbing her hands down the front of her linen trousers to smooth out the wrinkles. It seemed more symbolic than practical. I bade her farewell at the door. She offered a clammy handshake.

"Do you mind if I see the article before you send it off?" she asked.

"If you really want to, but I promise I won't mention the writer's block."

She winced at the 'block'. "Oh, don't worry. I think I do trust you. I'm sure it will be fine, and please call if you need any more quotes."

Strange, contradictory woman, I thought as I started up the Fiat and wound my way back to the village. I wondered why she had wanted to do the interview at all since there was no book yet to promote, unless she just wanted to stay onside with her publisher. I couldn't help but think that the writing drama was probably only part of her current problems. Maybe she was in some kind of menopausal ferment or poleaxed after a failed love affair. I'd probably find out in the autumn when the book still hadn't appeared and the news filtered through to the book review pages of the newspapers.

When I got home, I decided to email Sylvia Rainford again and tease out something about the book delay. The response was vague, all to do with the book probably taking longer because of research and so forth. It was interesting that Rainford hadn't mentioned any of this to start with. But I was sure she didn't know the real reason for the hold-up, and neither did the publisher. Perhaps they just thought Peregrine was keeping sloppy deadlines these days, bad enough though that was.

I also contacted an old colleague, Gloria, the books editor on The Alba, who knew a lot of people in the industry. While not giving too much away, I thought I'd sound Gloria out and see if any gossip was doing the rounds among the literary fraternity about Peregrine's procrastination.

6

There's something about Zeffy

Zeffy, the former bin boy, took to his new regime of daily walks like a Crufts wannabe. With his new collar and lead, his fur trimmed, his cockatoo crest gleaming white, he looked chipper. One day I took him into the village. Before we reached the outskirts, my heart did a queasy salsa when I saw the creep again on the scooter coming towards us. Had he moved into the village now? He stopped ahead of me on the other side of the road, the engine running. This was really too much! Zeffy started up a furious round of barking. He hadn't forgotten the man who hit him with the rock, the mark of which was still visible. As I got closer, the creep glared at me in his usual fashion. Then he laughed, pointed at the dog, and said something in Greek I couldn't understand. Zeffy didn't like the tone at least and was up on his back legs, straining against the lead, baring his teeth.

"*Fiye*," the creep shouted in Greek to the dog, with a wave of his hand that seemed to mean 'get lost'.

I pointed at the creep and shouted back, "You, *fiye*!"

He didn't respond for a moment, just stared hard. I wondered at the wisdom of being out here alone after that first encounter, telling him to push off. It crossed my mind that the creep knew where I lived now. It wouldn't be hard to find out in a small rural community. More reason never to walk this road alone in future.

"You not speak to me again, *xeni*, or ..." he said, without finishing the sentence, but he didn't have to. I got the picture but it was the dog he focused on now, pointing at it, spitting

54

something out in Greek, his face twisted in spite. It frightened me. There was no denying he had something nasty in mind. As if Zeffy sensed the danger, he started barking again and pulling on the lead. I slipped my mobile out of my pocket and fumbled for the camera icon but in the time it took to get it activated, the creep had roared off on his scooter and I got nothing, apart from a distant shot of him from behind looking unrecognisable. And there was no number plate on the scooter either, as I had suspected.

I continued to the village, faster this time. I felt shaken and angry. So, there was a threat this time. If I spoke out of turn again, the dog would be dealt with. Easier to threaten the dog than me. By the time I reached the Zefiros café, my mood was calmer. Elpida was surprised to see me with a dog, and all the details had to be supplied. Where did I get him, why, when, and was he living in Villa Anemos?

"Bronte, you rescued a street dog, really? Ah, you know I think I remember this filthy creature. The dirty fur, the funny patches. I threw him bits of food sometimes. He looks different now. Like he's been in the washing machine, yes?" She laughed, looking down at him as he sat nicely on the terrace between us. "What you call him?"

"You won't believe it, but I named him after your *kafeneio*. He's Zefiros, or Zeffy for short."

Her eyes went big and round.

"Why you do that?"

"Because I like it here. I like the name. And I found him just after the last time I was here."

"*Po, po, po,* Bronte!" she said, waving her arm around, as Greeks do when they hear something exceptional, frustrating, or plain crazy. I didn't know whether she liked the fact a dog was named after the *kafeneio* or not. One day it would surely all make sense to her. But I had something else to talk to her about.

"Elpida, remember recently when we saw some guys on their scooters parked on the road? You said you didn't like the look of them. One had long greasy hair, a long nose, mean eyes."

She rubbed her chin where a small bump gave it a kind of point. "I remember. Why you ask, Bronte?"

"You said you thought he was from further down the Mani. Do you know where he's from exactly?"

She sat quietly a moment, her lips pressed together with concentration. "I'm certain he's from the Mesa Mani, like I said. But which village, I don't know. Is he making you trouble?"

"Well … it's just that I keep seeing him on the road between here and the house. I wonder why he's hanging about so much. He's got a mean look and I don't like him," I said, not wanting to reveal all the details of the two incidents. Elpida was feisty enough to confront a trouble-maker. That would only make things worse, maybe for her as well.

Elpida rubbed her chin again and looked serious. "Okay, Bronte. I make some more enquiries for you. Someone here will know for sure who he is. No-one in Greece can hide for long," she said with a wink. "But why do you always walk that road. It's a long one. Why you don't drive here?"

"I never felt it was unsafe, until now."

She grimaced. "You be careful, okay. But good you have a dog to protect you now. Little Zefiros," she said, rubbing the air above his head, if not his head exactly, making the white crest rise with the static. She went inside the café and returned with some biscuits for him.

"What does Leonidas say about the dog?"

"He likes it a lot," I lied. "Who wouldn't?" I gave Zeffy a proprietorial grin as he worked over his biscuits.

Leonidas would have to be told this weekend. I felt sure he'd like the dog, even if it wasn't a poodle!

"What is that?" said Leonidas, pointing at Zeffy and crinkling his nose, when he saw us walking along the road from Myrto's farm.

It was Friday afternoon. He'd just turned up from Kalamata in his black four-wheel drive. He looked smart in a dark suit, carrying his medical bag.

"Myrto has given you a stray dog?" he said, his eyes growing dark and quizzical.

"No, of course not." But then I had to explain how I'd come across Zeffy with a head wound and took him to Dr Blacksnake. I didn't mention the creep just yet.

"He's just a young dog and all cleaned up now. Isn't he lovely? Go, say hello to Doctor Leonidas," I said to the dog, in a simpering voice. There will be trouble, I thought.

But Leonidas only stared at the dog, with its comical face patch and lovely chestnut brown eyes that had become big and pitiful, the default expression for dogs winning over humans.

"Okay, it's not a poodle. But are you keeping him for good, or just until you find him a real home?"

"For good."

He gave me a squinty look.

"You've got him inside Villa Anemos?"

I nodded. "Is that okay?"

Leonidas gently puffed air through his lips. Generally, rural Greeks don't like to keep dogs indoors. Outside in a doghouse, or on a stout chain, was usually good enough. But Leonidas was a city Greek as much as anything and I knew that some people in Kalamata kept pet dogs in their apartments. It wasn't completely uncharted territory.

"Don't worry, I've had him all fixed up, vaccinations, drops for the fleas, ticks. The lot. He won't be a bother. Trust me. And I won't bring him into Villa Ambelia." *Wouldn't dream of it*!

Then I explained what I'd called the dog. He laughed at least at the mad idea of naming a dog after a Greek *kafeneio*. Then he became more serious.

"Are you lonely, *agapi mou*, living out here at the edge of the village?" he said, his head slightly tipped to the side. He squeezed my arm gently, as if to prompt me.

"No … of course not. I've got Angus for company and I see other villagers. Myrto and Angelos are nearby. Why do you say that?"

"I just wondered," he said, narrowing his eyes.

"Look, it's like this. I wanted to save Zeffy because he saved me."

"What do you mean, Bronte?"

Time to confess. At least then Leonidas would feel more accepting of Zeffy.

He shook his head when I finished my story. "*Panayia mou!* Why didn't you tell me this before? This is serious."

"I didn't want to alarm you. Maybe it was just an accident. But very unpleasant. And look, that's how Zeffy got the mark on his head." I pulled aside his fur a bit where the scar was still visible. Leonidas bent down and looked at it.

"I see, but it's healing okay," he said, ruffling the dog's ear slightly.

"I've seen the scooter guy again, today, on the road. He didn't do anything. Just stared."

I thought it best not to mention the veiled threat – not yet. I didn't want to alarm Leonidas too much.

"I think this guy comes from further down the Mani but he keeps turning up here. It's part of the reason I wanted to keep the dog. It's safer and I like him."

Leonidas was quiet for a moment. He pinched his lower lip gently with his top teeth, which he often did when he was weighing up something.

"Take the dog home and come to my house. We'll talk there," he said, looking up and down the road, almost comically, before I turned and led Zeffy to Villa Anemos.

Angus was out. I fed the dog and told him to stay quiet. He went straight into his soft dog bed, which I'd bought at a Kalamata pet shop and placed just outside my bedroom door. I pondered what Leonidas had said about getting Zeffy because I was lonely. It was a curious observation. Yet Leonidas was smart and insightful. He'd seen something in me that I hadn't wanted to admit. I had everything I needed here. This was my dream life in Greece, the place I'd chosen to live, but a thought nagged like a stone in a shoe, that in a way I *was* a bit lonely. Lonely because I was still an outsider here, feeling my way, pleasant though it was most of the time, whereas Angus wasn't. He'd been here too long. Zeffy was an outsider, a ragged bin boy once, and still living on the fringes. We had a lot in common.

Leonidas had left the front door open for me at Villa Ambelia. I found him in the kitchen opening a bottle of white wine. We sat on the balcony, off the sitting room, which was on the top floor, to take advantage of the views. Our chairs were side by side. He pulled me close. His skin smelt of sea air and lemons.

"You must be more careful, Bronte. There are people about now who have been fired up because of the crisis. Extreme right-wing people, and many who live in the Mani. You know the party, Ellines Patriotes Enomeni? Greek Patriots United, as it's called in English."

I'd seen TV footage of demonstrations in Syntagma Square in Athens, of thugs dressed in black shirts holding flags with Nazi-style symbols and slogans. Angus had told me about them and stories were filtering into British newspapers as well, along with all the crisis reports. The EPE had been just a marginal party in the 1980s, full of right-wing agitators who were more of an annoyance than a force to be reckoned with. But during the 2012 elections they had won 21 seats in the Greek Parliament, appealing to the Greek electorate who opposed austerity and also the threat of increasing migration from the Middle East and India. With 7 per cent of the vote, this was a political development that shocked moderate Greeks and harked back to the days of the military-led junta of the 1960s and 70s.

"The EPE has had a lot of publicity since it gained seats in Parliament, which is a situation I still find incredible. I mean the fact they are actually in our Parliament," Leonidas said, running a hand through his curls.

"But isn't it the way much of Europe is going now – to the right?"

"Perhaps, but EPE is dangerous and it is increasing its influence here all the time, with many party supporters to help it carry out its propaganda against the European Union. It has support as well among the police force, in this region anyway. The party has started a campaign of beating up foreigners and communists, or anyone they don't like. They spread the idea that foreigners are the enemies of Greece. All foreigners, not just migrants from the Middle East. They want all of them out, British and other European settlers too. You see what a threat they are, my love."

He told me that in some of the towns and villages further down the Mani, where the party had a strong base, British expats had been targets for abuse. Cars and houses had been spray-painted with hate slogans and expats harassed.

"One of my patients, an Englishwoman, lives in the town of Areopolis. She has a small business there and she is frightened because of the rise in aggression towards foreigners. She has had a few small confrontations with EPE supporters and now she wants to sell her house and leave Greece. I cannot say more about her but she is a very strong woman and to come to this point is shameful. Those who intimidate are men mostly who don't have much work and plenty of time to go about causing trouble. Now I don't know if your creep is one of them, but be very careful. Perhaps take your car when you go out with Zeffy. Park it in the village and then walk the dog around where you can be seen. Or just take the dog the other way, past Myrto's land. She's always there, and Angelos. Okay?"

"Yes, I'll be careful. But I didn't think things were this bad, Leo."

"I don't want to frighten you, *agapi mou*. We have none of these people in Marathousa that I know of and most villagers here would be opposed to their ideas. Just be careful. Take your mobile always. If you can, get a photo of this man. If he bothers you again, we will go to the police. Not that they will do much probably, between you and me. They don't like coming down this far. But I have a friend in the Kalamata police. I can talk to him if you have more trouble."

I nodded.

Leonidas's warnings disturbed me but I was glad that he would now see the point of me having a dog. We sat for a while side by side, lost in our own thoughts, until he turned to me, his eyes narrowed with curiosity.

"Zeffy isn't that dog we heard last weekend barking like a crazy thing when we were in bed?"

"No, of course not. How could you even think that?" I said, looking away, towards the gulf where a northerly wind teased white caps out of the dark grey water.

Early on Monday morning, I woke to the sound of Leonidas whispering in my ear.

"I must leave now, my love. But stay here as long as you like." He kissed me softly and then left and I remembered with some disappointment that he had an early start, calling on a patient who lived in a hill village east of Kalamata. Despite the sounds of Marathousa waking – the donkeys braying, goat bells peeling through the still morning air, the odd clapped-out car juddering into the village – I had no urge to get up. I fell easily into a delicious sleep, sprawling on Leonidas's side of the bed, my head buried in his pillow as if to recapture the intoxicating essence of the night before.

It must have been mid-morning when I woke finally under a tangle of hot, sweaty top sheet with the sense that there was someone in the room – the sound of feet padding softly around the bed.

"Leonidas?" I said, pulling the sheet away, expecting he must have come back to the house again for some reason. But I was wrong.

The sight of a tall stranger looming over me made me cry out and grasp hold of the sheet again to cover my nakedness. A woman with very black eyes glared down at me as if I were a specimen on a petri dish.

"Who the hell are YOU?" I said, my heart bumping with apprehension.

"And who, my dear, are YOU?" she replied in not bad English.

She straightened up and stood beside the bed, hands on hips.

"And that's your business because…?"

She gave a derisory grunt. I wondered if Leonidas had a cleaner he hadn't told me about.

"You're the girlfriend?" she asked.

Then it dawned on me.

"Ah … and you must be Leo's aunt Thekla."

"Yes, and *xairo poli*," she said. The Greek expression means 'Good to meet you', but there was only sarcasm in her delivery.

I pulled the sheet up higher. "Do you always come into other people's houses unannounced?"

She cackled like an outraged hen. "I've been coming into this house a great many years. I have a key, you know." *Oh, great!*

She ambled around the room with proprietorial ease, glancing at my clothes piled on a chair, make-up on the dressing table. She ran a finger over the surface of the wood and then rubbed her finger and thumb together, as if to determine the quality of the dust. Strange woman.

I sat up in bed, leaning into the pillows, watching her.

"I came over to the house this morning to see Leo. I thought I would surprise him. I came to Marathousa very late last night. He must have left very early. When I knocked at the door there was no answer. Then I see that he has gone to work and left a side window open. I came in to close it and make sure all was well. But I see all is not." Hands on hips again and a face like a lemon harvest.

"Well, everything *is* fine here and, if you don't mind, I'd like to get up," I said, glancing towards the door, willing her towards it.

"Leonidas didn't tell me you were living here."

"I don't live here. I live next door with my father."

"Ah. Visiting then," she said with a sneery inspection of the rumpled bed.

I could tell that Thekla and I would not be bosom buddies. She was a curious mix of traditional village matron and something a bit more modern, from the years spent in Athens, no doubt. She wore a dark suit, as if she were about to go to church, and an elegant gold chain, with a thick gold cross on it. She had blonded hair, which was not a good match for the dark eyes and eyebrows, and a slightly sallow complexion. The hair was big, bouffant, as if it had been recently styled. She may have been beautiful once, with a long nose, a little like Leo's, and shapely lips, but in every way, she looked all of her 60-odd years. There was a flintiness about the eyes. When she stared at you, it felt like laser surgery on your emotions.

"Do you mind leaving me now while I get up?" I said.

She sniffed, turned on her heel and left. She wasn't in the house when I finally emerged from the shower and got dressed. I guessed she might not try a surprise house visit again. But she had her own key, for God's sake!

7

Aunts in your pants

"I've just met Leo's aunt," I said, walking into Angus's study. He was staring at his computer screen, the cursor winking at the top of a blank document.

"I didn't even know he had one," said Angus listlessly, picking up a heavy mug of tea and slurping it loudly.

I explained about the aunt and our dubious introduction.

He laughed. "Welcome to Greece, Bronte, where nothing is ever private. Did she ask to see the blood-stained bed-sheets?"

"Oh, please, don't be so gross!"

"Oh, don't be coy. That's what happened in traditional communities in the past, checking to make sure the deed was done, that progeny was assured," he said, smirking.

"You're talking about virginal brides, and can we please change the subject now."

But he barrelled on. "The real point is, the old dear will find it unsettling that her favourite nephew is shagging a foreigner in what she probably thinks of as her family home, or one of them anyway. And as a foreigner you will have no status anyway as far as the aunt's concerned. And Leo hasn't made a formal declaration of intent, has he?"

"I thought you liked Leo?"

"I do, very much. He's an outstanding Greek, but I thought by now that something more might have gelled." His eyes flickered in my direction, a slight hint of paternalism in the expression.

"You're talking like Thekla now," I said rolling my eyes at him. "Leo and I have been together six months. We're still getting to know each other. And how do I know it will work out? We're very different people, different cultures. We fell in love so quickly. Let's just see how we go without making big commitments yet."

I said that mostly out of pride and to scupper Angus's cynicism. I didn't want my father thinking I was a fool for love. And I adored Leonidas. He was the most charismatic, gorgeous man I'd ever met. Sexy from his curls to his Italian shoes. But even so, one part of me also enjoyed my independent, freewheeling life in Greece, even if I struggled with trying to learn the language and understand the customs, all in the heat of an economic crisis. I didn't need other parameters and pressures.

"It's none of my business anyway, Bronte. You're old enough to sort your own affairs. I meant that last word in its more general sense, of course."

I marvelled at how a conversation about Leonidas's pesky aunt had turned into an analysis of my love life. He turned back to his blank screen, his fingers softly strumming the keyboard. But he wasn't actually typing anything. I'd seen him a couple of times in the past week sitting just so at the computer, fiddling about.

"You haven't got a touch of writer's block?" I asked, smiling to myself. Writer's block seemed to be multiplying around me like a flu virus. I hoped I didn't catch it. I started straightening out his desk, as I often did, putting the books into piles, sorting the sheaf of papers he always had spread over the desk top – research notes and early drafts that he printed out and corrected by hand.

"No, I haven't. Just thinking," he said, writing the word 'when' at the top of the blank page. I felt quite sorry for him.

Angus's book was no mere whim. It had been his idea late in the previous year to write about the Battle of Kalamata, a calamitous conflict that took place in the southern Peloponnese in 1941. Although it had not been widely written about, not as much as the Greek campaign in Crete, it had been described by historians as the 'Greek Dunkirk', in which thousands of British soldiers and other allies gathered on Kalamata beach for several nights waiting to be evacuated by the Royal Navy as German troops invaded the city. But in the end, under a heavy Luftwaffe air assault, the navy ships had to depart, leaving some 8,000 troops behind. Hundreds tried to escape down the Mani. Many were never accounted for. Angus's father, Kieran McKnight, had been one of them.

It was to help Angus solve the mystery of what happened to Kieran after he fled down the Mani peninsula that had kept me in Greece the previous September, and not just the reason he'd first summoned me for – his heart problem. Kieran's fate had engaged us for a few months and we had been helped by many Greeks, including Leonidas. The mystery had overwhelmed our family since the Second World War, and Angus in particular. His father had died in the war, months before Angus was born, and because of lapses in postal communications, Kieran never found out his wife Lily was carrying his first and only child. Angus would spend a great deal of his life seeking closure for all this. The fact it was Greece that Angus headed to for his 10-year adventure seemed to bear this out. But at 71, with time running out, he'd made one valiant final effort to unpick the mystery of Kieran.

Kieran was a handsome 25-year-old when he was sent to Greece with the Royal Army Service Corps. He was sweet-faced with a thick head of wavy auburn hair, a family trait that I had also inherited. Kieran joined 60,000 British and allied troops during the Greek Campaign against the German invasion. When the allies were forced to retreat, many ended up in the southern Peloponnese, with the Germans close behind. While awaiting evacuation along Kalamata's beachfront, the allies engaged in a brave rearguard action against the advancing

German forces and under fierce bombing raids by the Luft-waffe, with virtually no RAF cover.

On April 28, 1941, the fighting had reached its peak when the Germans secured Kalamata city and the allies were gathered on the beach. Unlike Dunkirk, however, where a remarkable evacuation was carried out by British civilians in a flotilla of small boats crossing the English Channel, Kalamata was far more isolated, with the closest safe landing point being the island of Crete, almost 200 miles to the south.

The Greek evacuation strategy in Kalamata would be remembered as ill-fated and badly conceived. While many of the troops left behind were taken to POW camps, around 300 managed to escape down the Mani. From the small amount of research Angus had been able to do through the War Office and in later years online, all he discovered was that Kieran was one of the men who fled down the Mani, but whether he died on Greek soil or had made it out of the country, but perished later, was never known.

We unravelled the mystery in a difficult search that eventu-ally led us to a Taygetos mountain settlement. It was an amazing story that Angus had wanted to tell in a book, to highlight this infamous battle but mostly to pay tribute to his father's tragic war efforts. It had been a discovery that had changed both our lives irrevocably. It had brought us closer together and had rooted us to this part of Greece, where Kieran's remains were now buried – in Marathousa's graveyard.

Angus had been a talented, inspiring teacher in his former years in Scotland and he often said he wanted to write a book one day, as people do. But during the preceding winter he set to work, using the colder days, when storms raked down from the Taygetos mountains. His commitment and passion were valiant and he seemed to need little guidance on the writing, and so I let him be. But after a few months, his stamina had understandably flagged. Angus was smart but he was also no saint. He was a man who liked conviviality too, and all that went with it, in Greece. Long days at the computer were often punishing and the medication he took for his heart problems had also probably slowed him down.

"I've already written eight chapters, Bronte, and it's been enjoyable, but it needs discipline, I'll admit that," he said, with a long sigh.

"Can I read them yet?"

He girned a bit. "Later on. They need a bit of polishing. You'll pick holes in them, being a journo."

"Are you going to try for an agent when you've written a bit more?"

"Maybe later. If you've got any input there, I'd be glad to hear it."

I didn't, but I thought that one day I might contact Eve Peregrine for some input. That was probably a long way off.

"I need to read a bit of your opus first. But keep going – you'll get there. But if you get really stuck, I'll help you, you know that."

"Aye, I know. I'm just weary today. The old ticker slacks off sometimes."

"Take it easy, okay."

As I walked past him, I saw the cursor hovering over 'when' but nothing else joined it. I smiled in sympathy.

I made coffee, took him a mug and sat down at my own desk by the sitting room window. I watched as a car went by, towing a small trailer in which a farm worker was sitting, holding a wooden ladder aloft with one hand, talking on his mobile phone with the other. Most days I saw at least one marvel of Greek eccentricity spinning by me.

I spent a few hours that day writing up the interview with Eve Peregrine. It was an interesting, informative insight into expat life in Greece and enough to keep her millions of readers very happy, but there was very little humour in her observations. Maybe that's what writer's block did to you, sucked the fun out of your life.

About her latest book, I simply said it would be out by the autumn. Apart from the fact that it would be set in Scotland, I knew no more and had to embroider something about it probably being another best-seller with a rash, combustible hero and a heroine with a maverick taste for them. The features editor would be satisfied, I hoped. Then I started writing my column for the week. I'd already seen the first one in print under the title of The Greek Column, for which I had been given an amusing picture byline: an illustration of me leaning on a truncated piece of ancient column, possibly Ionian.

While it would be easy enough writing about life in Greece, as I approached my second column I realised that writing about villagers I knew would be more challenging. I was keen not to offend them, so I would have to fudge things or conflate people, apart from Myrto and Elpida, who wouldn't have cared what I wrote, I thought. And no-one should conflate those two anyway. But the problem was mostly academic. Although the paper had an online presence, not everything went on it, including some of the Saturday magazine articles, like my column. My scribblings would be safe, for now. I would have to be especially careful about the expats. Even though I didn't mix with them much, a few would have winkled out the fact I wrote for various British papers. If they even guessed I was writing about their village in a column they would not have been pleased.

"I hear you have met Thekla. She has already told me about it," Leonidas laughed, when he called me on his mobile phone one morning.

"It was slightly embarrassing."

"I am so sorry, Bronte. I don't know why she came into the house. She didn't have to, really. Ach, village women!"

"She's hardly a villager. She's much more an Athenian, isn't she?"

"Perhaps, but I always think of her as a village woman, but complicated."

"How so?"

"I can't really say," he trailed off.

Couldn't say, or wouldn't, I wondered. Why did so many people in Greece have complicated lives? And Myrto had told me on several occasions, "Villagers, Bronte. They all have their bladdy secrets!"

It occurred to me that perhaps Leonidas had conflicted feelings about Thekla and was too polite to say so, as she was on the flintier Maniot side of his family, his mother's side.

"You will like her, I think, when you get to know her."

"Yes, I'm sure I will," I said, with feigned optimism.

He changed the subject, asking me about the creep. Had I seen him again?

"Remember, I told you, we will go together to Kalamata to see my detective friend if you have any more trouble. Let me know. Okay? I miss you, *agapi mou*."

"I miss you too. I'm coming to Kalamata on Wednesday with Angus. He has a check-up with his cardiologist. Perhaps we can meet for a coffee?"

"Lovely. We will talk then."

Leonidas had invited me several times to stay over at his home in Kalamata. It was a stylish top-floor apartment close to the beachfront, though I had never stayed over. It had felt like his space and an extension of his life as a doctor. People were always phoning him and it was a place where he did some of his paperwork and after-hours consulting. At that point in our relationship, it didn't feel part of my life and I preferred the arrangement we had, even if it was sometimes lonelier.

Once I'd finished that week's column, I started to think again about Eve Peregrine, especially after an email pinged into my inbox from my books contact, Gloria, telling me she'd been in touch with some publishing contacts and discovered there had indeed been gossip doing the rounds about Peregrine's book delay, though how that got out I couldn't imagine, unless the agent had been bitching. The publisher was said to be nettled that the book would miss its summer launch.

"I heard the publisher has signed up a few other female romance novelists with hot new titles geared up for early next year. It may be that he's casting around for other stars to replace Peregrine if she stuffs up this book. But if you find out any more from Peregrine about the progress of the book, do let me know. I'm curious about it," wrote Gloria in her email.

I doubted I'd ever get another crumb out of Peregrine about the book, or anything else for that matter. Despite her proximity, Peregrine would probably keep a low profile at her villa, trying to channel the power of the mythological muses, to no avail. She never seemed to come up to the village for any reason and where she went to socialise, if she ever did, I had no idea.

She'd given me her mobile number, in case I needed to check any facts with her, but I doubted I'd ever need to call it.

8

Angus and the muse bulletin

The next morning before breakfast, I found Angus in his study again, at the computer, staring at a winking cursor. I sat down on the old rush-bottomed chair next to his desk.

"You're not still working? Have you been here all night?"

"No, pet. Does it look like that to you?"

"Yep. You look a bit bleary."

"I feel bleary."

"Maybe you had too much ouzo last night. You're supposed to cut back on it. Doesn't mix with the medication."

"Well, wine's a good mixer. No harm in that."

I laughed. "You're supposed to cut back on all of it."

"Don't start now. It's too early for gloom and doom."

Angus had been warned by the cardiologist that he had to take his medication religiously and cut back on alcohol and lipids, the fatty stuff. He knew all of that, yet there was a gremlin in his soul that bucked the medical regime. It was Leonidas who had helped Angus last year to get a private consultation with a Kalamatan specialist, which was the start of his treatment.

He sighed. "I wish Polly was here. She's always a positive influence."

"And I'm not?" I asked.

"No, I didn't mean that. Well, you know what I mean."

Angus constantly surprised me. In the past six months I'd learnt a lot about the father I'd been estranged from for 10 years as if he'd been Odysseus, away on long sea voyages, though his sirens and sea monsters were some-what tamer, like learning to tackle a foreign culture and learning Greek. When he first came here there was the initial challenge of easing himself into an expat lifestyle with a surfeit of souvlaki and local libations, until he tired of the expat culture, and his arteries rebelled. Then he worked for a few years as a private English tutor. It was during this part of his Greek odyssey he'd met Polly, short for Polyxenia, an attractive Greek woman in her fifties. She took English lessons from Angus and the two had become very close. Polly had acted as a translator during our search for Kieran but although the friendship with Angus grew stronger nothing more serious had come of the relationship. Now she was in Australia for a few months, where her daughter lived, married to an Australian. They had just had their first baby.

I too missed Polly, her laughing dark eyes, her wise counsel. I would miss her friendship in the coming few months and her sensible spin on the intricacies of Greek life.

"You couldn't make me a coffee? This writing malarkey, honestly! I've got nothing but respect for your scribbling efforts all these years. Have I said that before?"

"Not that I remember," I said, sarcastically.

"Well, I'm saying it now."

I went to the kitchen, fixed him a strong instant coffee and took it back.

"This is the second day you've been here working at the keyboard. What's the problem with the book then?"

"No problem. I just didn't realise when I started that you can get really skunnered, not with the writing, but just sitting at a computer when the sun's winking outside."

"Then go out on the balcony and write in a notebook for a bit."

"I think that might make it worse."

74

"Look, let's go to the village tonight for a meal. Take a break from the scribbling. It will do you good."

"That makes me feel better already," he said, sipping his coffee, leaning back in his chair, suddenly more relaxed. While we were chattering on about nothing in particular, we didn't notice Zeffy sloping into the room. He hovered around a coffee table, where Angus had put the plate of honey biscuits I'd brought with the coffee. In a split second, Zeffy had made a grab for the plate, overturning it, secreting a few of the remaining biscuits in his mouth.

"I hate it when he does that. Go on, bugger off!" Angus said, waving his arm around. Angus wasn't crazy about Zeffy being in the house but the dog was otherwise surprisingly good, given his previous homelessness. His main failing was that he stole food, a throwback to the days of raking in bins. What I didn't realise at first was that he didn't eat everything he stole. Like a magpie, he often hid food, like biscuits and treats, for later: in the corner of a room, in a shoe, under my bed. Even down the side of the sofa. It was quite touching but damned annoying when things were found, half eaten by other critters or in a crumbling state. But he was a good guard dog. If anyone was hovering around outside the house, he'd know about it.

The village taverna, the Kali Parea, always seemed to earn its title, meaning 'good company'. It was especially busy that night with a couple of large gatherings of Greek families outside. Miltiades the owner was in the middle of the paved square surrounded by tables. He was a stout man with a fat tummy and big meaty arms. He had wavy hair and dark, laughing eyes. On the square, he would often help the waiters take orders, but mostly, like Elpida, he wanted to chat to clients, collect some crumbs of gossip, have a laugh. He would trail from table to table in his convivial manner. With his big voice and mannerisms, he often resembled an opera singer about to break into a spirited aria.

Occasionally, when the music on the sound system was something he particularly liked, he'd dance as well. Often, late at night, when there was more of an empty space, he'd leap into a *zeibekiko* dance. This is a solo dance originating in Turkey but now iconically Greek. It's generally a macho performance with only one man dancing at a time and steps that can be as innovative as the dancer wishes but it's usually underscored with muted passion. Miltiades was surprisingly nimble for a big man and diners always showed their appreciation. I didn't think he'd dance that night, as the place was too busy, with several celebratory meals in progress, perhaps a name day or a baptism. It was unusual to see big gatherings any more, Angus had told me, as fewer people could afford to eat out regularly.

Miltiades always had time though to stop and chat with Angus or *Kirios Angoose*, Mr Angoose, as he always called him, unintentionally getting the pronunciation wrong. It always made me smile. Miltiades had been the one who offered to drive Angus to hospital the night last year he'd had chest pains – and he'd probably saved his life. No-one in rural Greece bothered to call out an ambulance. Most of the time there wasn't one to spare.

I felt there was a bond now between the two men. Miltiades would pat Angus on the back and ask about his health, admonish him for eating too much fat or drinking too much wine, which resulted in much cheeky banter in Greek between the pair, which I always enjoyed, partly because I never ceased to be surprised by how good Angus's Greek really was and how he had put it to good use the previous year when we were researching Kieran's fate. A night out at the Kali Parea, in any case, always put Angus in a good mood.

I ordered the specialty of cabbage leaves stuffed with meat and rice in a white lemony sauce. Angus, as usual, favoured something he wasn't supposed to have: pork souvlaki with chips, and a side order of ribbing from Miltiades about his diet. But he brought it for him anyway, with a complimentary jug of wine.

There was also a large group of expats that night, only a couple of whom I'd seen before, sitting at the edge of the square, at the back. It seemed a lively gathering. There was much talking and loud guffawing, with plenty of food and wine on the table. One couple were louder than the others: the man was tipsy, the woman had an irritatingly loud giggle, with a strange rising inflection. Angus pulled a face.

"That's Geraldine. I call her the cackling coat hanger. She's as thin as one, and always laughing, even when there's nothing funny." He shook his head in mild irritation.

"You don't like the expats, do you?"

"Look, they're okay. I saw enough of them when I first settled here, but the thing is, you're damned if you hang about with them – you get sucked into their bitching and moaning – and damned if you prefer the Greeks. The Brits will think you're letting the side down. Then there are people like Derek. He's over there," said Angus, dipping his head towards the table, "He's the one sitting quietly at the far end, with the goatee beard, not talking, but nothing is escaping his notice, I can assure you."

Derek was a miserable-looking man with a shiny bald head and doleful eyes. He refilled his squat wine glass at regular intervals. I didn't like the look of him much, but I couldn't say why.

"He's one of those expats who runs off to Greece, saying he hates Britain, then holes himself up on his rambling farm on the edge of the village like a hermit. But here's the thing: he knows everything that goes on in the UK, spends a lot of time apparently checking websites and putting comments on

77

expat forums. The expats here are harmless enough, really. The Greeks don't mind them, but I prefer to live a different kind of life here, that's all."

Before we went home, we stopped at the *kafeneio* for a nightcap. Its tables were set out just in front of the taverna's, bordering the road. On busy nights the two businesses melded into one and there was usually a genial, noisy vibe. Those who didn't want to partake, mostly groups of older Greek men, would hunker down in front of the TV inside to watch news programmes, argue over politics and play backgammon. This was one of Angus's favourite haunts as well, where he met the *paidia,* as he called them. *Paidia* is the literal word for children but it also means mates, guys, and these were Greeks with whom Angus had a strong, sometimes boozy, camaraderie. We sat at a table near the road. Elpida joined us for a chat.

"You looking real good now, Angus, with your new diet. Handsome without the pony's tail, eh Bronte?" she said, winking at me. I nodded in agreement.

"When I had the ponytail, Bronte used to say I looked like a Greek priest – without the stovepipe hat," said Angus, chortling.

Elpida wagged her finger at him. "You are much too naughty to be Greek priest."

We all laughed but then Elpida suddenly became serious, leaning into the table. She whispered, "Ah, before I forget, Bronte, I have found out for you, the man on the scooter. He's called Dionysos. He comes from the village of Glika Nera, down the Mani. Old wreck of a place, full of strange people now with crazy ideas." She made her hand into a claw shape and twisted it back and forth at the side of her head.

"What crazy ideas?" Angus asked her.

"Crazy political ideas. People on the Right who are for the Ellines Patriotes Enomeni party." She pulled a face. Angus frowned.

"My stomach is twitching over these people, Bronte," she said, tipping her head slightly to the one side and giving me a long, searching look. How well I remembered the day I'd first seen the creep Dionysos, with another man on the road. Elpida's stomach was doing a spirited cha-cha that day, and she was right.

"Don't worry, Elpida, we're on the case," said Angus, then he added something to her in Greek and they both looked at me.

"Translation, please! You're both making me nervous."

Angus said nothing but Elpida rubbed my shoulder. "Don't worry, *koritsara mou*, my girl, you got lots of friends here and you got your *babas*," she said, referring to Angus.

On the way home, Angus slipped his arm round mine.

"You didn't tell Elpida about the creep pushing me over, did you?" I asked him. Angus shook his head. "Because she'll get angry with him, and where will that lead?"

"No, not at all. I just told her to let me know if Dionysos comes prowling about again. Just so we know. But what this guy has against you exactly is a mystery, and also why he's hanging around this village so much. Maybe he's just a misogynistic thug. Next time I'm with the *paidia* I'll sound them out about this guy."

9

Chaos has no deadline

My mobile chirped on the table while Angus and I were eating breakfast on the balcony. It was Eve Peregrine's agent, Sylvia Rainford.

"Eve's disappeared," she blurted out, breathlessly.

"What do you mean disappeared?"

"She hasn't called or emailed since the day you spoke to her, which is over a week ago, and her mobile is always on voicemail."

"She doesn't call every day, does she?"

"No, but lately we have been in close contact because of the … err … book deadlines and so forth."

"Perhaps she's on her way back to the UK."

"She would have told me if that were the case. Anyway, she said this would be a longish stay in Greece this time."

I scratched my head. Angus was watching me with a quizzical look, buttering a large slab of hearty village bread.

"Was she all right the day you interviewed her? Did you upset her in some way?" the agent asked in a flappy voice.

"Me? Of course not. The interview was fine. She talked about Greece, as planned. Nothing contentious there. I did ask her about her book, but I've told you that already …."

Rainford cut over me. "The new book? I don't remember us discussing that."

"I emailed you after the interview. We talked about the delay, remember?"

"Oh, okay, yes, I kind of remember that. But was she upset about the book or anything else? Because something must

80

have sent her off the radar, and you're the last person to speak to her." There was a rising inflection of panic in her voice. I was glad I didn't have any kind of agent.

"Look, there's probably a simple explanation. Perhaps she's just cut herself a bit of slack," I said.

"You don't know Eve. She doesn't do slack."

"Then I don't know how I can help."

"Well, look, if Eve hasn't contacted me in the next couple of days perhaps you should report it to the police there. I mean, does anyone in the village there have a key to her house? Maybe she's in there. Maybe she's collapsed or something."

"That's a possibility, I suppose. Leave it with me and I'll check out the house."

"Thanks. It's all so unlike Eve."

Yet I got the opposite impression: that Peregrine always liked to do things her way, with a touch of high drama. I ended the call, shaking my head. Just when I thought I'd never have reason to think about her again, she'd legged it.

"What's all that about?" said Angus. He was still eating his bread and butter.

"Should you be eating all that butter?" I asked, noting how much he'd slapped on while I was on the phone.

"Don't worry about lipids right now. What's going on with this Eve woman?"

I told him about her disappearance.

"What should I do?" I asked him.

He dipped his knife into the pat of melting butter and spread it thickly on another fat slice of the volcanic-looking bread from the local bakery. Then he slathered the lot with fig jam, trying to eat and talk at the same time.

"Well, it looks like you've upset poor old Eve somehow. I mean … I've felt the nip of your razor tongue at times and wanted to leg it," he said, half-jokingly, referring to some heated arguments we had at the beginning when I came to Greece, before our relationship was ironed out.

"Oh, very funny. I'm being serious now."

"Well, why don't you go back to her house and nose around."

I had another week's column to write that day and didn't need a disappearing novelist to get angsty over. I might almost have taken umbrage over the agent's suggestion that I'd upset Peregrine but the fact was that she'd been very touchy about the work in progress and her blocky problem. And I remembered too that she'd said the whole thing had made her feel pretty low. Was she depressed perhaps? Had talking about the book stuff pushed her over the edge?

"Come with me to her house after breakfast, Angus. Maybe you can talk to the Greek neighbours for me."

"If you like," he said, with a lazy smile, as a man might when he's consumed half his body weight in low-density lipids.

Before we set off for Peregrine's villa, I tried her mobile number a few times but every call was diverted to voicemail. When we pulled up outside her house a bit later, Angus whistled lightly.

"Very smart little holiday hangout. I've passed it dozens of times coming up from the beach road and never thought for a minute Peregrine lived there. She keeps herself to herself anyway." Angus didn't read her books but I knew he remembered her from her early TV career.

There was no car parked outside, as there had been on the day of my interview: a small red rental car. We knocked on the front door. No answer. All the windows were shuttered. All was quiet. A side gate led to the back of the house. Surprisingly, the gate was unlocked. We went in. As we turned into the back garden, we both jumped when we saw the figure of a short woman in a navy dress, tipping soapy water into the flower beds. She looked uneasy when she saw us, wiping her sudsy hands on the sides of the dress. Angus spoke to her in Greek, then turned to me.

"This is Eve's cleaning lady. She comes on this day every week to clean the house. She doesn't know where Eve is. She doesn't have to. She has keys to the place and when Eve's not here she just does her cleaning and leaves."

"Ask her if Eve could be away on a trip, and where."

Angus rattled away for a bit. The woman shrugged.

"She has no idea, but if she's gone on some jaunt it would only be for a short while. Usually Eve tells this woman when she's off on a longer trip or going back to the UK."

"Ask the woman for her contact number, a mobile or something, in case we need to talk to her again."

I raked around in my bag for my notebook and Angus gave me a number for the woman, called Sophia.

"Give her yours, Angus, and ask her to call us when Eve gets back or, of course, if she doesn't in the next few days."

We were about to leave when I had another thought.

"Ask the woman if we could go inside a moment to see if everything looks okay. Tell her a good friend wanted us to check."

"Sophia says she's been in there. Nothing seems amiss."

"Tell her I'd like to see inside the house again, just to settle my mind that everything's like it was the day I was there."

Angus rattled away again. The woman eyed us both up suspiciously. There was a bit more discussion with Angus, then reluctantly she said yes, but insisted on coming with us. The back door led into the kitchen, which was very neat and clean, and then a dining room. I walked through to the sitting room. It looked just the same as it had on my first visit: very neat and tidy, as if no-one had lived here for a while. We walked about, with Sophia trailing behind us.

I looked again at the wall with the three large black and white prints. On a sideboard in front of them there were a couple of small neat piles of some of Peregrine's books, as if she were about to have a book signing of sorts. Everything looked to be in order, in fact too much so, as if it had been tidied in preparation for a long trip. I was certain she'd booked a flight back to the UK but had told no-one, not even Sophia.

"Everything looks okay," I told Angus.

The cleaning woman was visibly relieved when she saw us out the front door. She stood in the doorway and watched as we got into the car. As we wound our way up the hill towards the village, a sudden thought began to worm away in my head.

"You don't suppose it's got something to do with that weirdo Dionysos, who's been harassing me? Maybe he knows Eve's a foreigner too and he's maybe part of a gang of thugs, trying to drive out foreigners, especially well-heeled, classy-looking foreigners like Eve Peregrine. Maybe they've been casing her house."

"What, you mean like she's been kidnapped? That's a bit far-fetched. I agree there's a lot of sinister things going on in Greece at present, especially in rural areas. But picking on a high-profile kind of 'celebrity', if you like, would bring them a heap of trouble, wouldn't it?"

"Just a thought. But should we go to the police?"

Angus shook his head. "We've got no proof she's come to any grief. Maybe she just wanted to get away from it all, especially the whining agent."

"There's a bit more to it all than that." I told Angus about Peregrine's writer's block and the delay with the book. He guffawed.

"What's funny?"

"Sorry, pet. It's kind of comical; not what you expect from a high-rolling scribe. I mean, what's a block anyway? It just shows a lack of real talent. Imagine a top brain surgeon getting up one day and saying, 'I'm sorry but I can't seem to hold my scalpel straight any more. I've just forgotten how'."

"Well, your cynicism surprises me. I've seen you lately at your computer, dithering with a blank screen. You know how hard it is – writing."

"Yeah, I know it's torture sometimes but that's because I'm not really a writer. End of story."

"Why are you doing the book then?"

"Buggered if I know," he said petulantly.

I shot him an angry look. "Angus, I can't deal with your writerly jitters as well – not today."

"I was just winding you up, that's all."

"You're not though, are you? You're having a wee crisis of confidence yourself. Forget it, you *can* write. I've looked over your shoulder now and then at the computer."

"That's not fair!" he girned.

"Shh! Listen. You've got a passion for the subject and a great story to tell. That's pure gold for a writer. You're not Eve Peregrine."

"Whatever!" he said, smiling to himself and humming a tune as we neared the village.

"Don't you think we really should contact the police," I said when we stopped in front of Villa Anemos. "It does seem a bit strange for her to leg it without telling the cleaning woman."

Angus shook his head. "Not yet. The cops in this region can be pretty slack about following anything up. And think about it. If we go to the police, well, you're the last person to see her, it's true. It might look like you've had something to do with it. Awkward."

I hadn't thought that through properly. I might end up in a story about Peregrine instead of writing one. I bit on my bottom lip. Damn the woman for making my life complicated right now.

Back home, I got stuck into my column for the week and tried to forget about runaway Peregrine. I was writing a piece about the coping mechanisms of Greeks in crisis, without referring to the fact that some were failing to cope at all. It was never hard, at least, to find Greeks to comment on the crisis, or any subject. Unlike most interview subjects I'd ever met, Greeks were refreshingly candid and funny. Generous with their opinions. After I'd finished the column, I succumbed to an afternoon siesta. When I woke, I emailed Peregrine's agent and updated her on the house visit. She replied immediately and wasn't well pleased and emphasised yet again it was all out of character. I told her I'd definitely call the police if I didn't hear anything in another few days.

I rang Leonidas early in the evening. He was on his way back to his surgery for his evening consultations. He sounded tired, like he'd had no time to rest in the afternoon.

"Do you still have the dog Zeffy?"

"Of course. Strange that you should ask. Did you think I'd abandon it so quickly?"

"No, my love, I knew you wouldn't." I heard him laugh at least. The sound of his laughter always delighted me.

"You're not sorry I've still got him?"

"No, of course not. I like your sense of loyalty, Bronte."

"Don't worry, I never take him to your villa. I'd be scared he might break something."

"I'm scared he will do worse than that," he said with a derisory chuckle.

I told him about Eve Peregrine. I needed some other input. He was as mystified as I was.

"Should Angus and I go to the police?"

He sighed heavily. "I wouldn't do that yet. After all, wouldn't she be annoyed if she came back from her little trip and found the police running about her property, asking questions?"

"True enough. Maybe she's run off with a man," I said, chuckling because it somehow seemed unlikely.

"This is most intriguing, Bronte. But I am afraid I have to go now. I miss you very much, *agapi mou*. See you at the weekend."

That's another thing I loved about Leonidas. Although there was often a gremlin of mischief in his dark eyes that I knew so well now, at heart he was always sensible. Always the good doctor. He had a calming influence. He made me act sensibly. Oh yes, indeed!

"Angus, I've just had a great idea," I said as he emerged from his afternoon siesta. "Let's go out and look for Eve tomorrow."

"Are you mad, Bronte? Look where exactly?"

"Oh, I don't know. Somewhere. I have this terrible feeling that all is not well."

10

A date with Hades

We set off in the morning in the Fiat with Zeffy on the back seat, sitting in his soft dog bed, panting and excited about his first proper road trip. We drove the mountainous road south, zigzagging along endless hairpin bends with giddy views of the gulf and occasional roadside shrines with flickering candles dedicated to those ropey drivers who'd gambled with crumbing edges and sheer drops – and lost. I tried to explain to Angus my choice of destination – the Mesa Mani, the Deep Mani. I'd had a hunch the day before after we'd traipsed around Peregrine's house. Those black and white framed photos meant something to her; the way she'd directed me to them after the interview with strange enthusiasm. Hades at Cape Tainaron, Porto Kayio and the deserted village on the hill. And how she said the Mesa Mani was one of her favourite places – "a place to escape the rat race" – and she'd urged me to go. Was it a hint? For what exactly?

Angus said nothing as he watched the road and I chuntered on with my theory.

"The thing is, if she hasn't been abducted by aliens, rural pests, or obsessed fans, she might be hiding out somewhere at the bottom of this peninsula," I said.

"What? Just because of a few photos on the wall and because she likes places like Hades," he said, with a derisory grunt. "Seems appropriate somehow that the tormented one would be happier in Hades than anywhere else."

The thought had crossed my mind as well.

"Good of you to drive me down here though, and to go along with this ...."

"Fantasy?" he offered.

I laughed.

"Ah, well, Bronte, what else would I be doing today but trying to deal with my own writer's constipation."

"Your problem's different, Angus. When you see a blank screen on the computer, you automatically think of five other places you'd rather be, like down at the *kafeneio* with your *paidia,* scoffing a few more deadly lipids and a bottle of ouzo."

I made a mental note to email Polly and try to winkle out her plans; to see if she was coming back soon. Angus had seemed a lot more motivated when she was in our lives.

It took over two hours to get down to the bottom of the peninsula. In that time, we passed the whole spine of the Taygetos mountains and the Pentadaktylos (Five Fingers), the highest peaks. The range was also known as Kakovounia, the Bad Mountains, because of their glowering aspect and because they were near-impossible to cross. Even as they petered out further south into low barren humps, they remained an inhospitable, parched backdrop to land strewn with gorse and prickly pear. Offset with this High Noon vibe, however, there were deep sapphire coves overlooked by Byzantine chapels and tall, solitary stone towers. It was still only spring and yet the Mesa Mani seemed to sizzle, particularly at the point where a curiously-shaped promontory called Tigani, the frying pan, jutted into the sea.

Zeffy kept his face at the window, tongue lolling, filling the car with hot vibrant breath, as if the sight of the Deep Mani had ramped up a mortal thirst. A few times we stopped for cool drinks and to water the dog.

"When we get to the cape we have to go first to the cave of Hades. Peregrine talked about that a lot."

HOW GREEK IS YOUR LOVE?

I'd boned up on the cave of Hades and thought the mythology surrounding it would have piqued her sense of drama. This was the mythical portal to the underworld, where Hercules carried out his 12 labours and where he dragged out Cerberus, the feared three-headed Hound of Hades, who guarded the cave entrance and stopped dead souls from legging it. A portal to Hades is not just the figment of ancient imagination, it has a real entrance that is said to have been mentioned by Homer. According to my Mani guidebook, the entrance had long been identified as a cave near the water's edge beyond a temple in what was once ancient Tainaron.

When we reached the car park at Cape Tainaron, it felt like we'd reached not only the most southerly point of mainland Greece but had taken a passage into some hyper-visual outpost. The colours were indelible, like the blue of the water on the pebbled coves along the rocky treeless shore of the Bay of Asomatis, and the red hulls of two small boats pulled up on the shingle. A cluster of wild purple thistles seemed so perfect and vibrant as not to be real. The scene was stark yet beautiful, like nothing I'd ever seen. There were no people or animals. Where were they all? One narrow track led across a flat promontory to the cape's lighthouse, passing the remains of an ancient temple dedicated to Poseidon, with a mosaic featuring his mythical motif of rolling waves. I had read in my guide book that Ancient Tainaron was perhaps built over certain lay lines that had special mystical powers. Was this what had lured Eve Peregrine towards it?

The other track passed a sign for the Sanctuary and Nekromanteio (Death Oracle) of Poseidon, which was a stone ruin, once a Byzantine chapel, built over an ancient temple dedicated to Poseidon. It was nothing more than a single-vaulted room with a rough floor and large gaping holes in the roof. A weathered stone altar was covered in an array of modern votive junk: coins, plastic cups, one small leather sandal, a hammer – and then there was the *book*.

"Angus, come and look at this," I said, as I eased it out from under the hammer.

He trailed over and scoffed at the junk. "Looks like people come here and empty out their rucksacks of things they don't want. Clarty old nonsense."

"Yes, but look," I said, holding up the book that had a cover with a wind-blown, red-haired heroine standing on a clifftop: Against the Storm by Eve Peregrine.

"How weird is this?"

Angus laughed vibrantly. "Eve in Hell. Of course!"

"No, I mean this is spooky, isn't it? She shows me a photo of this place and I find one of her books here. What's the chance of that? She's obviously been here lately. This book's in good condition, so it's a sign."

"Of what?"

"I don't know … that I was right; she's down here and that she wants me to know that," I said, flicking quickly through the book in case there was a note, or some other cryptic scribble.

Angus gave me a mocking look.

"So, it's a sign … what … like Hansel and Gretel leaving a trail of crumbs in the forest so somebody will find them?"

"Yeah, something like that."

"If that's the case, what the hell's she playing at?"

"Don't know. But why would she go on about this place? And now this," I said, waving the book in the air.

Angus chortled. "Maybe this is Poseidon's remainders' pile. Eve really does need to lift her game."

"You old duffer!" I said, laughing and shoving the book into my shoulder bag. "Let's get to the cave of Hades then. Maybe she's there."

"Maybe Cerberus has already dealt with her. Better send Zeffy in first. He'll get things sorted." Angus was warming to his subject now, enjoying himself immensely.

"You know where it is, I take it?"

"It's years since I came here but, if I remember rightly, we need to scramble down a track just beyond the chapel and onto the cove below."

Zeffy was straining on his lead to get to the water. I could tell he wanted a swim. The dog was mad about the water, one of the things he hadn't enjoyed as a homeless waif, unless it was a night spent in the pouring rain. Since there was no-one about, I let him off the lead and he scarpered down the track to the beach and dived straight in. I could almost hear him sizzle like a hot pan hitting cold water and felt a twinge of jealously, so much so that I thought of taking off my clothes and skinny dipping, but thought better of it. Zeffy swam round and round in wide circles, barking madly and snapping at his watery slipstream, as if celebrating his own small life, enjoying perhaps for the first time ever, real animalistic joy.

We watched him with vicarious pleasure until he finally loped out of the water, shaking himself over the shingle beach. Angus looked about and scratched his chin.

"The entrance to Hades is supposed to be in a cave around here."

When we looked back towards the temple, we could see a bank of rock on the headland in a semi-circular shape, with a deep overhang and all obscured by a thick fringe of bushes.

Zeffy, fresh from the water, pushed through the greenery as if he sensed its significance and we followed him. There was a long, deep cave under the overhang, shaped like a gummy mouth, but high enough to walk into. It had an entrance of sorts – the remnants of two stubby ancient plinths that must have been part of a wall shielding the cave, which had since disappeared. Zeffy was quick to sniff out the cave wall, stopping at one corner where a round circle of embedded stones seemed to mark out a rim of sorts, filled in the middle with compacted earth, which Zeffy scratched at with little effect.

"Is that *the* portal to Hades?" I asked.

"It's a small one if it is, but then the ancients were small people, I imagine. Zeffy's got the scent of Cerberus, it would seem. Clever dog," Angus said, with a sardonic grin. "Cerberus used to guard the underworld, stopping the living from descending and the dead from legging it. Only demi gods like Iraklis – that's Hercules – were able to enter Hades and return to the living world again. It was here that Orpheus famously descended to retrieve his wife Eurydice, who'd been killed by a snake. Hades, the god of the underworld, had one condition when he decided to let her leave, that Orpheus wasn't to look back at her, which of course he did, and she was snatched back into the underworld again," Angus explained, enjoying his moment of instruction and reminding me how much he once loved teaching.

"I didn't know you were into ancient mythology. The things I'm learning about you."

"When you come to a place like this it brings all the great myths to life."

It summoned other thoughts as well. I remembered that when I'd boned up on Peregrine for the interview, I'd noticed she'd once starred in a modern theatre adaptation of the tale of Orpheus and Eurydice, to great acclaim. So, Hades was perhaps an emotive link to her past. Clearly, she wasn't around these parts at present, or maybe a few kilometres ahead of us, if this was really a scene from her disappearance gambit.

Zeffy was still scratching at the portal. I put him back on his lead for fear he might crack through into the underworld and drag us with him. We didn't hang about long. Although the patch of undergrowth right in front of the cave was bathed in sunshine, the place had a clammy, musty feel about it and we returned to the shingle beach and then walked back to the car park. A small taverna nearby was closed, with the tired look of abandoned buildings in Greece, as if no mortal had been there for decades.

"I think our next stop should be Porto Kayio, the second place Peregrine mentioned."

"I still don't believe for a minute she's down here, Bronte. I'm indulging you because it's great for you to see all these places, but honestly, that book in the chapel. It's just a whacky co-incidence."

"Maybe. We'll see."

He shook his head and we drove off to the next destination. It was slightly more hopeful, a peaceful settlement, nestling by a shingle beach with a stone jetty on one side of the narrow bay and a path leading up over a low gorsy hill. Like everything else here, it was a remote but pleasing outpost. There were a few tavernas and cafes along the beach, though none was particularly busy, as it was still early in the season. We stopped at the first taverna we came to, hungry after our excursion. We had a leisurely meal outside and shared a carafe of wine.

After lunch, I quizzed the waiter, who spoke reasonable English, about Peregrine and whether she'd come by here recently. I showed him the back cover of her book, with its author photo.

He considered it a moment and smiled. "Yes, she has been here a few times. And well ... this is *parakseno*, strange, I think you say ... wait a moment."

Angus raised a quizzical brow at me as the waiter sauntered into the taverna and came back holding a book. He handed it to me. It was another one of Peregrine's, entitled Fateful Journey, with a woman cresting a sun-drenched hillside dotted with cypress trees that looked like somewhere in Italy.

"She left this here?" I asked the waiter. He nodded.

I shot Angus a told-you-so look.

"Did she say that friends might be coming by?"

He frowned. "I don't think so. She left it inside where we keep a few little books near the counter for our clients."

"When was she here last, do you remember?"

He held his hands out a moment and grimaced with the effort of raking his memory.

"I can't say. A few weeks ago, or a few days perhaps."

Ah, Greeks and their time frames!

"Which is it?" offered Angus, gently.

"I have been away for three days at a wedding in Mani and started this morning."

"So, she might have come by a day or so ago but you weren't here?"

It made no sense. Angus sighed.

The waiter shrugged. "I don't know, my friends. I ask someone else for you?"

"No, it's okay. Can we take the book? Is that all right?"

"Yes, you take it and read on your holiday." Then he marched off to take another order.

"Are you collecting all her books, Bronte?"

"You never know, there may be a message secreted inside them."

Angus laughed heartily. "More crumbs?"

"Perhaps."

"You're going doolally now. Too much sun. You were never good in hot climates."

"I'm improving," I said, but he was right about that fact. My reluctance to come to Greece to help Angus out with his health problems at first was ramped up by my dislike of heat and sunbathing, especially with my colouring – my auburn hair and fair skin – but I had inherited my hazel eyes from Angus and not the pale blue of my mother, or her strawberry blonde hair, so with some persistence I did develop a tan in the end.

"I know you think my Peregrine theory is mad, but what else can all this mean?" I said, waving her book around.

"She goes for dramatic titles, doesn't she? Against the Storm, Fateful Journey," Angus said, sniggering.

I ignored the comment. "The thing is, she wants us to know that she's been here recently. Two books in two places. She knew I'd come looking for her. She'd already pointed me in this direction by showing me those black and white photos."

"But why would she do all that? Unless ..." he said, twisting his hand back and forth beside his forehead. The Greek sign for doolally.

"Be serious now, Angus."

"Oh, I would, Bronte, were seriousness at all required in this strange escapade," he said with a dramatic flourish.

"Maybe it's a cry for help. Eve's had a proper meltdown about the interview, about spilling the beans on the blocky thingy. Perhaps she's hiding out in an apartment somewhere here," I said, looking around the village, thinking maybe she was watching us right at that moment.

"But if Eve wanted you to follow her, with the book crumbs, as you say, why not just tell you where she is and request your company for a girlie rant-fest?"

"That would be too easy, wouldn't it?"

"Exactly. She's a luvvie and prefers to play games. And where will the next book crumb be, and what will it be called: Death on the Bad Mountains?" He sniggered.

"You're taking the piss now."

He nodded. "This is crazy stuff but it's a nice day out, I guess, away from the coalface. Shame about all the driving."

"I get what you're saying. I just have this feeling she's down here somewhere, honestly."

I was like Elpida at that moment, my guts twitching like crazy, and yet nothing felt very logical. As we drove out of Porto Kayio, I suggested we try the third and final place in the line-up of photos: Vathia.

"That's where she might be. That place with all those big high towers. She said it was her favourite place."

"Oh, aye! Vathia's a fantastic place but deserted now, Bronte. No-one lives there, apart from maybe the odd mad

Athenian with a half-finished holiday house who might come in the height of summer for a week. But even that would be pushing it."

"Let's swing by it anyway."

Vathia was a kind of citadel village built in the early 18th century across a high spine of rock to protect inhabitants from marauding pirates and Turks, but mostly from other Maniots intent on mischief. The Maniots in this southern region had always been a lawless, trigger-happy group formed into clans and clustered around fortified villages, like Vathia. They were fiercely territorial and uncompromising. In the past, the area was largely overlooked by the rest of Greece due to its remoteness, cut off by the Taygetos mountains and lack of decent roads. Even the Ottoman Turks, despite a few punitive raids, had no urge to take on these wild Maniots, so unlike the rest of the country, the Mani remained unoccupied during the 400 years of Turkish rule. In the 19th, century the Deep Mani was dominated by formidable and valiant clan chiefs, like Petros Mavromichalis, who gathered 3,000 men and marched them to Kalamata in 1821 to help kick off the Greek War of Independence against the Ottoman Turks.

All of this was easy to understand when we finally reached Vathia. Its slew of impregnable tower houses ranged across the hill like tall ragged teeth. Many of the towers were in a poor state, and several had lost the plot entirely, reduced to rubble with wild trees growing up through fallen masonry. Only a few looked like there had been some attempt at renovation, with fresh repointing and new doors and windows, all firmly shut. There were no signs of life, apart from the wind clawing at old shutters sagging on their hinges.

We parked the car on the deserted road near the village and took the narrow pathway that cut through the settlement. Although it was early afternoon, the height of the towers and the darkness of the old stone seemed to pitch the village into sunset. And it felt colder here.

"Honestly, pet, I can't imagine why Eve Peregrine would even want to come here, hiding out like some doolally Rapunzel," said Angus. "And if she's here, she'd have a car nearby, wouldn't she?"

At the end of the path was a view down to the sea over vast empty tracts of land covered in gorse and olive orchards. The tower at the very end was in reasonable condition, with brown painted shutters and a stout front door. A stone shed leaned up against one side of it, but with no door. It was empty. It was a strange place, where the wind strafed through the towers and moaned lightly. The place had its own raw beauty but all the same I was starting to feel dispirited. Even Zeffy, who had kept up a good pace all day, was walking with little enthusiasm.

"This was obviously a daft idea. She could be hiding out almost anywhere in Greece, couldn't she? Let's head back now," I said.

Angus's face brightened, but I knew the drive home wouldn't delight him much, with all the hairpin bends. It had been a worthwhile expedition for me to see these iconic places so many people had told me about. But when it came to the Peregrine disappearance, it was a folly. My instincts had been shot to pieces. We turned and plodded back along the pathway towards the road, but just before we got there something jagged my attention. I touched Angus on the arm.

"Can you hear an odd noise?"

"No, like what?"

"Oh, I don't know ... It's stopped now, I think." I stood gazing up at the towers we'd left behind. Perhaps it was the sound of the wind again, or branches brushing against the stone towers. I also had that strange sensation you get on the back of your neck when you're being watched.

"There it is again. Very faint but ..."

"What noise?" said Angus, looking impatient.

"I don't know … like … no, that couldn't be."

"What couldn't be," he said, shaking his head and marching ahead of me.

"Nothing," I said, shouting after him. Angus strode ahead to the road, quickly side-stepping an old woman dressed in black, bent over the dusty verge picking wild greens, like the sole survivor of a bombed-out village in a war zone. She was snapping off the greens with a short kitchen knife and piling them neatly into a wicker basket. Perhaps that was the noise I'd heard from the pathway, the constant snip of greenery.

Angus spoke to her and turned to me. "I asked her if there was anyone living here at present and she says no. Not that she knows of, anyway. She lives further down the road. She doesn't go into Vathia itself, she doesn't like the atmosphere. Can't say I do either."

On the roadside I decided to call Peregrine's mobile again, just in case. But I couldn't get a signal. Something to do with the towers perhaps, or a lack of reception in general. We sat in the car and sipped some water from the bottles we brought. There was something about the Mani that seemed to ramp up one's thirst, perhaps no surprise since the word Mani was supposed to have come from an old Greek word meaning a dry and treeless place.

"Let's think about all this for a minute, Angus. We've done the three places in the order Eve described them to me. Whatever order we did them in, I don't think we'd have had a different outcome. There's no book hidden around here to indicate she's been to Vathia. Maybe she skipped it. Maybe she went to Porto Kayio first and then Hades – in a depressed state of mind like, you know, to end it all."

"Now you're going real doolally. We didn't find her though, did we? And why leave a book in the temple? Why not a big note on the altar saying, 'Goodbye cruel world. I'm off to join Cerberus'. Or a trail of her books on the path to the deserted cape lighthouse, where she could have jumped off the cliff."

I laughed. "You're taking the piss again."

"I certainly am. Anyway, there are easier ways to top yourself than blundering around Cape Tainaron."

"But an actress, which is essentially what she is, would want total drama."

"Nah, I don't go for it. Anyway, we can't scour the whole area on the off-chance the crazy Rapunzel is here. Och, I'm weary, let's go."

I felt weary myself but I didn't feel I was done with the Deep Mani yet.

"I don't suppose you could swing by the village of Glika Nera, where that creep Dionysos lives?"

Angus had just started the car. "Why the hell do you want to do that?"

"Just want to see where he lives. What it's all about. Maybe get a feel for why he's harassing foreigners, me in particular."

Angus sighed. "We don't have time, Bronte. It's really out of our way, up a long winding road on the other side of this peninsula. We'll get back very late if we go there. We should get going now."

"Okay, I just thought that while we're down here …"

Angus didn't respond. I lay my head back on the headrest as we accelerated away from the deserted village. Glika Nera had been another daft idea but I doubted we'd come all the way back here in a very long time. But what I'd already learnt from the village Greeks was this: "When people make plans, God laughs."

As we drove towards the coast I turned and looked at Zeffy on the back seat. He was lying on his back, his legs straight up in the air, fast asleep. He looked content. I wondered if it ever crossed his mind how much he was living the life of Riley after his spell of rough sleeping? If anything ever did cross a dog's mind.

The day after our excursion, I left more calls on both Peregrine's home phone and mobile with brief messages asking her to call me, saying we were all worried about her sudden departure. Yet there was no reply. Either she was indulging in some attention-seeking prank, or was more likely holed up in a secret location trying to unblock her creative logjam. Or she'd been kidnapped and murdered by some Dionysos-like thug, given the toxic times we lived in, as everyone kept telling me.

Some days later, Sylvia Rainford phoned me, sounding frantic. Still no contact with Peregrine. She urged me to go to the police. I talked it over with Leonidas and he offered to set up an appointment with his detective friend at Kalamata police station, who would pass on the details if necessary to a uniformed officer for some exploratory checks. It would be better this way, he thought, than trying to explain the situation to one of the more junior constables.

I arranged to meet Leonidas in the old quarter of Kalamata at two o'clock after his morning surgery.

11

Vanishing act

Detective Nikos Vassanopoulos was tall, with wide shoulders and an angular face, dark greying hair and observant green eyes. He wore a scruffy leather jacket and black T-shirt. He gave Leonidas a warm handshake and ushered us to a battered desk piled up with paperwork, files, plenty of rubber stamps and ink pads. The desks were arranged in an L-shape, with old filing cabinets along one wall. One was hanging open and I could see it was stuffed with dog-eared manila folders. Only one other detective was present, sitting nearby and barking down the phone like a constipated walrus. While there were a few ancient-looking computers on desks, I got the feeling that things were still done the old-fashioned way, with plenty of form-filling and rubber-stamping. The detective was smoking, his ashtray overflowing with cigarette butts and a takeaway coffee cup beside it. There were remnants of cake on a cardboard plate crossed by a plastic fork.

Leonidas spoke to the detective in Greek, explaining the apparent disappearance of Eve Peregrine, whose name was fired out at regular intervals like Morse code. The detective scratched out notes, glancing at me now and then with a narrow-eyed stare, as if I were the main suspect in this possible misdemeanour. The detective spoke some English and only questioned me briefly about my relationship with Peregrine. He didn't say much but his eyebrows flickered slightly when I told him I was a journalist.

"I hope you do not scare the tourists away from Greece, Miss McKnight, writing too much about our terrible economic crisis for your British newspapers," he said, with a forced smile.

"No, of course not," I said, giving Leonidas a meaningful look. He smiled faintly, a mere twitch at the side of his mouth.

More chatter in Greek, then the detective turned to me, snapping his notebook shut.

"Miss McKnight, there is probably nothing to worry about here. I am sure your friend will return, but we will do some checks in case an unidentified person has been reported." I was sure he meant unidentified 'body', which was something I didn't want to think about. He shook my hand before we left, a strong finger-bending handshake, then he slapped Leonidas on the back with laddish affection. People were loitering in the corridors, some in uniform. It was noisy, the air was thick with worry and cigarette smoke, and I was glad to be back out on the street again.

After we left the police station, Leonidas drove back to town and parked near his surgery. We had a coffee nearby, but didn't talk much. He seemed a bit thoughtful, as he often was these days.

"How do you know this detective?" I asked, amused at the thought of two people who couldn't have been more different.

"He is married to one of my cousins on my father's side, so really we're related in Greek terms, though I don't see him much."

But it was useful, I had no doubt, having a cop in the family in a country where I was beginning to understand that to do anything quickly and easily you need contacts, something to ease your way in life.

"Thanks for taking me to see him today, but I don't think it will achieve much, do you?"

He shook his head. "Probably not. The worst that will happen is your friend will turn up after a disastrous end, an

103

accident perhaps," he said in the perfunctory way that doctors have in explaining difficult subjects.

I shuddered. He smiled, his dark eyes crinkling at the corners, but there was none of the usual sparkle in this gesture.

"Is there something troubling you today, Leo? You look preoccupied."

He tipped his head slightly to the side and gave me a sweet but searching look.

"I had a difficult morning in the surgery. Same worries as usual. I struggle to help people these days when patients can't get the necessary drugs from the pharmacies when there are shortages. Just this morning I saw a patient suffering from cancer. He has seen his oncologist and needs to continue with a course of chemotherapy and yet he can't source the drugs here in Kalamata now. He will have to go to Athens to source them, and he is tired and sick. Ach! It's tormenting. Every day brings a fresh challenge."

He rubbed his hand over his chin. I tried to imagine what it would be like here, having cancer, and having to schlep about from place to place searching for life-saving drugs. These stories always made me anxious about Angus. I wondered what would happen with his heart condition if he couldn't get hold of his medication.

"Sorry, Bronte. I should spare you these details. It must be depressing for foreigners to see what a mess our country is in at the moment."

"Don't worry. It's nothing I haven't already heard from Angus or seen on TV."

Angus always updated me on the state of the crisis and every night we watched the evening news on the TV when we were home together. He would translate relevant parts to me. I had already begun to learn rudimentary Greek from books Angus had given me, and I had the Greek alphabet under my belt at least. I tried to read the subtitled news headlines that always accompanied most news programmes and only now and then did I recognise a word. Most regularly I saw the word 'thriller' – as in political thriller – in Greek script, which was part of the media lexicon now. I saw footage every night of people demonstrating over political and social issues, but even still, the lack of serious language skills often made me feel I was living in a parallel world from most other people, which seemed wrong. As if I were in most respects immune to everything that others suffered.

Leonidas and I sat in silence for a moment, finishing our coffee. Along with all his other worries, I was sure the visit to Kalamata police station couldn't have lifted his mood much. When I saw him looking so thoughtful, I felt such tenderness towards him.

"If you're free this afternoon, why not come back to the village for a while. We can go out to a taverna later," I said.

"I don't think so, *agapi mou,*" he said, squeezing my hand. "I have a lot of paperwork to do tonight. I am sorry."

"Okay, we'll see each other tomorrow night anyway. Perhaps on Saturday we could go for a drive somewhere or have a swim; just have a nice chill-out time. What do you say?"

He didn't answer at first but glanced at his mobile phones, scrolling emails on one of them. He always carried two: one just for patients, the other was personal.

"Actually, Bronte … I can't come this weekend at all. I have some important family things to attend to," he said, still looking at one of his phones, reading a message.

"Oh, that's such a pity," I said, struggling to mask my disappointment.

He looked up at me, a consoling tilt of his head, his lips pressed gently together. It was the kind of look a parent would use to comfort a child after delivering bad news. And it *was* bad news indeed because I lived for the weekends when he came back to the village. And there had been no weekends I could remember when he hadn't made it back to Marathousa. Before we said goodbye at the café, he hugged me tightly and kissed me. I had the nagging sensation that he hadn't quite told me the truth; that something was wrong but he didn't want to share it – not yet.

"Look, my love. Maybe if I can, I will drive to the village on Sunday afternoon for a few hours, but I won't promise. I will call you though."

He kissed me again and I turned quickly away before he saw the glimmer of tears. A childish overreaction, no doubt, but they were tears of confusion and frustration, reminding me that amid the joy of living a dream life in Greece, notwithstanding the crisis, I was still like a stranger in paradise.

I'd borrowed Angus's Fiat for my trip to Kalamata and walked back to the narrow side street where I'd parked the car, flanked by badly positioned, beaten-up wrecks. On the walk I'd managed to scupper my poor mood somewhat, reminding myself that falling in love with a Greek doctor, pulled in different directions during this crisis, was never going to be easy. I may have been treading water hard but my love for this man was the important thing. And there were small gains in this new, complicated life, I thought, as I got behind the wheel of the Fiat.

I never thought I'd ever be driving in Greece, and not in Angus's old bomb. It had taken weeks of practice to get used to the left-hand drive, the roads, the way Greeks didn't bother with road rules; the way they could drive, drink coffee, text on their phones, all at the same time. Just that morning I had seen a guy on a scooter wearing a regimental uniform, a trombone balanced over his knee as if it were the most natural thing in the world.

As I roared out into the narrow street I thought, well, if I can drive in Greece and stay in one piece, I could conquer any setbacks.

Angus went to Kalamata on the Friday on 'business', as he liked to call it. I knew he often did research for his book at the public library in Aristomenous Street, but I suspected that later he would meet some of his old drinking buddies in the cafes and ouzeries of the city. He'd shown me the ouzeries, a remnant of an older era, that were minimalist, sometimes raucous, male hangouts, in side streets, where shelves were decorated with empty ouzo and wine bottles from decades past and men were hunched over metal tables, moaning about life. There was an exotic aura of the Levant about these places and although I rarely went inside with Angus, I did hope they'd survive the worst of the crisis.

I phoned Eve Peregrine again but still there was no answer. I also called her agent, Rainford, to update her and report that I'd been to the police station and was certain they were keeping Peregrine on their radar. Angus had told me he doubted anything would come of the visit, as the force was reeling from budget cuts and staff shortages during the crisis.

Rainford, however, was still playing the same old scratchy record. "I can't fathom it. It's all so unlike Eve to do this. I can't even contemplate that something terrible has happened. But *something* must have upset her in an extraordinary fashion for her to disappear like this."

I sensed the veiled accusation again, that it was all because of my interview, benign as it was. However, I promised to update Rainford the minute I knew anything. If I thought that would be the end of things for a bit, I was wrong. Peregrine was catapulted right back into my life that afternoon when I got a call from The Daily Messenger. This time it was the news editor.

"We have your feature on Peregrine, and thanks for that. It's fine and we'll run it as and when," said a youngish-sounding Londoner, who spoke fast, gobbling up his words, in a perishing hurry with deadlines, no doubt. I was ready to hang up when he rushed me through another idea, telling me the paper now wanted Peregrine for something quite different. While I listened to him outlining what it was about, I marvelled at how so many people were in such dire need of Peregrine just at a point in her life where she had no intention of being accessible.

This particular piece concerned a Tory MP called Douglas Markham, who'd been prosecuted for sexual assault and had now been convicted and given a six-month jail sentence. As it happened, Peregrine had had a volatile two-year relationship with Markham 15 years earlier. There had been plenty of stories and pictures online about their relationship, which I'd found while researching Peregrine for my first piece, though I'd only glanced at most of them. However, I'd gleaned that Peregrine and Markham were a dazzling power couple in their time, she as a popular TV star, just before she gave up acting for writing. He was a good-looking, ambitious but high-handed backbencher, obviously heading for greater things in politics and finding his niche in recent years as a cabinet minister. Throughout his career, however, Markham, already divorced with one child, was better known for romantic scandals and a lack of personal judgement.

Now he'd have a criminal record to add to his exploits, convicted of sexual assault on a young parliamentary worker, a fact that would trounce his career. I can't say I'd followed his case with much interest since I'd left the UK. I might have, if I'd known the Messenger would one day task me with interviewing Peregrine about the whole sorry business rather than the benign feature on being an expat in crisis-hit Greece.

"We're planning a few spreads on Markham," said the editor, "now he's been sentenced. We want to get in quick with some strong coverage before everyone else does. And how perfect that you live near Peregrine in Greece. So, here's the thing: get her to talk about their fiery life together, what he was like, scandals, sex, drugs, whatever! Everyone remembers them as a pair and the fact there was a very public, acrimonious split. Okay?"

I marvelled at how news editors could brief you with the expectation you will tease out impossibly candid stuff as a matter of course. Even if I could actually find her, I had doubts that the guarded and somewhat flaky Peregrine would spill that many beans. But as if he'd tuned into my silent worries, he added, "Peregrine will talk, don't worry. The publicity won't do any harm at all, especially with a new book coming out soon, yes?"

Yes, yes, but not to the book coming out any time soon.

"Sure. Leave it with me," I said, sounding chipper. How could I not when the fee he quoted was ridiculously generous?

"And we'd like it ASAP, in the next day or so. Thanks."

I gulped. As if!

"If you hook this in nicely," the news editor said, "the Messenger will get you to do more stuff from Greece if you want it. You know, with the crisis and all." Then he hung up.

So, here was a large carrot. The Messenger, despite leaning more to the right than I was comfortable with, was always a paper that freelance journalists gravitated towards because it valued decent reporting and was thorough, and best of all it paid well. It didn't look shabby on your CV either.

I sat at my desk, staring through the window at the crags of the Taygetos. What the hell was I doing though, agreeing to interview a woman I'd just reported missing to the local police? In another few days if Peregrine didn't turn up and the police had no leads, I'd have to contact the British Embassy and hand the problem over to them. I'd be writing a very different kind of news piece then. But if she was still alive and hiding out somewhere, as I hoped she was, I'd have to find her before someone else did.

Angus came back early, looking rosy-cheeked and glassy-eyed, as if he'd had a fair nip of alcohol. I'd cooked pieces of chicken in the oven and made a salad. He sat down at the table to eat and poured himself a glass of beer. I told him about my latest commission.

"You're going to write another piece for that crappy right-wing rag!" was all he said, slicing into a chicken leg.

"Yeah, okay, but it's the biggest-selling quality tabloid in the UK. Who am I to turn up my nose at that?"

"Oh well, work's work, isn't it?" he said with a sour face. I had the impression there wasn't a newspaper left that Angus liked much, apart from one or two Greek ones, but I wasn't about to start a discussion on the rights and wrongs of modern journalism.

"Pity you get this big commission and the subject's just legged it," he said, chortling darkly.

"Yes, trust me!" I said, slugging from a bottle of beer, thinking what a dismal weekend this was going to be. No Leonidas, Peregrine lost, and Angus being his usual cheeky self.

"So, we've got to put our thinking hats on and really find Eve this time."

"We? Och, Bronte," he said, putting down his fork, "we've done all that; followed your hunches down the Mani, in and out of Hades, and everywhere else. What do you suggest now? Oh, I know, let's drive north and go see the Oracle of Delphi. She'll know where the tormented scribe's hanging out."

"No need for that. Elpida's the next best thing – the Oracle of Marathousa, I call her. And maybe she'd be as good as anyone," I said, trying to make light of my misery. But if anyone had seen Peregrine in the vicinity or heard some report about her, it would probably be Elpida.

Angus gave me a squinty look. "I hope you're joking, pet, about finding Peregrine. She could be anywhere in Greece."

110

"I know, I know."

"How soon does the Daily Mess want this piece?"

"Soon as possible."

He shook his head. "Is all this angst really worth the money? If you're short, I'll give you some."

"It's not just about the money, Angus. I want to make a success of freelancing. I didn't give up mainstream journalism in Scotland to sit in Greece swinging worry beads around and working on a suntan."

He smirked. "Sounds good to me. Look, you can try to find this damn woman but if you can't, just tell The Mess. You can't comb a brick after all."

"Is that one of your village sayings?"

"You get my drift. I mean, have you got any idea where to start, or are you just going to wing this completely?"

"Wing it, yes."

He drained the beer bottle and went to the fridge for another. "Why don't I call the cleaning woman on her mobile and see if she's heard anything. That's a start, eh?"

"Good thinking. Any other good ideas? Happy to hear them."

"Not at present, but I've got something else to talk to you about, Bronte," he said, not looking at me and absently twisting the base of his beer bottle on the table.

"If it's not urgent, keep hold of it. I've got to concentrate on this for now."

"It's not urgent, but it could be," he said, glancing up at me.

"About your health?"

"No, something else."

"Okay, sounds ominous, but can we talk later?"

He nodded and dialled a number on his phone. He spoke in Greek, rolling his eyes at me before hanging up.

"The cleaning woman knows nothing. She's as mystified as everyone else."

After dinner, my stomach was churning with worry. I sat at my desk and flipped to a fresh page in my notebook. I started planning who I could phone, even though I'd run out of ideas. I began with Sylvia Rainford, to tease out the name of any contact Peregrine might have in Greece, to help track her down. It drew a blank. While I'd avoided any mention of Markham, it was Rainford who brought up the subject.

"Eve and Markham were quite an item once, though you'll probably know that of course," she said. "It might seem a long shot but I'm beginning to think that Eve has run off somewhere to avoid talking about it. I guess that would make some sense. She'd have known his sentencing was coming up and would expect the press to hound her for comments, given the pair's past relationship. And I've had calls about it already; papers requesting interviews with Eve."

"Really?" I replied. "But why would Eve do a runner? She's off the radar in Greece anyway. Hardly anyone knows her exact location and it's fairly remote, I can assure you. No-one will have her mobile number, except you and a few other trusted people. I can't see papers sending reporters out for this. It's not *that* big a story, is it?" I felt guilty about my own commission. But needs must. "What are you telling the journalists who call?" I asked her.

"Just that Eve's in Greece but out of contact at the moment. Sounds thin, but what else can I say? Can't tell them the truth, can I? Not yet. Not unless."

Rainford didn't finish the sentence but I knew too well what she was thinking.

"Eve should have contacted me by now, at least for some advice on how to handle the Markham sentencing. It's all so ODD!" she moaned.

After that, I decided to call Elpida at the *kafeneio*. That's how much faith I had in her gut instincts and sleuthing abilities. Though she'd never met the 'famous hermit', as she put it, who lived down the hill, she'd heard of her at least and promised to keep her ear to the ground in case one of her customers mentioned anything that could be significant. It was a mighty long shot, but that was the point I was at. I didn't expect to find Peregrine until she was ready to be found and I'd probably have to make that call to the Messenger in the next few days to fess up.

Angus was pecking at his keyboard when I went downstairs to shower. I didn't disturb him but went back to my room to read for a while, propped up against my pillow, with Zeffy lying at the bottom of the bed. He yawned three or four times, making a funny squeaking noise with it, as if his jaw was rusty. It made me laugh. First laugh I'd had all day. A short while later, Angus knocked on the door. He came in slowly and sat on the edge of the bed.

"I thought Zeffy wasn't allowed to sleep on beds," he grumbled.

"I never said that, did I? Anyway, it's comforting having him nearby. I know if he hears anything strange in the night, he'll wake immediately and go to check it out. That's why I always leave the door ajar now."

"He's loyal at least, and that counts for something," Angus said, looking thoughtful, running a hand through his hair. I noticed his hair was getting long again, as if he were gearing up for another ponytail like the one he'd worn when I first came to Greece and which Polly had persuaded him to cut. He was lucky to have so few grey hairs, despite his age, and his hair was thick and healthy, one of his best features, along with his hazel eyes. For a man in his early 70s I thought him to be quite handsome.

"Tell me now about the other thing you mentioned."

He chewed on his bottom lip. "I don't want to add to your woes, but I can't keep it to myself, sorry."

"Okay, tell me," I said, putting down my book, with a sense of foreboding. Even Zeffy lifted his head up and gave Angus a bug-eyed stare.

"Today I went to see an old mate in a bar on Aristomenous Street." This location had the city's central square, lined with cafes and bars, and was the best place to people-watch. "We had a table outside under the awning. While we were there, I saw Leonidas walking by with someone."

"Who?"

Angus looked straight at me. "You won't believe it. It was Phaedra."

"Phaedra! Are you sure?"

"Yeah, I'm sure. Polly pointed her out to me once in Kalamata. Sexy thing with long black hair."

Phaedra was the ex-girlfriend of Leonidas, now living in England.

"Well, it's probably nothing," I said. "She always comes back here about a week before Greek Easter to see her family. Polly told me that once."

"Well, perhaps, but that's not the whole story. It's just that … see …. he had his arm around her back, a kind of comforting gesture, I thought. They were so engrossed, Leo didn't see me sitting there. Anyway, they were walking very slowly, so much so I even managed a picture of them," he said, pulling his mobile out of his pocket.

I was surprised. Angus was someone who hated using a mobile phone when I first came to Greece. He'd rather have used a homing pigeon. For him to bother taking a picture of Phaedra – well, it had to be bad. My stomach was feeling queasy.

"Here it is," he said, turning the screen towards me. It was a slightly hazy shot but there was no mistaking that it was Phaedra turned side-on to Leonidas, gazing into his eyes. A tender moment, you could call it, that didn't delight me.

"Okay, so she's back and they meet up for some reason. They were together for a while. No big deal perhaps," I said, though I didn't believe that.

"Yeah, sure. Maybe. But you told me yesterday Leo said he couldn't come this weekend because he had family stuff to do, right?"

I nodded. How could I have forgotten?

"Seems to me that it wasn't family stuff after all and Phaedra was the real reason."

"It does look that way, doesn't it?" I said, putting my book on the bedside table and slipping down the bed a bit. Zeffy was fast asleep now. I stared at the ceiling, feeling mortally tired myself.

"I don't know what to say, pet. Looks a bit off, doesn't it? I mean, did he mention he was going to see her when she came back?"

"No. But there will be an explanation for them being together. Leo's a decent guy, you know that."

"Yes, I do, and I like Leo a lot, so just ask him what's going on and …."

He didn't finish the sentence but squeezed the top of my bent knee. I remembered vividly then that when I was a kid and I'd had an upset he always came and sat on the side of the bed and tweaked my knee like that. It was his paternalistic way of saying everything would be fine. But would it?

"Okay, Angus. We'll talk about it in the morning. I don't know what's going on but the worst-case scenario is that she's maybe angling to come back to Greece, because …"

"She wants him back, right? And why not? He's a great catch and anyway … it was her silly fault legging it to England in the first place."

"Or maybe he wants *her* back." I hadn't wanted to go that far yet but the thought had bubbled up and I couldn't suppress it. And I remembered how moody he'd been the previous day, after we'd been to the police station.

"You've got to confront him, Bronte, otherwise I will."

I smiled. "Thanks for your loyalty. Appreciate it."

He patted my knee again and got up, still looking thoughtful.

"Sleep well, if you can. Sorry to bring you grief, but I thought it should be said."

"Night-night," I said, as he turned to go to bed.

I lay awake a long while thinking about Phaedra, a problem I didn't need right now. Leonidas had been going out with Phaedra when I first met him and they had been close to an engagement. But with the crisis beginning in Greece and the expectation that things would get bad in this country for everyone, they had hatched a plan to move to Britain, like thousands of other Greek professionals. Phaedra was to organise a job first in England. As a dentist, with a good practice in Kalamata, she had little trouble in scoring a position in a thriving practice in Brighton. Leonidas had applied for jobs as a GP in health centres in the same area, and one or two were very interested.

He was to follow a year or so later, as he had much to finalise in Greece, not least the fact that he had a nine-year-old son, Adonis, from a former marriage to a local actress, now based in Athens. With his current work schedule, he only managed a quick trip to Athens every couple of months, but the issue of not seeing his son much at all if he moved to England had put a dampener on the plan. Then he met me and that completely scuppered it. Phaedra stayed in England and Leonidas confirmed his commitment to Greece.

I never feared the love affair with Phaedra would fire up again. Until today, I had never doubted his loyalty. He was not a deceitful man or a philanderer. But perhaps the old ties to Phaedra, the family connections, the cultural similarities he once told me had drawn them together were stronger than they both thought. And the reality was that I still knew so little about this man – as much as I loved him. I understood so little of life and love in Greece. I would need to bone up on all these things – and soon.

I finally managed to fall asleep in the early hours of the morning but woke abruptly at seven with a vivid thought that I couldn't shift. Had I dreamt it? And it was nothing to do with Leonidas and Phaedra. I was thinking of Eve Peregrine. And Vathia. Something had been nagging at me like a stone in a shoe since we'd gone to the village: the faint noise I'd heard when we were walking back along the pathway to the car. I couldn't quite grasp it – until now.

12
Working hard for the Mani

I leapt out of bed on Saturday morning and went to Angus's room, shaking him gently awake. He turned a bleary face towards me and pulled the sheet over his head.

"Sorry to wake you," I said. He groaned. "We've got to drive back down to Vathia, Angus. I've worked it out. Peregrine's definitely hiding out in one of those towers."

He pulled the sheet away from his face. "Jeezy peeps!" he said, using a funny Scottish exclamation. "You've really lost it!"

He shut his eyes again. I went to the kitchen and made some coffee, bringing two mugs back to his room and sitting down on his bed. He pulled up his pillows against the headboard and hauled himself into a slumping position, rubbing his eyes. Poor man, right that minute he looked his age.

"Please explain," he said, slurping his coffee and grimacing.

"Remember I told you at Vathia I'd heard a peculiar noise I couldn't quite fathom? I finally realised what it was: the faint tapping sound of an old-fashioned manual typewriter. Someone was up in one of those Maniot towers, typing away on one. I'm sure of it."

He gave me a vague, tired look. "I don't remember hearing a typewriter."

"It wasn't going on continually, that's the thing, but I should have picked it up straight away. It's just sometimes, you know, how you don't recognise a particular noise because the context's all wrong. It's not every day you hear an old typewriter, especially not in a deserted village on a Greek hillside."

"So you think it was Peregrine in one of the towers?"

"Exactly!"

"That's a stretch, Bronte."

"Think about it. Those black and white prints she was so keen to show me; the books left in particular places. She's down there all right and she's in Vathia. The day we were there, I think she was in that last tower, the one with the nice shutters. She was trying to work on that damned book and get it finished. What else could it be?"

"What, on an old manual typewriter?" He leaned into his pillow and laughed.

"Why not? It looked like most of the towers had no electricity. She'd have to use a manual."

He shrugged. "But why hide away in Vathia, of all places? She could have stayed at home. Home is pretty chic and remote enough, isn't it?"

I told him about the agent's theory that Peregrine wanted to leg it so she wouldn't have to play ball with the press over Markham.

"Well, she won't want to play with you either, even *if* she started out leaving you clues – books, crumbs, whatever – for some other daft reason. This is different now. She absolutely won't want to talk to you now."

I chewed at my lower lip. "I agree, but we still have to get down there and flush her out. I have to show willing for this interview. That's how it works in newspapers. If she won't talk, fine. At least I'll have tried. Look, I can go myself if you're tired. About time I took on a bigger driving challenge. Zeffy can come with me."

"Is he going to navigate?"

I laughed at the thought of Zeffy in the front seat with the road map.

"I know the way now."

"It's a long drive and the roads are tortuous in places. You saw that last time."

"I'll be all right."

He stared at the ceiling. "Oh Jeez! ... Okay, I'll come. I mean, I dragged you up a mountain last year when we went on that wild goose chase to find Kieran."

"That's true," I said, smiling with relief that I didn't have to do the drive myself.

"But if she's not in one of those blasted towers, that's it, we're heading straight back, okay?"

"Okay. It's a deal. And thanks," I said, leaning over and kissing him on the forehead.

We were ready in half an hour, Zeffy fizzing with joy for another drive. He was good company and a great guard dog, should we need him to be. We packed the car again with Zeffy's bed on the back seat and a few provisions, then drove off. As we came level with Villa Ambelia, Angus slowed the car a bit. Thekla was just coming out of the front door. She stood on the steps watching us, her big blonded hair swaying in the wind. I fancied she had a sly look on her face and it occurred to me that she would know about Phaedra coming back. She knew everything! She probably even approved of the meet-up with Leonidas. Egged them on, perhaps. My thoughts were spiralling downwards when Angus remarked, "I don't know what it is, but that witch always gives me the heebie-jeebies."

He gunned the car, as much as a battered Fiat can be, and we drove off without a nod or a wave to Thekla. As soon as we were on the road south, I put the issue about Leonidas out of my mind. There was time enough to fester over it and right now I had to sort out Eve Peregrine.

When we finally arrived at Vathia and parked, I noticed there was only one other car around. It had German number plates and we assumed there would be a few tourists perhaps picking their way around the ghost village today, yet we saw no-one as we trailed along the main path again, Zeffy walking behind us, sniffing the village air.

At the wooden door of the last tall tower, we stopped a moment. There it was again, the sound of the typewriter, louder this time, with a window upstairs apparently open, the shutters pinned back against the wall. It wasn't a manic, in-full-flow-clickety-clack typing but a slower pecking sound. The muse was sluggish. I looked at Angus. He winked.

"It's got to be her," I whispered.

The door had a brass knocker of a clenched hand and a small spy window above it with a wrought iron grille in front of the glass. I rapped the knocker a couple of times. The typing stopped. A minute or so later, the small window opened and a face peered out through the grille. The wisps of strawberry blonde hair were unmistakeable.

"Oh," a voice said and then the heavy wooden door creaked open.

Eve Peregrine stood before us, dressed in baggy trousers and a T-shirt. Her hair was scraped back, twisted and pinned with a tortoiseshell clasp on top, the ends sticking up a bit like Zeffy's cockatoo crest, and fanning out chaotically.

"Well, I'm surprised," she said with a petulant expression, cross perhaps at the intrusion. Then she glanced towards Angus.

"My father and driver." He dipped his head, flippantly.

"I never expected to see you two back again. You better come in," she said, turning quickly inside.

"Again?" I mouthed at Angus. His eyebrows flipped up.

"You mean you saw us down here the other day?"

"Yes, from a top-floor window," she tittered a bit now. "Sorry, but I just wasn't in the mood for company then." She wheeled around just as Angus was pulling a massive face. I nudged him with my elbow.

"You could have saved us this drive today, if you'd called out," I grizzled.

She offered a shrug of mock repentance. "Come in then and I'll make you coffee."

She glanced at Zeffy. "Must he come too?"

"Yes," I said in a way that brooked no opposition.

The dog sloped inside, his ears low and his cockatoo crest flopping. The tower was narrow and quite dark and seemed to have a few levels. There was a small kitchen on the ground floor where she led us, offering some rattan chairs around a wooden table. There were a few candles on it and on the window sills. Zeffy sniffed at the stone wall near the table and slumped against it with a dismal air.

"There's no electricity here, I'm afraid."

"How do you manage?" I asked her, wondering what the fascination was for this lonely outpost stuck in another century.

"It's absolutely fine. I don't need electricity that much. I do some basic cooking on the *petrogazi* here," she said, filling a small saucepan with water and placing it on one of the rings of the small metal cooker standing on a work top, a rubber tube connecting it to a gas bottle.

"Anyway, this is a good place to write. It's very secure and quiet. These tower houses were impenetrable, and still are, except when it comes to curious journalists." She laughed but there was scant humour in her eyes. She turned and took down three mugs from a shelf that had a frill tacked along the front of it, such as you might see in replicas of old kitchens in folk museums. It couldn't have been further from her gleaming white villa. She prepared the coffees. Angus sat quietly, saying nothing, though I could tell from his eyes he was just as bemused as I was, meeting this one-time TV star in this peculiar setting.

"If you don't mind me asking, Eve, why the hell did you disappear like that? Your agent has been frantic."

"Oh, what a fuss!" she said with a sigh, observing me over the top of her coffee mug as she sipped.

I bristled slightly. "Well ... your agent said you'd never gone off the radar before and she thought something might have happened to you. So did we. We even went back to your house, talked to your cleaner. You told her nothing."

She looked surprised. "Why should I? Sophia knows what to do. I don't need to be there all the time. This is Greece. We have longer reins here, remember," she said with a faint sneer.

Angus chortled slightly at the 'Greece' comment. It was something they might agree on. I guessed that Eve was also someone who didn't like to follow rules, which might explain her decision to move part-time to Greece, the place that abhors most rules.

"Did you not think to tell *anyone* where you were going?"

"Obviously not," she snapped. I noticed her eyes were red-tinged and tired. Too much typing?

"It might have helped. Your agent contacted me a few times and wanted to involve the police, and I admit it was starting to look like a good idea."

"And did you?"

"Yes, a detective at Kalamata police station, in case you'd come to some kind of harm."

She groaned. "Oh dear!"

I could sense Angus squirming in the chair next to me. "If I can just add, Miss Peregrine, that Bronte cared about your welfare. She was trying to do the right thing," he said firmly.

"Of course, I appreciate everyone has worried about me, but I do hope it doesn't mean I'll be called into the cop shop to explain myself."

Angus sniggered. "I wouldn't think so. The cops don't do much in the Mani. They think we're all cowboys here and they won't waste their time trying to find you. Trust me on that!"

"Charming!" she drawled.

Angus shrugged.

"Honestly, I haven't disappeared, as you put it. Every time I come to Greece I go off on little jaunts. My agent knows that."

"Sorry, but that's not the impression I got," I said.

"Well, next time Julia calls, could you perhaps tell her I'm having a little holiday down here, but don't be specific. I'll call her when I can. There's usually no phone signal up here. But, honestly, can't a woman disappear for a while without other people causing an uproar?"

Angus and I looked at each other, stunned, that it was we who were made to feel inconsiderate, instead of the other way around. I had a sense then, as I had on our first meeting, that beneath the charming, careful exterior, Eve Peregrine was a self-absorbed little minx. And while I quite liked her, or at least had after our interview, when she relaxed and we'd shared a few wines, I suddenly had little sympathy for her, or her writer's constipation.

"Tell me one thing, Bronte. I'm curious. Why did you think to come *here* of all places looking for me – twice?"

"Don't you remember how you showed me the black and white prints in your house and explained them? How you raved about the Mesa Mani: Cape Tainaron, Porto Kayio, this place? I assumed you might be down here somewhere."

"I must say I'm impressed you took so much notice of my décor, the prints etcetera, and I don't mean that to be as sarcastic as it sounds." She smiled, showing her straight white teeth and small dimples at the sides of her lips.

"I really thought you were leaving me clues, if you like, before you disappeared, so we'd know where you were."

"That's bizarre! Why would I do that?" she said, smoothing a wisp of hair behind her ear.

"No idea, but it seemed as if you left a few here and there."

"Like what?" she said, her eyes saucer-like with curiosity.

I glanced at Angus. He looked puzzled, like someone lost in a maze with no idea where the exit was. I was beginning to feel the same.

"Well … you left one of your books at the temple of Poseidon, on the old altar."

She laughed. "Ah, I can see how you may have thought that was a clue, and I had been there recently. But I left the book there as a votive offering to the god Poseidon, thinking he might work a little magic with my latest opus."

Votive offering! I glanced at Angus. He had a tense, funny look, like someone trying to hold back an outburst of giggling. I didn't have the heart to tell her I'd lifted the book and it was on my 'to be read' pile. She had no chance with old Poseidon.

"And you left another book with the waiter at a taverna in Porto Kayio."

"Ah, well that's easy to explain. I go there a lot and I leave old books of mine on their bookcase. Everyone does – you know, for other tourists to read. It helps spread the word, too."

"So you weren't leaving us clues?" I said, feeling a bit ridiculous now.

"No, I don't believe I was, but it's an intriguing idea. Unless I was doing it unconsciously. I can see it in a plot sometime though. But full marks to you, Bronte, for working out I was in Vathia at least," she said.

"As well as the 'clues', I also heard the typewriter noise the first time we were here, though unfortunately I didn't realise exactly what it was until we were back home. But it confirmed the fact you were here."

"Bronte's not a journalist for nothing," said Angus, with a proprietorial lift of his chin that I found endearing.

"Indeed," Peregrine said, giving Angus a sobering look. "This is all very interesting, but I didn't want to be found at all. I was looking for some solitude so I could get on with my novel. The thing is with this tower, in this remote part of the Mani, there's no landline phone, no wifi, and no mobile phone reception. I have to use a manual typewriter, that's true, but it's like another world here. Total isolation. It's bliss. I don't get harangued by my publisher or agent. Or anyone …. no offence, Bronte. And normally my agent doesn't get this hysterical when I go off on a little trip. I don't know what's got into her."

But we all knew.

"So how *is* the novel going?"

"Oh … coming along just fine," she said, her eyes flickering sideways. I knew she was lying.

"I'm sorry we're disturbing you then. But there's something else I wanted to talk to you about. It's a story for the London Daily Messenger again, something different."

She took a while to respond. Then her lips went lemony. "So my welfare wasn't the only motivation for this dash down the Mani?"

"Yes, it was, the first time we were here."

She gave me a long, searching look and finished the rest of her coffee before replying, "Why do I have the feeling, Bronte, you're probably here because of Douglas Markham, now he's been sentenced. Am I right?"

"Yes. But how did you know that's just happened? No internet, right?"

"I do have to go out occasionally to buy food. And I was in a café the other day, taking a break from writing and using their wifi, and I read a news report about Markham's sentencing."

"Look, you can say no if you like but the Messenger just wanted a few quotes from you about Markham for a feature they're running. That's if you feel like talking." And I imagined she didn't.

She was playing with her rings, twisting them about.

"Six months in prison," she said, without looking up. "So it will be open slather with stories for a while."

"I imagine, yes. People have certain expectations of politicians and it's only right to let the public know what kind of man he really is. That's where you come in."

"Oh yes, public interest and all that. How worthy!" she said sarcastically. More ring fiddling and silence.

My eyes flicked towards Angus. One of his eyebrows twitched almost imperceptibly but it was amazing to me how I could read it exactly. I don't know how he mastered that subtle brow-comment but I knew what he was thinking at that moment, just as I was. *She's about to bottle out.*

But then she surprised both of us.

"Well, since you've chased me all about the Mani, I suppose I can give you something. If I don't talk to you, someone else will try to corner me anyway," she grizzled. "Let's go up to the sitting room, it's more comfortable, and get this done as quickly as we can."

She took the coffee cups to the sink and while her back was turned Angus jerked his thumb towards the door.

"If you don't mind, Bronte," said Angus, "I'll let you both have some time to yourselves. I'll take the dog and explore for a bit round here. What if I come back in say ... an hour, that should ..."?

Peregrine cut him off. "Yes, more than enough time."

Angus got up and Zeffy bolted for the door ahead of him. I sensed he hadn't liked the tower's atmosphere and had sat by the wall with a sulky face. After the pair had gone, Peregrine led the way up the first of the series of steep wooden staircases that connected four floors. They were no more than stout wooden ladders with broad 'treads', set close to the stonework, with thin wooden handrails attached to the wall.

The two floors above were bedrooms, with the sitting room at the top, a minimalist but a pleasant space with Ottoman-style boxed-in seating covered in long padded cushions and more embroidered cushions for backrests. The views from the small windows were stunning, right down to the gulf over the olive groves.

There was a small wooden table wedged in front of one window. The manual typewriter was there, with a sheath of plain paper beside it. I glanced quickly at the page in the typewriter and saw nothing but a few short paragraphs at the top. Not a great output, I thought. When I recalled the sound of her typing, it now seemed fetching: the lonely writer in her tower fighting with a damnable block, distracted by an award-winning view. And a Maniot tower at that, the kind of stronghold where rebel householders a few centuries ago could scope out interlopers for miles around and then either shoot them or toss a vat of boiling oil over their heads when they arrived. I imagined in the past week or so, Peregrine must have been mindful of the village's violent struggles, though I got the sense that in this room there was more writerly hysteria rather than history going on.

"I can see the appeal of the tower. It's rather, em ..."

"Monastic?" she offered.

"You could say that."

"How did you find it?"

"The landlord lives in Athens. He's a lawyer. He also has a house in London, which is how I know him. He comes to Vathia maybe once a year. Rents it out sometimes. He rents it out to me whenever I want it. I collect a key from a friend down by the coast. I leave money for him. It's all very easy. I never tell anyone I'm here. It's my secret tower."

I smiled as I recalled Angus's earlier reference to Rapunzel. It suited her perfectly. But I still sensed there was a bit more to all this than she was letting on.

"So, let's talk about Markham," she said, reaching up and unpinning her hair, letting it dangle around her shoulders; charmingly messy. She seemed more relaxed now. "You thought I'd spit the dummy over an interview on Markham ... is that right?

"Not really," I lied. I opened my notebook.

"Well, I'm not thrilled exactly to be talking about him, but since you've come all the way down here ... I don't want to be churlish. As for Markham, I don't care a fig about him and I don't owe *him* any favours at all. He's got exactly what he deserves. So, what do you want to know?"

"Tell me what he's really like. And did you ever think he was capable of sexual assault?"

She sniffed a little when she said, "I'm afraid that Douglas has always had a problem with women. He's a danger to women in every way, actually. He was devastatingly handsome when I first met him, when he was a young backbencher in politics. He was very ambitious, driven, conceited, all that. We had a serious relationship for about two years. That was all. He'd just come out of a difficult marriage and I was single and I've never married, as you will know. We were quite the glamorous couple of our day; he a politician and I a successful actress. There were always photos of us in the papers, magazines, at various events. It was all quite thrilling. And we were in love. Well I was, at least. You could never be sure with Douglas because while he seemed ardent, he still managed to squeeze in a few affairs. It never came out till later.

"But the truth is, deep down, I never really trusted him. If an attractive woman roamed into his sphere, he couldn't keep his hands to himself, so the current mess he's in is no surprise to me. What surprises me is that for someone as ambitious as he is, and smart, he'd let these urges ruin his life. It's almost like a sex addiction. And he was good in bed, as you might imagine – virile, athletic," she said, with a lascivious glimmer in her eyes. "He may even have been up to much more than everyone realises. Back then, it was easier for sexual predators to cover their tracks, and women were less forthright than now."

I scribbled away. This was better than I'd hoped for. It occurred to me that meeting Markham must have been serendipitous for someone who secretly yearned to be a novelist one day. He must have provided a rich seam of discord and character flaws for her to plunder, not to mention the steamy sex. I was sure most of the male characters in her novels were a colourful pastiche of him.

"I read all the stuff about the sexual assault on the young parliamentary worker. Okay, it wasn't actually rape but it was close enough; a lot of shabby stuff, you know, pushing her around, groping her breasts, a hand up the skirt, all that, on more than one occasion, it appears. It's pitiful for someone of his intellect. I think he really needs help with this and he needs to sort out his drinking as well. He always drank too much, and one thing leads to another. And I believe the drink problem has only got worse."

She stopped a moment, leaning back into the cushions. Her cheeks had coloured slightly and I had the strong impression it was from the unexpected pleasure at being about to talk about the virile bad boy of her younger life and to get even with him at the same time, as their relationship had allegedly ended with great acrimony. Without much prompting she continued on for another 10 minutes or so, talking about some of his more memorable indiscretions, some of which had not been exposed before. All in all, I had more than enough material. I glanced at my watch. Angus would be back soon.

"Thanks for talking about this, Eve, and sorry for intruding on your …"

"Creative endeavours," she cut in, with a strangely sardonic smile, which only confirmed there was little flowing out of the typewriter on the table.

"Oh well. You're a fellow Grecophile and neighbour. What can I do?" she said with a smile that finally seemed warm. "Let's wait downstairs for your father. We'll need time anyway to negotiate the ladders."

I noticed on the wall of the sitting room another black and white picture, but this time it seemed to be the tower in a former crumbling state, with holes in the walls and shutters hanging off at jaunty angles.

"That's how it looked before Konstantinos renovated it about 10 years ago. It's an old family property. Wonderful to inherit this, isn't it?"

I nodded and thought that inheriting such a monolith of history would be great – but not all the torment that went with it. On the wall there was also an old rifle, which Peregrine told me dated from the 1820s, the period of the Greek War of Independence.

"Konstantinos found this behind one of the walls when he was renovating, along with a cache of weapons. The Maniots were always fighting," she said, laughing.

While we waited in the kitchen for Angus to return, chatting about nothing in particular, I warmed to her a tiny bit more despite the fuss she'd caused over her 'disappearance', which she denied was any kind of a faff. "Sometimes the world needs to cut you some slack. That's all I can say", was her defence. I did feel she could have been more contrite about worrying everyone, especially her agent. Perhaps she didn't do contrition but I couldn't leave without a dig at her least favourite subject.

I waited until her back was turned and she was tidying the kitchen.

"So, any idea yet when your book might now be finished?"

A few heartbeats of silence and then she said, addressing the wall, "No, Bronte. And, really, I hate it when people keep asking. It will be finished when it's finished." Then she turned and gave me a dazzling smile. A top performance.

Angus rapped on the front door and I was keen to leave now. She said goodbye as she saw me out and the heavy door boomed behind me.

As Angus and I trudged along the pathway back to the car, I made him stop for a few moments just to see if the typewriter noise would start up again, but there was nothing, only the noise of wind fingering shutters and loose doors.

"So, did she spill any beans?"

"Yes! Good stuff, actually; some cracking quotes. So, mission accomplished."

"Was she nippy about it though?"

"Not really. The only thing that makes her nippy is any mention of that damned book. She's been holed up in that tower and the book's still in a rut."

"Maybe it's not about the book. Maybe it's some other personal U-bend she's stuck in," Angus said.

"Could be, and the disappearing trick wasn't a call for help after all, was it?" I said, laughing. "So much for my mad theory about her leaving signs all over the place. And contrary to what her agent said, she wasn't running away from having to talk about Douglas Markham. Sheesh, she seemed to be gagging to talk about him!"

"Revenge is sweet, pet," Angus said.

I nodded in agreement.

At least some of my other outlandish theories had been ground to dust: her being kidnapped, murdered, or abducted by aliens. Finding her had been a good result though. Depending on how long she hid out in the tower, I'd probably not see her again before she returned to London.

But Eve Peregrine and I were fated to be stuck together for a while, like the honeyed layers in a Greek baklava sweet, the one with the crushed nuts. Oh yes, there would be nuts!

13

Sweet waters run deep

"There's one thing I wanted to ask Eve and forgot. How does she get around here when there's no car parked nearby and it's miles to the sea?" I said as Angus drove away from Vathia.

"I know," he said with a wink. "The lean-to shed beside the tower? I explored a bit when I left you two, and behind the shed, guess what, she's got a very nice red scooter parked there. She must have driven it down from her villa, or she's parked her car by the coast and maybe hires the scooter. All a bit crazy, but everything is a bit doolally with her, isn't it?"

"You didn't like her, did you?"

"Well, she's good-looking and glamorous, like she was on the telly. Great to meet a TV star and all that, but she's a bit self-absorbed for my liking, and tense. Jeez! She's as tense as a sack full of overwound clocks."

I laughed. Angus had a skewed slant on life but he amused me when I always needed it. "You're right there. And she's certainly had a few wild strops with journalists over the years, so I'm dead lucky, I guess."

We lapsed into weary silence for a while. Zeffy was sleeping on the back seat. His legs were twitching. Dreaming of some spirited flight from trouble? From the creep? And that's when I thought about the village of Glika Nera again.

"You know how last time we were here, I wanted you to go to Glika Nera to scope out Dionysos the creep ?"

"Don't tell me you want to go there."

"Can we? We've got the whole afternoon."

He sighed. "Okay, but let's not hang around too long. I don't like the sound of the place, or the creep either."

Zeffy had suddenly woken and was sitting bolt upright, watching me with his pretty brown eyes. I felt sure he knew what 'creep' was by now. I'd said it often enough.

Glika Nera (Sweet Waters) was a small village on the right-hand side of the peninsula, heading north. It had an old Byzantine church in the square but otherwise not much else that was memorable. Outside a *kafeneio* two old guys were drinking ouzo and grizzling over something. Clearly location was everything here, as it was near the sea and protected on one side by a high promontory covered in olive trees.

We parked the car near a grocery store, where we bought some small bottles of water, and Angus suggested we walk down to the seashore with Zeffy. I hadn't thought about actually walking around the place and at first it was pleasant, but after a while I felt nervous.

"What if Dionysos is actually here and he sees us? Foreigners in his miserable patch. It might ramp up his grudge," I said.

"If we see him, I can ask him why he keeps stirring up trouble in Marathousa."

"You're kidding, right?"

Angus didn't answer. I hoped he was joking. We trailed down a narrow street past a row of houses in a poor state. A radio somewhere played a mournful wail of a song like an old woman keening. A couple were bickering, a baby crying fitfully, the smell of roasting chicken filled the air. On the street a bone-thin black dog nosed an empty food carton, looked up and then vanished over a low wall. At the end of the street on the corner was a stone chapel overhung with trees. A whitewashed perimeter wall had graffiti scrawled on it. Angus told me it had "Ellines Patriotes Enomeni" painted at the top with its logo and a line that Angus translated: 'Greece for Greeks only'.

"Well, this is obviously the place that sired your creep, and plenty more of them. They will blame all Greece's current problems on incomers. Typical of the extreme right," said Angus.

Also taped to the wall was something that looked like a small flyer with EPE along the top and underneath the word *Oxi* (No) in bold type and the lines that Angus translated as: 'No to austerity, no to poverty, no to the sell-out of our homeland'.

"That looks like an old election flyer," said Angus. "I seem to remember it was pinned up around the Mani last year during the general election. The party has a clutch of MPs in parliament now. Absolutely outrageous."

When we came to the beach, we found it deserted, with a few houses along the narrow road in front. Zeffy wanted to swim but we kept him on the lead. The sea was clear and very blue and obviously earned the village its name, but everything else was jaded. Just as we were about to turn and leave, a man came rushing out of a small white house towards a car. When he saw us, he stopped and glowered, narrowing his eyes at the dog. Zeffy responded with a low growl. The man yammered in Greek and Angus replied. They had a short exchange. I heard the man use the word *xenoi*, foreigners. I knew that word by now. Then he jumped in the old banger, slamming its door, and drove off, watching us in the rear-view mirror, from which a set of worry beads jangled.

"What was that all about?"

Angus shook his head. "He wanted to know if we were lost. Asked if we were foreigners. You probably got that bit. I said, 'Yes, is that a problem?' He didn't answer, just gave me that stare. Visit's over. Short but hardly sweet, like the water."

"I can't believe you provoked him like that, Angus. He could have got really nasty."

Angus just shrugged. Once we were back in the car, he drove fast out of the place. But as we slowed down near the intersection for the main road, we saw another *kafeneio* we hadn't taken much notice of the first time. It was on its own, with a derelict building hunched against it on one side. There were a few metal tables outside under a sun-faded awning. I was shocked to see Dionysos sitting at one of the tables, drinking and smoking, playing the board game *tavli*. Angus glanced at the men but didn't know Dionysos was one of them because he'd never seen him. But I recognised him straight away: the long greasy hair, the malevolent black eyes. He looked up and saw me. I flinched. Zeffy saw him too and started to bark at the thug who'd wounded his head.

"What's Zeffy barking at?" asked Angus.

"Nothing, let's go."

When we were well on the road north, I told Angus I'd seen Dionysos at the last *kafeneio* with a few cronies.

"You should have told me."

"After your exchange with that other guy at the beach I thought you'd jump out of the car and give the creep a right bollocking. That wouldn't have helped."

"Nah. I just wanted to see what he looked like for future reference. I'd rather do the lambada with Thekla than take on those numpties."

I smiled at the vision of Thekla doing Latin American dancing.

Angus sighed. "I don't know if we did ourselves any favours by going to Glika Nera, but it's good to know what we're up against, what we're all up against, if this party gets any more powerful in Greece. Some Greeks actually fear a return of the junta era of the 1960s and 70s. They're getting wound up. I hear them in the *kafeneia*, the old boys, talking about tanks rumbling down the streets again. But I don't think we'll ever get to that point. I hope we don't."

At least now I had a better sense of what dark conspiracies were being silently spun here in this backwater.

"Why does Dionysos keep coming to Marathousa? It's a long way away," I asked.

"You saw Glika Nera. There's not much happening, is there? I imagine most of the men in the village are unemployed now. Not their fault and there's not much arable land and not that much tourism either, and the crisis has ramped up the hopelessness. No expats here to hassle though, are there? Dionysos probably goes to other places in the Mani where he knows there's expats – Brits, Germans, whatever. Marathousa has its fair share. He probably has a few mates in Marathousa."

We got back late in the afternoon, tired from the trip, but at least I had the Peregrine interview under my belt. Just as we pushed open the gate and walked down the path, I saw Thekla in the front garden, bending over, snipping green things yet again and putting them in a plastic bag, much like the woman at Vathia, except Thekla cut an odder figure; better dressed than the village women, her hair well-coiffed, as usual.

"What next?" Angus said in a hoarse whisper.

"You could ask her for a spirited rumba round the herb beds."

He guffawed. "In your dreams!"

She straightened up when she saw us.

"I hope you don't mind. I called by to gather some *horta* from the garden," she said with proprietorial ease, as if everything within a few miles' radius belonged to her. Angus eyed her with impatience.

"This is my father, Angus, by the way." He nodded and fumbled for his door key, not waiting to exchange pleasantries.

"We've just driven up from Cape Tainaron, *Kyria* Thekla," I said. Angus had recently taught me to address women with whom I was on a more formal footing with the honorific *Kyria*, Mrs. I did it with her now for a touch of irony. I certainly didn't need to be formal with her. The first time we'd met, I was lying naked in her nephew's bed.

"You're welcome to come in for a drink of something," I said, with no great enthusiasm, but she was Leo's aunt after all. She eyed Zeffy suspiciously when I walked inside with him on the lead.

"Leo tells me the house was freshened up in the winter and I am looking forward to seeing what he has done," she said.

I went off to make some hot drinks. She wanted camomile tea. Angus wanted instant coffee, though I imagined he'd have liked something stronger. She wandered around the house, gazing at everything, touching furniture, books, running a finger along the dusty bookcase and wincing.

"The kitchen is very nice," she said, walking around the small space, turning on the mixer tap, admiring cupboards. The kitchen had been an old drab space but now it looked modern with sage green cupboards, grey tiles and a new cooker. We sat at the dining table, sipping our drinks. She eyed me a lot, the way some Greek women often do, in a kind of brazen way, with unsmiling eyes.

"Leo tells me you are a journalist, Bronte. What things do you write?"

"Stories about Greece, that's all."

She didn't probe further, for which I was relieved.

"Leo tells me you're quite good friends with Myrto next door."

I nodded.

"Ah, Myrto. Now *she* has stories. She tells many of them, as we would say, much embroidered, I think."

I realised there was no love lost between them. Angus gave me a pained look over the top of his coffee cup.

"What do you do with your time here?" I asked. "It must be quite dull for you after Athens."

"Pah! Athens. Nothing but troubles, riots. So many tensions. I am so relieved to be in the village. I work in my garden a little. It has gone wild since last year. I meet with old village friends. I do things for church. This morning we had a special celebration before *Megali Evdomada,* the Holy Week of Easter. You would have liked it. It celebrates the miracle of the raising of Lazarus," she said, with a look of sour reprimand, as if I should have made the effort to be there. I had completely forgotten that the coming week was the start of Greek Easter, I'd been so obsessed with finding Eve Peregrine.

"Did Leonidas go to the service?" I asked.

"Not here," she sniffed. "He went to the church in Kalamata. He will not be coming to Marathousa at all this weekend."

"Yes, I know that," I said, without missing a beat. "I meant in Kalamata."

She glanced at me, cat-like. So, she knew already that Leonidas would be busy with 'family things' in the city this weekend. Of course. She would have applauded this on-going connection with the Tooth Fairy, as I had once jokingly christened Phaedra the dentist. I gave Angus a knowing look. He rolled his eyes at me. I got up and whisked the cups over to the sink. A hint we wanted her to go now.

Once she was out the door, clutching her bag of greens, I walked back to the kitchen. Angus was holding two bottles of beer.

"You might need this," he said, handing me a bottle.

I slugged some beer, the cold liquid fizzing down my throat. A few more gulps and I felt better. It had been a day of surprises and sleuthing amid the ghostly towers of Vathia, and revulsion in Glika Nera, but all of it had deflected my attention from Leonidas and Phaedra. Now I'd have to think about them.

"Damn Thekla! She knew all along that Phaedra was back in town," I said, finishing off the beer and fetching another bottle from the fridge.

"You're drinking too much, pet," said Angus, with mock concern. It was the kind of thing I usually said to him.

"I haven't even started yet," I said, winking.

"Get used to Thekla. Greek families – tight as two coats of paint. It's nice mostly. They're all loyal to each other and mostly kind to a fault, but now and then it can also be brutal, especially for an outsider when there's honour at stake or family cohesion. I know you're daft about Leonidas, and I like him too, as I keep saying, but if you were ever to get really serious, if you were to marry him, you'd be joined to people like Thekla as well – it all comes with the territory."

Holy Mother! Was this what it would be like marrying a Greek – if that were actually on the cards – with all the layers of traditional and cultural differences? I could barely speak Greek, let alone fathom everything else. Angus tapped the back of my hand. "Don't you worry about Thekla though. Beneath all that arch bluster I'm sure she's a quivering Bambi."

I laughed. "Hardly!" I said, skulling beer. "But Thekla might not be in the village for the long haul. She'll get bored and want to go back to Athens."

"Not so fast, Bronte. A Greek friend of mine who does odd bits of building work around the village says she's getting him to do some repairs and work on her garden and the stone wall on the perimeter, which has collapsed in a few places. It's a big garden, it'll take time. She wants to supervise it."

My heart sank with chilly foreboding. I would need to go out and buy one of those small blue glass beads that Greeks wear to ward off evil beings.

14

Trees have ears

That evening I called Leonidas, just out of curiosity. He had indeed been to the special church service for Lazarus.

"Did you go with your family?" I asked him sweetly.

"Yes, I did. My mother, Eleni, particularly likes it. I would have invited you, Bronte, but I don't know if you're quite ready to meet all my family yet. They might frighten you off," he chortled. If they were like Thekla, they probably would. I wanted to come right out with it. What about Phaedra, was she there? This was a time when I wanted Polly back in Kalamata. She had been such a brilliant confidante and knew everything that was going on in Kalamata. She would know what to do about Phaedra. I had recently sent her an email and had been disappointed to learn she wouldn't be back until weeks after Easter.

"So, you're still not coming back this weekend. No time?" I asked.

"No, *agapi mou*. I have family things, as I said. I am so sorry. But next weekend is very important here. We have a big service on Saturday night after the Holy Week. Although I will go to the cathedral in Kalamata for that, as I usually do, I will be in the village on Sunday. Everyone celebrates on this day with a big family feast. This year I will arrange a barbecue at Villa Ambelia for a nice group of people, locals mostly, not all the family, as they will celebrate in Kalamata. You can invite a few people too, perhaps Myrto. I know you like her a lot. Or whoever you like. Okay? You will like the lunch. It will be very nice."

When I hung up, I felt marginally better. No Phaedra, at least. Polly once told me she always went back to Koroni, on the opposite peninsula, where her parents came from and had a large villa, for all the main Greek celebrations.

I updated Angus about my phone call to Leonidas. "Why didn't you just ask him straight out about Phaedra? You have to know for sure," he piped up.

"I want to stay cool, you know. There may be nothing in it."

"I hope not. If he's back with Phaedra, I'll banjo him, I promise, Bronte." I laughed, even though it wasn't the least bit amusing.

Less amusing was the fact that Leonidas hadn't mentioned her at all, not even in passing. It nipped at me constantly. Maybe I just had to get a bit real about things.

The next day I found Myrto in her farm, sitting under the fig tree, sewing up a hole in a sock. There was a small goat tied to a tree and Zeus the donkey nearby as well, also tethered. He was making a great heehaw noise over a pile of unappealing black things, which I later found out were carob pods, supposedly an animal delicacy, if you could even describe something that looks like it's been cremated on a barbecue as such.

"Where you been, my girl?" she asked, patting a plastic chair next to her.

"What are you doing, mending socks?"

She laughed. "Good job, eh?" she said, holding one up for me. The hole in the blue sock had been stitched with red thread. It was like something a child might have done at play school.

"Sock belongs to Angelos. Now I'm like his mother, doing all the little jobs for him."

"You get on well together, working the land here. That's so nice. It was a good idea of Leonidas's, wasn't it?"

"Yeah, it's worked out good."

Angelos was a bright young man of 25 who'd had a promising job in advertising in Athens but lost it during the crisis. His father, Leonidas's brother, had suggested Angelos should go back to Kalamata to look for other work and to be with the family at least. When no other jobs eventuated, he agreed it would be a good thing to return to his roots and work the land for a year or so. Leonidas then arranged for Angelos to work with Myrto, who never had enough workers to help with the olive harvest on her 600 trees, most of which had been left to grow wild.

"Where is Angelos?" I asked her.

"Over in the other field doing some hard yakka on my trees," she said, using the colourful Aussie word for work. I still laughed at her curious English and how she stitched in Aussie slang, bits of Greek, and anything else to hand, a bit like the way she darned socks.

We talked for a while about our news. I told Myrto about visiting Glika Nera and about Dionysos, the creep. I told her to keep an eye out for him.

"If he comes from Glika Nera, he'll be no good. They all have crazy ideas there."

I talked to her about Thekla, digging her heels into Marathousa. I didn't say much though, as I'd already learnt that most Greeks didn't like to criticise other villagers. In the past it had been a matter of loyalty but also survival. When the Ottoman Turks and other interlopers were snapping at their heels, villagers everywhere needed all the friends they could get. But Myrto was a bit more candid, some might say reckless, than many other Greeks, probably from her years in Australia.

"That old *kourouna!* You think the old crow seems real nice and polite, nice clothes, nice hair – BIG!" she said, her hands shooting up vertically past her ears. "But deep down, Bronte, she's a scorpion. Stings when you don't expect." She chuckled, digging her needle into another sock.

I laughed at her description, from a crow to a scorpion. It kind of hit the spot.

"Funny I call her a scorpion because she has big fear of the scorpion. *Po, po, po!* Let me tell you! She has a small olive grove behind her house. Once I help her during harvest and a big black scorpion falls out of the tree onto her head. She goes craaazy, rushing around like a woman on fire, and screaming. Was real funny, now I remember." Myrto laughed while she darned.

I made a mental note of Thekla and scorpions. Who knew when that could be useful? Myrto finished the socks, snipping the cotton thread with her teeth and putting her sewing kit away in a plastic bag.

"We go see what Angelos is doing, eh? It's just a little walk over there," she said, pointing to the other field.

Angelos was in the middle of a thick copse of olive trees, his maroon flatbed truck parked nearby, near a stout metal gate. He had a pile of olive tree branches he'd cut and cleaned up that day and was stacking them on to the truck to take away to store for later in the year, when they'd be sold for winter fuel. He was dressed in old torn jeans and a T-shirt that was sticking to his chest with sweat from his efforts. Myrto brought him a fresh bottle of water and some biscuits, which he wolfed down.

I remembered then that I'd promised Myrto once that I would help in the field one day, gathering branches, clearing up. It was repayment for her keeping Zeffy in the beginning, but she'd never insisted on the work and I felt relieved. When I saw how Angelos was toiling over the land I knew I'd be useless. I was sure it had been one of Myrto's little wind-ups.

I had only ever seen Angelos fleetingly, as he was always in one or other of the fields, harvesting, pruning trees, clearing the ground or shifting rocks and rubble. He seemed to enjoy the work. He was a good-looking young man, very similar to Leonidas, with black wavy hair. Not as curly as his uncle's, but it was one of his better features, as well as his fine dark eyes. He seemed to be good-natured as well, much like Leonidas. A bit younger and he could easily have passed for his son.

Myrto and he had a conversation in Greek, in which she seemed to be directing him about other jobs to be done. At one point she became quite animated and I couldn't tell whether they were having a small disagreement or not. He turned to me and winked, as if to emphasise he had the measure of Myrto and knew how to handle her. But in some ways, she was charmed by him and I saw her hand Angelos the bag of darned socks, which he put in the back of his truck.

"I go back to my house, Bronte, but you stay and chatter with Angelos. He's nearly finished here now. We talk later," she said, rubbing my arm sweetly before marching back to her farm.

"Have a seat, Bronte. I apologise that it's very basic, though," Angelos said, pointing to a kind of bench he'd fashioned out of a long plank of wood set over two rocks. It was very rustic.

"Your English is very good," I said.

"I used my English a lot when I was in advertising in Athens. I don't use it so much now I'm working here, but it's nice to keep it in practice," he said, sounding slightly earnest, in the way that Leonidas had done when I first met him. It made me smile.

I wondered what he thought of my relationship with his uncle. There was no hiding anything in Greece, especially not in a rural village, and everyone in Marathousa knew about us, as we often went together to the taverna, the *kafeneio* and sometimes to services at the church of the Anastasi beside the *plateia*.

"How do you like living in this village?" he asked.

"I like it a lot. I'm loving my time in Greece, actually. And my father lives here too, as you will know. I can keep my eye on him."

"And what about you? How do you like working here," I asked him. "It must be quite a change from Athens?"

He leaned against his truck and laughed. "Yes, it sure is, but Athens is difficult now with the crisis. Many problems there. I love Athens but right now I'd rather be here," he said, his eyes trailing towards Mount Kalathio, the closest peak of the Taygetos to Kalamata, with its small village at the top and a severe zigzag road leading up, which locals called the Traumatic Road. But there was no hardship in the view, at least.

"How do you get on with Myrto?" I asked.

"She's a funny lady, isn't she? Has a temper sometimes, *panayia mou!* But she's helped me a lot to understand harvesting the olives, the trees. No-one knows the trees like Myrto: which ones are too old, too new, too weak. How to prune, when not to prune. It's interesting. I may not be a farmer forever but right now it's nice healthy work."

"I hear that lots of people are coming back to the villages because of the crisis."

"Yes, like Thekla, my great-aunt. How do you manage with her?" he asked, with a knowing grin.

"Oh, very well, though I don't see her much." *Thank God!*

"She's a good person, but she likes to interfere with things. Just ignore her if she gets too ..." he started reeling off a few Greek words, searching for the English equivalent.

"Bossy," I offered.

He laughed. "Yes, that's the right word, I think."

He swigged quickly from the bottle he was still holding, a small gush of water spilling onto his already soaked T-shirt.

"Is Leonidas coming to the village today, do you know? I haven't seen him for a while." Funny he should ask but I remembered that Angelos's father had a small house closer to the village that he rarely used any more and he'd offered it to his son.

I shook my head at his question but said nothing, following the Greek habit. I think I even felt my brows twitching upwards, the 'no comment' gesture. But he must have read the disappointment there.

"Can I say something to you, Bronte, if you don't mind?"

"Sure," I said, surprised at his forthright manner.

"I love my uncle Leonidas. I also admire him greatly, but you mustn't be … em disappointed sometimes that he might seem a little aloof, or too preoccupied with his work."

"He has to be, he's a doctor, and I do know something about the crisis and the medical pressures," I said.

"Leo's a great doctor, one of the best in Kalamata, but he can sometimes be so focused he might forget there is a world out there beyond medicine, and you can't ignore it. Maybe that was the problem for his marriage. I mean, his former wife's an actress and she's …" he puffed out his lips and waved his arm windmill-style, which I took to mean the ex-wife was drop-dead gorgeous.

"Sorry, I am being too candid, if that's the right word." I nodded. "But you know what I mean. And I hope he doesn't forget about you sometimes while the crisis is weighing him down. That would be a tragedy," he said with a warm, appealing smile. "Be patient with him."

"Oh, I am. And I also admire him very much. He's a wonderful man."

I stood up to go, feeling a bit strange talking about Leonidas to someone I didn't know that well yet, as if that mattered in a Greek village, where everyone seemed to know everything about everyone. As Leonidas always said, "In Greece, the trees have ears." Or as Elpida liked to say quite often, "The secret that two villagers share will be known by everyone." Another one of those old village sayings.

Angelos seemed to sense my disquiet. As I said goodbye, he put his hand on my shoulder and squeezed it gently, smiling at me.

"I can see how Leo has fallen in love with you, Bronte, and you must be strong. These are difficult times for all of us. Have faith and all will be very well."

His words were touching towards a foreigner in their midst. While I mulled over his comment, a black shape caught my eye through the olive trees. It was Thekla, standing quite still on the stretch of road where she often took a daily walk. She was watching us, her hands on her hips and a squinty strange look on her face. Angelos saw my expression and turned towards her, but she quickly moved off. He pulled a face but said nothing.

"Thanks for the talk, Angelos. I must go now."

I turned to walk away, then had a sudden thought.

"Are you going to Leo's lunch for Easter Sunday?" I asked.

"I usually have the lunch with my father in Kalamata, but I can change my plan. Why not? Leo always has very nice lunches at his villa."

Good, I thought. More people to offset the creeping antipathy of Thekla. And Angelos was so charming anyway.

As I left, Angelos went back to work, piling the last of the branches into the back of his truck. I thought again about his words. "Have faith". Was he referring to Phaedra perhaps and her Lazarus-like return? Was he trying to boost my morale?

I planned to spend most of the Easter week working. On the Monday I finished writing the feature on Eve Peregrine and Douglas Markham and I was pleased at how revealing it had turned out. I filed it to the Messenger and it was due to run any day now. Easter gave me rich pickings for my latest column and I lingered over the national obsession with the daily church services that ran through the Holy Week, most of which I'd managed to attend, if not to the bitter end, as most lasted three hours. It was a solemn sequence that advanced the story of Christ's capture to his crucifixion, and on *Megalo Savato*, Holy Saturday was the rousing climax, the resurrection service at midnight. These were all highly dramatic services which, despite the earnest-ness of priests and congregation, briefly went awry now and then with props misbehaving; sound systems failing; candles held too high, threatening festive decorations; *psaltes*, choristers, admonished for the odd lapse of attention over their ancient hymn books.

It was also curious to me that services during this week appeared to be a cue for village women to refresh their looks, for reasons I couldn't fathom. I noted one villager who hitherto had black straight hair now had a gingery mop of curls, which didn't suit her at all. Another sported a short back and sides where her hair had once been luxurious. Thekla's hair had, if that were possible, gone even bigger to the point of being nesty, even though her black outfits were severe. It was all unexpectedly intriguing.

Angus refused to come to these services, saying if he had to get up and down for three hours every time the priest came out of the sanctuary (which was often) he'd wreck a knee cartilage. Easter gave me much to write about.

I thought about Peregrine during those days and wondered – now that she was back in her villa and all was well, according to her much-relieved agent anyway – why she never had the merest curiosity about village life, and Easter especially. I wondered if she'd dam-busted her writing blockage yet and how she spent her lonely evenings, if in fact she was alone. Even so, I felt just a bit sorry for her, and that, combined with gratitude for her candidness over the

Markham piece, prompted me to contact her at the end of the week to invite her to Leo's Sunday lunch.

When I called her mobile, she answered right away and seemed pleased to hear from me. Had she seen the feature, I asked her, which had now run in the paper?

"My agent sent me a link. What can I say? I'm not a great fan of press exposés, but it's fine. I've had a few requests through my agent for more interviews about Markham, which you may be pleased to know I haven't taken up. I've had quite a few emails too: people from the past, wondering why I'm hiding away in Greece scribbling books when I was once a TV star. Ho, hum! If only I *were* scribbling, Bronte!" she said, with a tired edge to her voice. However, the invitation to Leo's Sunday lunch seemed to lift her mood.

"Ah, the Greek doctor. I'm curious to meet him," she said, with girlish enthusiasm.

"The rest will be locals: Greeks, no expats."

"That's a relief," she said. "I won't have to sign autographs then. I'm very touched that you've asked me, Bronte. It's kind of you to want a cantankerous old trout like me along, especially after I seem to have worried you all to death with my flight to Vathia."

I laughed. Well, the cantankerous was spot on. I was relieved there was a bit more levity between us.

"Tell me, what's the dress code for this Easter lunch?"

"It's just a barbecue, but it can be whatever you want really. The older folk will be in their Sunday best."

"What are you wearing?" she asked.

"I don't know. A sundress perhaps. It will be warm on Sunday. Why do you ask?"

"It's just that I have far too many clothes here and some wonderful dresses I never wear. I've put on weight. All the olive oil, I expect. I just thought you might like to have one of my dresses. They're all practically new and you're about the size I was a month ago. It's my gift to you for putting up with my gruff behaviour at Vathia and also for having to chase me around the Mani when you thought I'd been murdered by unknown assailants," she said, with a hint of sarcasm.

"I don't think I really believed you'd been murdered, but it's kind of you to offer a dress," I said, taken aback by her generosity.

I did panic a bit over what kind of dress she had in mind but I was curious to have another glimpse into her secretive life. I promised to come over to her villa in the late afternoon.

"Wonderful. We'll have a glass of wine as well. I have something too that I want to discuss with you."

"Oh, that sounds intriguing."

"That's one way to describe it," she said, with a laugh that rang hollow down the phone.

Just when I thought she was in a better mood than previously, getting on top of her writer's block, here was another drama perhaps. But would it send her rushing off to a Maniot tower again?

15

All about Eve

When Eve answered the door that Friday afternoon, I couldn't see any evidence of fresh pandemonium in her life. She looked radiant, fiery even, with the bright afternoon light streaming in from the balcony, catching the tendrils of her strawberry blonde hair. She was dressed in loose white trousers and a flattering pale pink T-shirt.

"First things first. Let's check out those dresses."

Eve led the way into her bedroom and opened a large built-in wardrobe to reveal a row of dresses in eye-catching designs and colours.

"I'm a woman with a thing about dresses – not shoes. But I hardly wear them and don't know why I keep bringing them on trips. Now I have this collection. Do you like 50s-style dresses – you know, little waist with belts and slightly full skirts?"

Before I could answer she'd pulled one out. It was just as she'd described, with a bold pattern in dazzling shades of blue and purple. I think I gasped.

"This was a hugely expensive designer label and I haven't worn it. Pity!"

She pulled out a few more, in very much the same style. I was overwhelmed. She watched me, smiling, enjoying a rare girly moment.

"I don't want you to think I'm a total recluse, Bronte. I do have a social life in London and I go to a lot of events. But here in Greece, it's different. I do know a few people in

Kalamata but mostly I seek solitude. But look, let's have that drink and you can decide later about the dress."

She led me into the sitting room and drew the curtains to block some of the light and heat from the balcony. We each sat on one of the comfortable cream sofas. She brought white wine in tall crystal glasses and a plate of small Greek appetisers.

"Tell me about this man of yours, if that's not too nosey of me," she said, popping a small stuffed vine leaf into her mouth.

"What can I say? He's a GP in Kalamata, a lovely man, very kind, and amusing."

"And sexy, I imagine."

"I think so."

Leonidas, I thought, was the kind of man who would appeal to her. While she had never married and appeared to live like a Carmelite nun these days, I knew from her talk about Douglas Markham that she had an appetite for men who were sexy and confident. But Leonidas was a different kind of sexy, to my mind; someone who seemed never to be conscious of it and who didn't use it to manipulate the world around him.

I also told her how we'd met. About our search for my late grandfather Kieran. She was a good listener.

"How amazing, Bronte, and you say your father is writing a book about all this?"

"Trying to. He's not a writer, so it's going fairly slowly."

"Yes, I can appreciate the problem exactly," she said with a heavy sigh. "But Leonidas sounds divine."

Then I couldn't help telling her about Phaedra, and about her return. About how Angus had seen them together in the city. I didn't think I was close enough to Eve to confess any of this. Yet I felt I needed another woman to bounce ideas off, especially with Polly away in Australia, although Polly had maternal qualities I felt Eve lacked.

"Oh," she said, pouting. "I can see how that might alarm you, but she's simply come back for the Easter holiday and, okay, they met. So what? He didn't mention meeting her because he didn't want to worry you because it meant nothing. Yes?"

"Maybe, but Kalamata is just like a big village, I think you'll agree. Everyone knows everything and sees everything, and he must have known that sooner or later I'd find out."

"Oh, my dear. It's not worth worrying about, unless you get more proof he's switched teams." She popped another appetiser in her mouth and chewed delicately. We drank another glass of wine. It had been good to talk about the Phaedra situation but I felt I'd chattered too much.

"Is there no-one in your life right now?" I probed, since we were in a girly mood.

"There was someone recently. He's an actor I used to work with about 16 years ago. I was mad about him then, but he was married. Now he's divorced. We got together several months ago, met at a luvvie kind of function, but it didn't last. You can't reclaim the past easily. Some of the magic had gone. I'll admit I'm not the easiest person to live with. I'm very egotistical, like most actors and writers ..." she said, trailing off. The business of writing was like a running sore.

"Perhaps the disappointment over this romance has taken some of your motivation away in general," I said, trying to be helpful.

"Well, I'll admit, I was in a dark place for a while, but it was something else that happened around the same time that has overwhelmed everything, most especially the writing. It's quite a story, to me anyway, if you want to hear it, because it's the main reason I asked you to come today."

Nothing grabs a journalist's interest more than the words "quite a story".

"Of course," I said.

154

"Well, first of all, I don't know why I feel I can be so candid with you, Bronte, no offence meant by that. It's just I've never trusted journalists. But you feel more like a friend, and I feel you might be able to help in some way."

"I'll try," I said.

She poured more wine. She seemed calm and composed, and yet I saw her hand tremble slightly when she lifted her glass to her lips.

"What I'm going to tell you is strictly off the record. It would do me irreparable harm if this story got out. Okay?"

"Yes, of course," I said. Now she had my whole attention.

"Well ... the writer's block I've mentioned – it's not really a writer's block as such. As you know, my latest book isn't finished and I won't make the summer deadline – or even the autumn one at this rate. The publisher is nettled with me. My agent is trying to be supportive but her patience is also wearing thin. They don't know what the delay's all about. Whenever they ask, I fudge things and go on about having to do more research. No point in wittering on about a writer's block. The problem is, you see ... I'm not a writer!" She clasped her hands together in her lap and tipped her head lightly to the side, as if to gauge the effect of her strange comment.

"I don't know what you mean. You've penned 12 bestselling novels."

"Yes, that part's true, and I'm grateful for the books' huge success. But the fact is ... I didn't write them," she said, looking pained. She leaned forward for her wine again. Her hand shook more visibly this time and she had to put down the glass after one sip.

I gasped. "Okay ... you have a ghost writer to help you, is that what you mean? Quite a few celebrities do."

It had briefly crossed my mind once, I admit, that Eve may have had a lot of help with the writing in the beginning as an actress turned author, but I'd never heard any rumours that she had a ghost writer, and these things always seep out in the end.

She sighed heavily and I saw the start of a sweaty sheen on her smooth forehead. She dabbed at it with her unused serviette. "Let me explain if I can. There *was* someone, someone special, working on those 12 books, but whether she would be classed as a ghost writer, I don't know. She's certainly a ghost."

"A ghost?"

"Yes," she said, mournfully. "She died two months ago. No-one but me knows who she is, and no-one knows the whole story. That's why I can't finish this book, or ever write another. The writer has departed and I'm a creative husk, that's all I am. But apart from her writing gifts, she was a great friend, and I do miss her terribly."

She sat quietly for a moment, as if collating her thoughts. I was stunned. I hadn't seen this coming.

"Before I left acting which, by the way, I enjoyed but felt a little unfulfilled with in the end ... I think it was the cop series. Poor choice really and hardly the height of thespian achievement. But as I was saying ... I had always had an ambition to write. It went back to childhood. I had loads of ideas and was very creative but I hadn't the patience to apply myself. That sums me up actually, as I have a very low boredom threshold and I'm terribly impatient. But once acting swept me up I forgot about writing. Then I went to Tuscany one summer, where I got the idea for a novel. It fell into my head, just like that," she said, clicking her fingers. "I worked out the plot and the characters and I thought it was great. All I had to do was write it up."

She wrinkled her face at me. "Harder than I thought! Harder than any role I've taken on, but I worked at it for many months, wrote several drafts, until I was finally pleased with it. First real piece of writing I'd ever properly finished. But before I sent it off to an agent or publisher, I wanted another set of eyes to look it over. In the apartment building where I live in north London was a woman called Grace Phimister. A wonderful woman, very down-to-earth but well-educated. She had spent her working life in secretarial positions, which seemed beneath her abilities, I always thought. Her income would have been quite modest, I imagine, but she'd managed to get by in London because her apartment had been left to her by a family member years before. It's one of the more expensive ones in the building and on the top floor. And she also did some freelance work in the evenings: proof-reading and editing, which I think was more out of interest than a financial consideration. She lived a frugal kind of life. So we became great friends. She was unmarried with not much family left and perhaps she treated me as a bit of a surrogate daughter. She was also a fan of all my acting work.

"Grace was also an obsessive reader of fiction, so I decided to give her my manuscript to read. Dear me, but she was very direct! She loved the plot, but she thought the writing wasn't up to scratch. It was laboured. No real surprise there, I guess, since my forte had always been ideas. She seemed to know what she was talking about, so I offered to pay her to knock it into shape before I approached a publisher because in those days it wasn't quite as easy for celebrities to get a publishing deal just because they were well-known, like it is now.

"Grace actually rewrote the story and the version she came up with was brilliant. In fact, it was almost unrecognisable from the one I'd written. She had brought it to life. She obviously had a gift for writing but had never done anything with it, which is remarkable. So the novel that became Five Nights in Tuscany was sent to a few publishers, and Greyfriars and Perryman, whom I'm still with, published it to great acclaim. Grace didn't want to be recognised as the writer, or indeed the ghost writer. She was quite happy to be in the background. That's how she was. Very unassuming and generous.

"So that was the start of a long collaboration that neither of us really expected. I had the ideas, Grace wrote the stories. We both played to our strengths and I gave her an increasingly larger cut of the royalties as well, enough for her to retire from full-time work after a couple of years. We were both very happy and thriving. I never thought of the future; what might happen, even though she was 20 years older than me. I thought we would just go on forever like that, turning out book after book. And then Grace died suddenly."

She stopped a moment to see how I was taking her revelations. I was pretty shocked, and mostly by the fact she'd managed to pull off the deception for so many years without anyone winkling out the truth. But then, essentially, she was an actress and she'd probably just acted the role of best-selling author with all the usual foibles, and ego turns, many of which came naturally to her anyway. She'd pulled it off perfectly, now better known as a writer than an actor. She must have noticed my slightly disapproving look.

"Don't misunderstand me, Bronte. In the beginning I never thought this would go on for so long. I thought, okay, I'll do a few books, fulfil that childhood ambition and get on with acting. But we both got swept along with the success of the venture. It wasn't just a business collaboration either. Grace and I had great fun with all of this and it changed our lives completely. She was like family to me for those 15 or so years, especially since I don't have much family left and what I have aren't particularly supportive. I'm devastated that Grace is gone."

Eve stopped a moment and I thought I saw her eyes gleam with tears. I hoped it was sincere.

"How did Grace die?"

"A sudden heart attack. No warning signs in the weeks beforehand. She'd just come back from a short holiday in

Scotland, where she went every year. She never came here, by the way. She was one of those Brits who hates to go abroad. It was one thing we didn't have in common. Anyway, she was out shopping and died on the bus home. Quite terrible really," she said, lapsing into silence.

Friendship apart, it was a pity Grace hadn't finished the book before she died, was all I could think of. No doubt that thought must have secretly nagged at Eve, though she'd never say it.

"What will you do with your book then? Finish it yourself?"

She shrugged in the Greek way, arms out, eyes closed a moment. It was painful to watch.

"I don't know, Bronte. That's the thing. Grace was about two-thirds of the way through the first draft when she died – though her first drafts were always pretty clean, I must say. But there's no way I can finish it. I know the plot, of course, but I can't write the rest in her style and I certainly can't do it in mine. Readers are very sophisticated. They'd know it was different. And I've tried, believe me. Up in that Vathia tower with the manual typewriter, I had a go at it. I mean, I really tried for a few days solid, but the results were absolute *bollocks!*" she said with emphasis. I had to stifle a snort of laugher by pretending a cough. As her agent would have said, it was so unlike Eve Peregrine.

She sipped a lot more wine, then slumped back onto the sofa, lightly hugging her chest. I thought about Vathia. It meant that the tapping I'd heard from the tower was her writing nonsense, or perhaps just a long and complicated shopping list.

"Well, Eve. That's quite a story! I'm gobsmacked you were able to do what you did for so long without coming unstuck, you and Grace. It's a huge achievement. But now, basically ... you're fucked, if you don't mind my saying that!" *No point in beating about the bush,* I thought.

She smiled lightly "No, I don't, and you're right. I can't see any way around this problem."

"What about your publisher? You've known him a long time, can't you tell him … well not the whole truth, but tell him you've got serious writer's block, or burn-out or something? Maybe he could find a proper ghost writer to discretely finish the novel – just this once. There are loads of writers making a living this way."

"Ha!" she said, flicking her hand in the air with impatience. "My publisher's a miserable old goat! He's become worse over the years. Okay, he's not been bad in publicising the books and all that but he's already petulant over this delay and if I told him I couldn't finish the book at all he'd go mad. Even if I could fudge some kind of excuse for the delay, claim a temporary mental health issue or something, he might be cunning and tease out the real story. It would make its way into every British tabloid. I'd have to move to Greece permanently. So, you see, unless a miracle befalls me, there won't be a book coming out this year, or any year."

She gave a mournful stare and rubbed her long fingers nervously up and down one of her forearms. I sensed the hairs on it were standing on end. Mine were.

"Bronte, I'm telling you all this because, for one thing, it's such a blessed relief to get it off my chest. But since you're a writer you might have some idea what I can do. I'm at my wit's end."

"One thing that occurs to me is … I'm assuming Grace wrote the books on computer, right? And you have access to it and that's where you found the incomplete first draft?" I asked.

"Yes, of course. I had a key to her apartment and access to her desk drawers and the computer, though I'd never had any reason to do that when she was alive."

"Did you check all her computer documents in case she had, for some reason, written the rest of the book on a separate document?"

160

"I checked *all* her documents. Grace was very meticulous. If the last part of the book was there, on a separate document, I would have found it. Also, she regularly backed up her work onto small storage discs and I found one in her desk drawer. The book manuscript was on it, but again, only two-thirds finished. When I came to Greece, she always gave me a small storage disc so I could read through the current manuscript on my laptop and make any changes while here. When I told you I came here every year to write, that's what I was really doing, reading the manuscripts, and creating new plots of course."

We both became silent a moment with the sheer hopelessness of the situation. Finally, she gave me a pleading kind of look.

"Can I ask, Bronte, have you ever written a novel?"

I shook my head. I feared this was where the conversation had been heading, but I had no desire to be her ghost writer, or another ghost.

"Lots of journalists toy with the idea of writing a book but I'm afraid I'm not one of them, Eve. Not at this point anyway."

She pouted with disappointed. "I quite understand."

"So, what will you do?"

"What can I do?"

"One thing's clear. You're going to have to tell the publisher soon that you can't finish the book, and let him sort it out. What's the worst that can happen? The book remains incomplete. You have to give your advance back, endure a mighty strop, some bitching in the press and so forth. At least you can just stay in Greece until the furore dies down."

She reached forward, poured more wine into our glasses, finishing off the bottle, and said, with a wry smile, "Retreat to Vathia, I'd say. But first of all, I have to go back to London soon, and not for the publisher. Grace left her apartment to me, as it happens, which was very generous of her. She didn't have much surviving family, as I said, and was only in contact really with one of them, Imogen the niece. According to Grace's will, she wanted most of her personal possessions, excluding the computer and desk contents, and family mementoes to go to Imogen, or whatever she wants of them. When I'm in London again I must arrange for her to come to the apartment to look through Grace's things. I just hope Grace never let on to Imogen she was actually writing my books. But Grace was very tight-lipped about our arrangement, I'm sure of that, but I'll never know. Inheriting her apartment right now has been a godsend because, although I've made a lot of money from the books, apart from the ongoing royalties, I will have no more regular income."

She slumped back on the sofa cushions, a pale shadow of the feisty woman I'd first seen at the house. I felt a bit sorry for her. But only a bit, because now I'd heard all of the story, I could never forget the fact she'd spun this literary mess herself and deceived millions of loyal readers in the process. I seemed to remember from my research that she'd won a major Best Romantic Novel prize a few years ago, and had been shortlisted for others. And she'd been quite brazen in lying to the press all these years, including myself, to start with at least.

"You could always go back to acting," I suggested.

She pulled a face. "That might be hard. Who wants to hire an actress at 50 who hasn't had a decent role in years?"

"Well, okay," I said, wearily, feeling sucked into the vortex of her desperation. "Then the only thing I can suggest is that you try again to squeeze out the last part of the novel yourself. I'm sure you must have picked up a lot more from Grace over the years than you think – like her authorial voice. Have a go!"

Another face pulled. More wizened than before.

"Maybe, and if I do, perhaps you might cast your eye over my efforts. No more than that."

"Yes, I'd be glad to do that." What else could I say? But I doubted she'd get that far. Trapped in the Rapunzel tower for ever more.

"Thanks, Bronte. Now let's sort out your dress. It's the least I can do for you."

She ushered me back to her bedroom, where all the dresses she pulled out were draped over the bed, but it was the purple and blue number that my eyes kept trailing over.

"Try it on and if you like it, take it," Eve said, as she wandered off to check her mobile phone.

I tried on the purple dress. I don't think I'd every worn anything as brilliantly cut and styled in my life. It was nipped in at the waist, with a deep V neckline that showed a bit of cleavage, and a full, but not too billowy skirt. And it suited my colouring and long curly auburn hair perfectly.

When she returned to the bedroom, she gasped. "Bronte, you look sexy. It suits your curvy figure perfectly. It was made for you."

"Thanks. I love it!" I said, twirling round, wondering if it was quite the right thing for a rural barbecue in Greece. I expressed that thought and she shook her head in mild frustration.

"If you've got the least suspicion that this Phaedra woman is out to snatch the doctor back, you need to go in with all your big guns this weekend. And by the way, I can't believe she's glamorous and also a dentist. That doesn't quite figure, does it?" She winked.

"Phaedra won't be at the lunch at least. She has Easter Sunday with her family."

"Excellent! The doctor can concentrate his mind on you, my dear. And you must make a big splash, if you see what I mean."

Later on, I would have good cause to laugh at that last remark.

When I got back early in the evening, I found Angus sitting on the balcony, drinking beer. He'd been to Kalamata that afternoon to see the cardiologist again for some test results.

"How did you get on? What did the doc say?"

"Same old thing. I have to watch what I eat and drink and live like a monk on Mount Athos," he said, skulling his beer with evident enjoyment.

"I keep telling you, it's not rocket science, is it?"

I told Angus about my meeting with Eve and about her 'secret'. I know I'd promised to keep it to myself but Angus was completely reliable. I just had to tell someone else. He threw back his head and roared with laughter.

"Oh dear, oh dear, what a clusterfuck! So that's what the typing in the tower was all about. She probably didn't even have any paper in the typewriter."

I laughed. "Don't breathe a word, Angus. If this got out it would be a car crash, believe me."

"It's a crash already, by the sounds of it. But don't worry, I won't say a word. But I may extract something from you one day in return."

"Don't even think about it, Angus, or I'll extract something from you, and it will hurt." He winced. We often bantered on in this manner, a hangover from our earlier slightly petulant relationship when I came to Greece last year. Although we had happily overcome our former problems, we had stuck to our same wind-ups and pretend-bickering because they were generally amusing diversions in our little Greek rural life.

"There was I, telling you one day that real writers don't get writer's block, remember? Boy, I was right on the money with that." He chortled a bit more.

"By the way, I've invited Eve to Leo's lunch on Sunday, and she's given me a gorgeous dress to wear." I fetched it from the posh shopping bag Eve had put it in.

He whistled. "Is that how she buys your silence?"

"She trusts me. And she should, even though I've told you. Just don't get blootered at lunch and get a case of loose lips. I'm warning you. And by the way, I've noticed you're drinking a lot these days. I worry about that."

"Drinking too much, ha!" he scoffed. "I don't think I ever drink nearly enough!"

He rubbed his hands together with glee. "Well, I must say, this barbecue sounds a lot more interesting than hitherto. We've got an actress with the devil of all writing disasters, the mad aunty Thekla who, were she in a classic English novel would be locked up in the attic and the house blown up, and Myrto for rural colour and Aussie larrikinism. I wouldn't miss it for the world."

But, oh, we would end up having much more fun than all that!

16

May contain dogs

There was a fizz of excitement in the back garden of Villa Ambelia and the delightful aroma of roast lamb. We arrived at noon, carrying a cake in a beribboned box, as it was customary, Angus told me, to bring a dessert to a celebratory meal. I also had Zeffy on a lead as an experiment to see how he would behave at a gathering, though I had a pact with Angus that if he played up, one of us would take him straight back to the house. He was washed and brushed and unrecognisable from the rough sleeper I'd saved.

Tables had been arranged in one long line, covered with crisp white tablecloths and set with plates and cutlery under three Italian-style sun umbrellas. There were already a few villagers huddled at the far end, whom I didn't know well but recognised as people who frequented the Anastasi church and whom I often saw in the *plateia*. The barbecue for spit-roasting the lamb had been positioned near the kitchen on the lower floor that was part of a guest studio but useful for summer parties.

One older guy in a baseball cap sat beside the barbecue on a rush-bottomed chair, tasked with basting the meat at regular intervals with oil and herbs. I recognised him as Adonis, an elder of the church. I left Zeffy with Angus and went into the kitchen, where two women were chopping up salad and preparing vegetables for lunch. Leonidas was also there, wearing an apron and waving a set of tongs. He didn't see me come in, so I enjoyed the sight of this cheery domesticity.

When he turned, he looked surprised.

"Good morning, *agapi mou*," he said, taking my cake and placing it on a kitchen bench top. He embraced me and kissed me on both cheeks. "And *Christos Anesti* too." This is the common salutation in the hours, and even days, after the Easter Saturday service, meaning Christ is Risen. Leonidas stepped back a moment to look at me.

"You look very beautiful, Bronte, in this dress. And the style is magnificent." I liked the way his eyes caressed its lines for a moment too long.

I never thought a dress could actually give a woman a glow but that was how I felt – glowing. There was just something about this dress. Because it had fifties' glamour, curiously, it made me feel slightly removed from the ordinariness of my rural life. I felt as if I should have had a red Vespa parked outside so that I could leap on it later and scoot along the coast, with some Latin love song as the soundtrack. Despite the fifties allure, I wanted to appear cool because I hadn't forgiven him yet for not fessing up about Phaedra the Tooth Fairy. Now, however, I was anything but, especially when he leaned in close, whispering, "It's been too long since I've seen you, Bronte." The teasing puff of hot breath in my ear made my back muscles twitch pleasantly –but it was short-lived.

What a cheek! The absence between us was all his fault, I thought, as a peculiar vision of Phaedra assaulted me unbidden. Her in a white coat, with killer heels, clutching a dental drill. I knew what I'd like to do with her drill if I ever caught up with her, but mercifully she wasn't around. And hopefully with it being near the end of the main Easter festivities I imagined she would sashay back to the UK soon enough. Root canals were calling! Once she was at a safer distance I could better face up to Leonidas and assess the damage.

"I invited Eve Peregrine here today. I thought she might be lonely at her villa."

167

"Ah, the lady we reported missing at Kalamata police station," he said sarcastically. Had anyone told the police to stop looking? I wondered. I'd already explained to Leonidas about Angus and me going down the Mani and finding her, but not all the pertinent details.

"The Greeks will like having a famous actress and writer for lunch. No, not for lunch. For lunch we have the lamb."

I laughed at his little joke. He turned and spoke to the two female helpers and must have told them about their famous guest. They both waved their chopping knives around, going, "*Po, po, po!*", the Greek equivalent of 'bloody hell'. Indeed!

"I've brought Zeffy. He's outside. I hope you don't mind." Leonidas wrinkled his brow.

"He won't be a bother. He'll sleep most of the day, especially if he gets a little treat of lamb perhaps?" I crooned.

"Okay, my love, but don't let him go crazy in the garden. Not all Greeks like the recreational dogs."

I laughed. It sounded like 'recreational drugs'. He gave me a quizzical look. No time to explain though.

"Don't worry, Zeffy will be fine," I said, not knowing if that would be true. "By the way, can I help here?"

"No, not in your lovely dress. No Bronte, you are to sit down and relax. We have everything taken care of. I have had a whole lamb roasting for hours and there are plenty of lemon potatoes in the oven too. I will bring you a drink very soon. How is Angus? Will he take a beer?"

"Two or three, I should think," I said, as I fluttered away.

I sat down at the far end of the long table with Angus. Zeffy was lying under the table but I hooked the end loop of his lead under the leg of my chair, for added security. I'd already seen a few surly looks from a couple of villagers when we first walked in with the dog. No doubt some might see through Zeffy's elegant make-over and rumble him for his former homelessness. It would confirm what most rural

Greeks felt about foreigners: that when it came to animals, we were all barking mad.

Not long afterwards Myrto arrived with Angelos. She was wearing a summery dress with long sleeves and a set of pearls, her hair loose. It had been cut in a kind of bob and had a light wave to it. She was wearing a small amount of make-up and looked good. You would never have known that ordinarily she spent her day pruning trees, sorting through cremated carob pods and assessing the virtues of edible weeds. It was miraculous.

"You look nice," I said as she sat beside me. I caught an aroma of herbs and something a little French with floral top notes.

"There's more to Myrto than you know, Bronte. I'm not always the raw prawn," she said, mangling an Aussie expression.

Angelos shook my hand firmly. "*Christos Anesti*," he said. I smiled at how handsome he looked when scrubbed and clean, without a flatbed truck to load. He was wearing jeans and a crisp white shirt. He was disturbingly like Leonidas but without the intensity and the boomerang ex-girlfriend, and he would have greatly accessorised my fantasy Vespa on the trip along the coast in other circumstances. While I daydreamed, he wandered off to talk to Leonidas, which was just as well.

I'd almost forgotten that Eve was coming to this lunch, and how could I really? She was slightly late, as befits a thespian. By the time she arrived, knocking on the side gate, and was led into the garden by Leonidas, everyone was seated at the long table with drinks, eating *meze*, appetisers. Leonidas arched his brows at me as she sat down, slightly hot and breathless. It was a mark of her sensitivity perhaps that she hadn't chosen to wear one of the many other fifties' dresses she had, similar to mine. Her dress was glamorous all the same: a sixties' knee-length, white clingy sleeveless dress with fuchsia-coloured beads. It had a scoop neck showing a modest amount of cleavage and she wore a fuchsia chiffon wrap around her shoulders. With her blonde hair loosely curled and hanging round her shoulders she looked like an edible confection.

Leonidas introduced her loudly to everyone, thinking the villagers would be suitably impressed. They all turned and stared appreciatively – the men, particularly, and the women just so they could spin it later into some kind of rural gossip.

Eve sat on one side of me, Myrto on the other, and Angus beside her. Having the two women in close proximity seemed bizarre, as they were so completely different. The elegant 'celebrity' and the farming goddess who eschewed anything close to haute couture in favour of *horta*-couture while she worked in her compound. In her inimitable fashion, however, it was Myrto who was more at ease, chatting to Eve, wanting to know: Who was she? Why was she here? How famous? On TV? How much did they pay her? But Eve seemed just as curious about Myrto and her strange English/Aussie patois. Before long, I feared, Myrto would be baptised with a glamour gown of her own.

During a quiet moment Eve leaned towards me and whispered, "By the way, Bronte, I know I've already said it but you look divine in that dress and you've put a bit more make-up on. It suits you." She winked.

Eve was a complex creature. Although she claimed not to be particularly sociable, and admitted she could be difficult and thorny – as I'd seen myself – at this Easter lunch she was nothing but affable and charming. Or was it an act? I couldn't decide but I began to like her more and more, especially now I knew her whole story.

Angelos, who had been standing with some of the villagers at the other end of the table, was drinking a beer. I noticed he was surreptitiously watching Eve quietly over the top of his glass, as entranced by her as everyone else. I imagined he hadn't a clue about her age, and today she looked about 40 – not such a big difference in their ages on this occasion.

"Come now, *paidia*, have some more appetisers," said Leonidas, striding out of the kitchen and placing a large platter of barbecued octopus and stuffed vine leaves on the table. I saw Eve's eyelids flutter slightly in his direction before he turned back to the kitchen.

"Leonidas is just the way you described him, Bronte. Lucky, lucky you!" she stage-whispered in my ear. "And the young man over there is one of his relatives? I see a stunning resemblance," she said, her eyes flitting towards Angelos.

"His nephew."

"Pity he's so young," she said, biting into a small tentacle of octopus.

Good job he was, I thought to myself, smiling.

The men at the other end of the table were in very good spirits with a few glasses of wine or ouzo under their belts already. Every now and then they clashed glasses together and chorused, "*Yeia mas!*" To our health!

But where was Thekla? No-one mentioned her and as the clock ticked on, I wondered if God had smiled on me and she'd been called away on some errand, some weed-picking convention, some scorpion-detainment project, an AA group for embroidery addicts. Everything felt perfect: a warm day, the air full of the aroma of spit-roasted lamb, the table full of loud happy chatter.

At one point Eve and I found ourselves cut off from a gust of Greek conversation around us.

"Thank you so much for inviting me here today, Bronte. Better than staying at home alone, fighting with a typewriter," Eve said with a wry smile, sipping wine.

"Do you know many people in this region?" I asked.

"I know a few people in Kalamata: artsy people, some actors and musicians I've been introduced to over the years. Very nice, actually."

"Greek?"

"Some of them, yes. I meet up now and then for a drink, a meal, but I'm not especially close to anyone. As I keep saying, I'm a hermit when I'm here."

Looking at her today, as lovely as she was, I had trouble understanding why.

"Has there not been a Greek guy on the horizon, I mean since you've had your house here?"

"Now and then there's been a discreet dalliance," she said, her eyes sliding unconsciously in the direction of Angelos, which was an interesting slip.

"But I've never had the urge to get really serious with someone who's language I don't speak much of, or whose culture is still a mystery to me – mostly."

"I know what you mean. It's challenging," I said.

"I admire you, Bronte, for following your heart and going beyond your comfort zone with a different culture and way of life."

"That's kind, Eve, but sometimes I must seem like a cliché – falling for a Greek after only a few weeks and then walking away from my former life."

She tipped her head to the side in a gesture of sympathy. "As I see it, you're obviously very much in love, and I don't blame you. And I suppose that's the key; to have the passion and commitment to make it work."

"I am in love, but can you learn to love the country and the culture as much as the man?" I said, glancing at the others around me, conscious I was becoming too candid. Possibly the wine was kicking in. I was a person who expected frankness in my interview subjects, not the other way round. She didn't answer, or perhaps she thought it was just a rhetorical piece of musing. Yet it was anything but.

"Before I forget, Bronte, can I thank you again for listening to my story the other day. It was so good to talk about it, you can't imagine," she said.

I looked over at Angus, who had been chatting with Myrto, about what I couldn't imagine. Now he seemed to be lugging into our conversation. His mouth twitched at the side, usually a precursor to a cheeky quip, but he stayed silent. I thought how nice he looked that day, his hair shiny and neat, his skin tanned and fresh for someone who'd just a few months ago been on the threshold of a heart attack. If only Polly had been here too!

"Have you thought any more about what to do?" I asked Eve.

She sighed heavily and lowered her voice. "Not really. I did take your point about having a go myself, with the writing, but I don't hold out much hope."

Might as well boil a stone, as the villagers would say.

Leonidas announced that the lamb would be ready soon. He was looking hot now, walking to and fro, serving food and drinks with no-one to help him, apart from the two women, who seemed tireless. I admired his dedication to being host and chef and making the afternoon a success. Everything was going well, even Zeffy had remained quiet under the table, though I suspected the smell of roast lamb was driving him crazy.

In a lull just before we were ready to start lunch properly, we saw the garden gate open slowly and Thekla appeared in a fitted black dress, her hair big and slightly more blonded; expensive gold earrings and a string of pearls. She looked like one of the mythical Greek Sirens, wrinkled and pensioned-off now, though living comfortably, and only her towering hair nudging a memory of how women can crash ships and drown sailors if they have a mind to. In short, she looked like trouble – and trouble wasn't far behind. As she held the gate open, the next person to step into the garden was Phaedra, the Tooth Fairy!

17

Easter was never this hot

I heard someone at the table gasp. Perhaps it was me. Everyone turned to look at Phaedra, some with a modicum of confusion, one or two with amusement. Obviously, everyone in the village knew the whole story of Leonidas and Phaedra, their engagement once, their split and the arrival of the foreigner interloper.

Leonidas was still in his apron, holding barbecue tongs. I had hoped he might have looked mildly shocked or surprised but his face was a picture of calm. Only his eyes were just slightly narrowed in concentration. This was no doubt the 'medical stare' sworn to along with the Hippocratic Oath, with which a doctor could deal with all kinds of mayhem. I only saw his eyes flicker briefly in my direction, once.

Myrto hissed, "*Panayia mou!*"

Angus stared at Phaedra, then tapped my shoulder and leaned towards me behind Myrto's back. "Here's another clusterfuck about to happen, pet," he whispered.

Eve looked around in confusion. "Am I missing something?" she said quietly.

"The older woman is Thekla, Leonidas's aunt, and the other is Phaedra, Leo's ex-girlfriend, the woman I told you about."

"He invited her here, today?"

I shrugged. "Could be."

I thought of the irony of my chat with Eve moments earlier about following one's heart and love overcoming cultural challenges. I wondered how love would get around this damnable intrusion.

Phaedra was dressed in tight white trousers, well cut, and a turquoise silk top, cut low with a hint of a lacy kind of bra underneath; a clutch of pearls at her neck. Very chic and sexy. Her straight black hair shimmered like midnight as she walked into the garden. Thekla led the way and as she passed she fixed me with her evil button eyes. Just for a second but they burnt into my soul. Leonidas dashed calmly into damage limitation and kissed them both briefly on the cheek. He spoke to them in Greek. All very affable-sounding. He sat the pair in the middle of the long table, far enough away.

With the initial shock of seeing Phaedra, I had the urge to get up and leave, but good sense prevailed. It would hardly look cool to leg it in a huff, not in this glorious dress. Thekla had a look of entitlement, head up, smoothing a wisp of hair behind one of her big fleshy ears. I laughed, more of a nervous cackle. Angus nudged me with his elbow and gave me a warning look. But the cackle couldn't be silenced yet. I was remembering the story Myrto had told me about the scorpion landing on Thekla's head during an olive harvest. I had a vision in my mind then of Thekla with a scorpion's nest in her big hairdo, and running about in fiery circles. How could I get hold of a scorpion before the lunch was out? The thought had already hit me. It was probably Thekla who engineered this Easter surprise all by herself. A piece of spite ramped up by seeing Angelos and me in Myrto's field. Well, that's what I preferred to believe, otherwise it was Leo's idea. That was another kind of scorpion's nest.

Myrto leaned towards me and said in a hoarse whisper, "Leonidas lining up all the sheilas now, eh?"

Another cackle escaped me. Angus laughed, but only briefly. Phaedra's eyes flicked towards us and then away.

Angus leaned towards me again, whispering, "Do you want me to go and talk to Leo, Bronte, and tell him he's a feckin' toerag doing this?"

"No. He probably didn't know." I dipped my head towards Thekla, who was piling her plate with barbecued octopus.

"Ah, I get it. She had to get even with you for snaring her favourite," said Angus, his eyebrows bunching with intent to commit some kind of felony.

I nodded. "Maybe, but let's all keep calm," I said, dousing my rising stomach acid with a quick gulp of water.

Underneath the table I heard Zeffy growl lightly. Perhaps he'd picked up a change in mood and didn't like it, or the roast lamb had awakened his senses. Then he growled louder.

Thekla pulled up the tablecloth.

"*Panayia mou*! You have that *vromiko* dog under the table, Bronte?" she said with a grimace.

"Yes, and that's where he's staying. And he's not filthy as you say," I snapped.

Phaedra flipped up the tablecloth and glanced at the dog. More cautious than critical, I thought. Trying to catch a glimpse of his molars perhaps. Eve was daintily eating her appetisers and quaffing wine, occasionally giving me a sisterly smile. I saw her appraising Phaedra from time to time, as if wondering how she might one day work her into the plot of a romantic thriller of some kind, if she could actually ever write one.

I skulled a half glass of white wine, poured another and smoothed my dress over my knees, trying to gather my thoughts. But whatever I did, I knew the afternoon was finished now. I watched as Adonis at the spit started to carve lamb onto two large platters and one of the women brought them over to the long table. Bowls of salad and baskets of bread were also brought and we tucked into lunch. Leonidas chose to sit at his own small table near the kitchen, sharing it with the women and the lamb carver, safe for now.

The lamb was delicious and despite momentarily having lost my appetite, I was suddenly starving and decided to at least enjoy the food, and most especially the wine. Zeffy was getting restive again and when no-one was watching, I took some of the grisly morsels from the platter that no-one else wanted and slipped them under the table. That was a mistake, of course, because it made him want more.

After the main meal, the village women offered the plates of dessert, the things that everyone had brought: *galaktoboureko* (custard pie), sticky baklava and plates of fruit. It was quite a feast. Now and then I saw Leonidas in the distance enjoying his lunch and laughing with the villagers. He was always easy with most people, able to fit in. It was one of the things I'd always loved about him up until now, and his essential goodness. He never spoke to Phaedra, who kept a vigil by Thekla's side. Beauty and the beast.

With a lull in the proceedings, I wandered over to ask Adonis if I might have some of the leftover bits for the '*skilos*'. I thought he'd pull a face, but as there was plenty of meat left over, and some of it less edible, he was only too happy to pile a small paper plate with meat and a piece of the barbecued *kokoretsi*. This is a Greek specialty for these occasions, a long sausage construction stuffed with different bits of offal, like a kind of Hellenic haggis. I wandered back to the table and made sure that Thekla saw the pile of meat as I slipped it under the table for the dog. I could hear Zeffy sluicing it down. Only the piece of *kokoretsi* was left. I should have kept that back for later – that was my biggest mistake. I momentarily forgot about Zeffy's habit of hiding food, like an obsessive magpie. Often, I found food in the house in odd places, in corners, under furniture – once I discovered a chicken bone hidden inside a vase.

When he got to the *kokoretsi* there was no turning back. He bolted out from under the table so fast that his collar came off and it lay on the ground at the end of the lead, trapped under the leg of my chair. He dashed into the garden, with the *kokoretsi* clamped in his mouth like a trophy.

Everyone looked up to see what the dog was doing. Thekla mouthed something in Greek. Leonidas turned and gave me a disapproving look. Angus was mumbling about more clusterfucks. Myrto was laughing.

"Better than an Aussie barbie this one, Bronte," she said, slapping her knees with mirth.

I ran down the garden after the dog, feeling like one of those bad mothers in a British supermarket, chasing a tearaway kid down the aisles. When I got near him, where he was sheltering under a vibrant orange tree, he thought this was some kind of game and leapt about, the ends of the sausage flapping. I chased him, my kitten heels gouging out divots on a patch of pristine lawn. I cursed loudly. I began to regret having brought Zeffy at all.

"Come here, Zeffy," I cajoled. I knew I wouldn't catch him. He was too young and wily. He took off back up the garden towards the pool while everyone watched. I noticed Thekla with her pinched eyes. Other Greeks were harrumphing with annoyance. How nice it must have been for everyone to see the *xeni* woman making a spectacle of herself while the woman who rightfully should have been at the head of the table, in their view perhaps, was skulking prettily on the side lines. I saw Angus making towards Zeffy with the lead and collar in his hand.

Zeffy stopped at the edge of the pool, the *kokoretsi* still in his mouth. He was staring at the second thing in the world he loved most: a big body of water, something to swim in. Oh no, he wouldn't, surely! But what he did was so much more. In the middle of the pool was a blow-up plastic lilo, which Leonidas had put there, thinking some guest would actually want to dip in the pool today, apart from the dog. Zeffy launched himself off the side of the pool with a big belly-flop, which sent an arc of water my way, splashing the front of my lovely dress, soaking my shoes. Sharp intake of breath from the diners. With the *kokoretsi* still clamped in his mouth he paddled to the lilo and clambered onto it. Safe from human killjoys, he devoured the treat in a few satisfied gulps as everyone looked on in disgust. Dogs in Greece were barely tolerated in the sea, definitely not in posh swimming pools.

"*Poli kako*, bad dog, Zeffy," I shouted, more for my self-respect than anything else. But despite my soaking, there was a bit of me that now applauded Zeffy's spirit, his paw up to the established view of canines. It all seemed amusing until he decided that a proper swim was now in order and belly-flopped straight back into the water, swimming around in big circles, barking at anyone who came near or attempted an expulsion. Out of the corner of my eye I saw Leonidas bounce from his chair and rush over. He'd lost his cool and looked angry. Not something I'd seen often.

"Really, Bronte, I can't have the dog in the water. I asked you to keep him under control," he said angrily.

Angus was at the side of the pool, bending down, trying to grab Zeffy as he streamed past. Round and round he swam, enjoying his moment in the sun, a 'catch me if you can' expression flashing in his brown eyes, celebrating his new liberated life.

Leonidas gave me a look of sharp entreaty.

"Well, I'm not going in for him, if that's what you're thinking," I snapped back at him.

Leonidas walked off towards a small shed under the house, to find something long, I assumed, to hoist Zeffy out of the pool. It was Adonis who had the most sense, and seemed to be the only one of the Greeks enjoying this impromptu entertainment. He brought me over a chunk of lamb and pointed to the dog. Brilliant. I held it up for Zeffy and in seconds he had managed to scramble out of the pool but not before he'd given himself one last almighty shake, which sent plumes of water over some of the Greeks at the table, splashing me across the face. As soon as I dropped the meat in front of him, he'd downed it, and Angus managed to slip the collar over his head, grabbed the lead and took him back to the table.

"Can you keep a hold of him, Angus? I need to clean up a bit," I said, sitting down for a moment as I fetched my handbag from under the table.

"You're fine as you are, Bronte." He gave me an expression of comical paternalism, then flicked his eyes in Phaedra's direction and pulled a sour face.

Eve hadn't said very much but I could tell she was soaking up the antics of the day with certain mirth.

"My dress is soaked down the front. You'll be sorry you gave it to me," I said to her.

"Don't worry, Bronte, there are more dresses where that came from. And I'm just loving the entertainment. I didn't know Greek Easter could be this lively," she said quite loudly, for a bit of benign mischief of her own, I thought.

That made me smile as I strode off to the house just as Leonidas was walking out with a net on a long pole, as if on some doomed fishing expedition.

"Don't worry, it's all sorted now," I said, waving my arm airily towards the pool. He gave me a chilly look.

I made my way up to the main bathroom in the villa. The house was cool and quiet with its light marble floors and pale furniture. Despite having chosen to live in Villa Anemos with Angus, I did like the solitude and quietness of Villa Ambelia and it was especially welcome then, far from the chaos below. In the bathroom I managed to pat the dress dry. No damage there. I wiped my face, reapplied some make-up and sorted my hair. When I left the bathroom, I found Leonidas sitting in the living room, waiting for me.

"Sit here for a minute, Bronte," he said quietly. His mood had lightened, but not much. I sat on the opposite sofa, brushing my hand over the dress nervously.

He was about to say something but I rushed in first. "Don't criticise the dog, please. It's not his fault."

"You didn't have to bring him though."

I held up my hands. "I like the dog. My choice. You didn't have to invite Phaedra."

He ran a hand through his hair. "I didn't. Thekla must have gone to the church in Kalamata for the Sunday service. She must have seen Phaedra and invited her back here. I don't have the whole story but it's not an issue, Bronte. Today, everyone socialises."

"But Phaedra didn't have to come …" It occurred to me that she should have been in church in Koroni, where her family and she were always supposed to celebrate Easter together, or so Polly had once told me. But I let the point go.

"Phaedra wouldn't have come if she didn't think she was welcome; if you two weren't still comfortable together," I said, petulantly.

"We're not together at all," he replied impatiently.

"Angus saw you both together in the city, looking very friendly. He even took a photo, with his mobile."

"Really!" he said, more surprised, I thought, that Angus – who'd always been a Luddite with mobiles – had actually taken a photo.

"Yes. It's a very cosy image."

He sighed. "But pictures can be deceiving."

"Maybe. Look, it's no big deal. But the fact is you've kept all this a secret."

"Phaedra came for Easter and wanted to see me, to talk. She has some problems with her life in England. She wanted to talk to me about them."

"What problems?"

"I cannot say, Bronte. She wouldn't want that. It is confidential."

"Can't you give me a clue?"

He was quiet a moment, his face turned towards the view from the window, as if collecting his thoughts, but when he looked back at me, I could see his eyes beginning to simmer with annoyance. Why all this faff and secrecy over Phaedra's problems? I wondered. Were they matters of national security?

Then the thought plopped into my head.

"Perhaps the issue is ... she wants to come back to Greece. She misses her family, her life here? Am I right?"

"In the middle of this economic crisis?"

"Maybe."

I could tell he wasn't enjoying this much and the less he said, the more I tried to fill in the gaps out of frustration.

"Isn't it the case that it's not Greece she wants, it's you! Maybe you've both decided you made a mistake – splitting up. It was all very sudden."

"I haven't made a mistake, Bronte. And you know how I feel about you."

I said nothing. He came out with a torrent of Greek and I was clueless, except for the word 'Thekla', several times. I hoped he was damning her to hell.

"The point is, Leo, you told me you had family business to sort out last weekend. You lied – it was all about Phaedra."

"In a way, but I wanted to give her advice quietly before she left for England."

"And have you?"

"I think so."

There are some expressions in the English language I don't like because they are 'leaky' in my mind, never quite embracing the truth, and 'I think so' is up there with them. It's an expression that sounds reassuring but it's often a giant get-out clause that leaves the way open for a change of heart.

I took a deep breath to calm my mind. I felt weary all of a sudden.

"Maybe it's more complicated than we all know," I said quietly. "Maybe you should examine your heart a bit more, Leo. As I should perhaps. And I think it would be best if I don't see you just for a bit. I want time to think things through."

He sighed with annoyance. "Think what through? Ach, Bronte. Don't let Phaedra's problems come between us. It's nothing you should be worried about, trust me!"

"But the problems have come between us already. Whoever invited Phaedra, she's here now and it looks bad," I said, getting up and smoothing out the front of my dress again, like some Sorority Princess who's had a bad night at the Prom. He stood up as well and came towards me, trying to give me a hug. But I pulled away.

"Let's talk later on today, when everyone's gone," he said.

"I've got nothing more to say right now. Maybe we'll talk next weekend," I said, turning and walking out of the room.

On the way down the stairs I saw Phaedra ascending quickly, like a smooth homing pigeon. There was no way to avoid her. I was a couple of steps above her. She smiled. It was perfunctory but I got a sharp view of very white straight teeth, as you'd expect of a dentist, and attractive dark eyes.

I didn't want to play the wounded heroine so I said, "Hi, Phaedra. Leo tells me you're working in Brighton."

She looked uncomfortable and took a moment to answer. "Yes, I've been there well over a year now," she said in perfect English.

"That's nice," I said stepping down a stair, ready to bolt, but she continued, "It's very strange, is it not, that you are living in my country now and I am living in yours. The crisis has …"

I cut across her. "Yes, curious, but I am *loving* your country despite the crisis."

"And I *yours*," she added, looking comically shocked.

Liar, I thought, as I bade her farewell and dashed down the stairs, out of the house and into the garden. Now the only real thing I'd ever remember favourably about Phaedra was her teeth.

I got back to the table to find Angelos sitting on the other side of Eve, having a laugh over something, their shoulders slightly hunched together, which didn't surprise me at all. He was young and attractive and Eve was at her charming best. I glanced quickly around the assembled guests and knew that the image of the pair would cause a frisson of interest, no more probably. But Thekla, who was communing with one of the village women, noticed everything. She had eyes like a fly that seemed to look everywhere at once and I knew they were darting towards Eve and Angelos frequently. I wondered if Eve, despite her years of coming and going to Greece, really understood the dynamics of the Greek village. Perhaps not. Or maybe she simply didn't care. Myrto looked a bit tipsy. Angus also.

I kissed Eve on the cheek. "I'll be off now, if you don't mind. I must change anyway. I'm so annoyed that Zeffy splashed the dress."

She whispered in my ear, "Pity you have to leave but I quite understand, Bronte. I'd do the same. And what a brass neck, that minx turning up at lunch."

I nodded.

"Come over and see me one day soon," she said, before turning back to Angelos. I caught his glance just before I turned to go.

"Bye, Bronte. Thank you for the invite today. It was fun!" he said, with a faltering look in his eyes, before he carried on his chatter with Eve. It was that look that children get when they've been caught out doing a slightly naughty thing. Ach, it wasn't my problem, but I'd been here long enough to know that, actually, it probably was.

18

A woman and her mangas

Angus decided to leave with me, saying he was tired with all the excitement, but I knew he was doing it out of a sense of loyalty, which was sweet, especially as I knew some of the Greeks were his regular drinking buddies. Adonis rushed over to say goodbye before we left, handing over a bag with more leftovers. He was laughing and pointing at Zeffy. "*O skilos, einai poli mangas.*"

Angus laughed and slapped the man on the back.

"What did Adonis say?" I asked as we walked towards Villa Anemos. I slipped my arm through his.

"The dog's a *mangas*, a real character, a daredevil, that kind of thing. A compliment."

"He's right. Zeffy knows how to stir up the disapproving masses."

"He's Greek. You don't spend months on the street without becoming a rebel."

"So it seems."

"By the way, pet, I don't know if I said it before but you looked absolutely beautiful today in that dress. You just glowed. Still do, despite your baptism by Zeffy. I was proud of you."

"Thanks, Angus, that means a lot coming from you," I said, my eyes prickling a bit with tears. "I should have stayed longer at the lunch. Leaving looks like total defeat, but I couldn't stay. I would've lost my temper in the end."

"You did the right thing, Bronte. Sometimes keeping your dignity means more than winning."

Back home, we sat on the kitchen balcony. It was still hot and the gulf was calm, with serried rows of fluffy clouds scudding overhead. Now and then we could hear a peal of laughter from Villa Ambelia and the sound of Greek music drifting up from the pool area. I dreaded the lunch would morph into a party in our absence, with singing and dancing, which would ramp up my resentment even more.

Angus went inside and returned with a bottle of white wine.

"Might as well have another drink," he said, pouring two glasses. "I hope you got stuck into Leonidas for the Phaedra fuck-up," he said, not-so-delicately.

"Not really. And anyway, he denies having anything to do with it." Angus rolled his eyes. "But I told him I was cooling things for a week or two. I need time to think."

"Oh dear! I know how much you like Leo, but if you don't mind me saying … maybe it's just a kind of holiday affair after all."

I was shocked. "It wasn't just a holiday affair to me."

"You know what I mean. It was the circumstances, wasn't it? Our search for Kieran. The high emotions of that time. And Leo helped us. I mean, he's a great guy. I like him, but as a potential husband … It's the Greek thing, the pitfalls of another culture."

"Polly always said Greek men have a huge sense of entitlement."

"Polly's right. They get spoilt rotten by their mothers. And here's another thing, Bronte, I'd have thought you'd have met his parents by now. They live in Kalamata, don't they?"

I nodded.

"Well, why have you never been taken over to meet them if he's so in love with you?"

"I don't know. Perhaps Leo's worried they won't like their son being in a relationship with a foreigner. Maybe they're like Thekla, and I'm better off not meeting them yet."

186

"Well, if they've got strong feelings about their son hooking up with a foreigner then it doesn't bode well for the long run, does it?"

"Maybe," I said.

We lapsed into silence. A song with Levantine mournfulness rode on currents of hot air from Villa Ambelia. It seemed to chime with the downbeat conversation we'd just had.

Finally, Angus squeezed my arm and said, "You know, pet, you don't have to stay in Greece if you don't want to."

"That's a strange thing to say right now. And I know that anyway. I'm not a prisoner here."

"Don't you miss your life in Scotland, in journalism? I often wonder if this is enough for you. I mean, I love the fact you're here and how you helped me sort out my health problems, and the situation with Kieran, but I don't want to keep you here if you think you'd be better off back home. You're not my carer."

"I've never thought of myself as that, Angus. You don't actually need one – yet. As for the other bit, you're always saying Scottish journalism's going down the pan. You told me last year when I left The Alba and took redundancy that it was the best thing I could have done."

"It was, but there's always London. There's plenty more on offer if you want it. You've got good contacts. You could build on that. Your friend Eve has contacts in London in publishing, and journalism, I'm sure."

"She has and she's already told me she can help me to get more work if I want it – freelance that is. But I wouldn't have to leave Edinburgh for that."

"Well, think about it. I'm sure you miss the excitement of your old life. And you're a good journalist."

"I miss seeing Marcella and Shona. I miss some of my friends, of course, but honestly, I can't believe we're having this conversation. I don't give up on things that easily, you know that. And I love Leonidas. I would miss him dreadfully if I sloped off back to Scotland."

Angus had his chin leaning on his hand, staring over the gulf, looking a bit distracted.

"Tell me, Angus, do *you* miss Scotland? I mean, if you wanted to return, I'd go back with you, at least till you settled."

He turned and looked at me with startled eyes. In the light outside I could see how hazel they were, with flecks of green and pale brown. It was a combination of colours that changed according to the place and the mood. Now they looked browner, darker.

"I don't want to go back to Scotland. Not because I don't love it. I do. And there are lots of things I miss, like those baldy wet hills we used to struggle up, remember? I miss having a blether with old friends in the pub. Apart from that, and Shona of course, and the grandkids, there's nothing for me over there now. I can't pull up stumps and start again, not at my age. And I love it here too. My heart may be Scottish and falling apart, but my soul is Greek."

I smiled at that. I think he was right. He was as Greek perhaps as a foreigner can be. Angus had told me the ancient Greeks believed that if you spoke Greek, you were Greek – and he spoke Greek well enough.

"I don't know what's wrong with us today, we're awfully moody and reflective. It's all Thekla's fault. She's stuck her witch's broom into everything," I said.

"What was she like today, with that muckle big hair and dripping in gold!"

We laughed heartily. I hoped the noise would carry down to Villa Ambelia.

"What we need, Bronte, is to conjure up a plan to put Thekla off village life and send her scuttling back to Athens, where she belongs."

"Okay, let's think of something, and soon," I said, more to humour him because I feared it would take a miracle to lever her out of Marathousa.

I left him sitting at the table, staring into the distance. I could tell by the set of his mouth and his eyes narrowed in concentration he was already hatching some crazy plan.

Later that night when I went to bed, I lay for a while thinking about what Angus had said – about going back to Scotland. It seemed unimaginable, a few days ago at least. I had walked away from my career, and the country I had always thought of as my home, and my family and friends, and mostly because of my love for Leonidas. I was infatuated with Greece too, little by little. But perhaps it was time to consider that my existence here was just an entertaining experiment in living abroad, and that I might have to slope off one day with nothing but my modest victories and failures packed up like disparate souvenirs, like some of the framed images that now adorned my chest of drawers.

There was the picture of Kieran that was precious to me, in his Royal Army Service Corps uniform, his hair thick, dark and wavy with its widow's peak above the forehead, his eyes hazel like Angus's. He looked happy. When we uncovered his fate in Greece, it meant finding Kieran for the first time in my life; fleshing out a grandfather who had been little more than a ghost up to that point. That was my greatest achievement here at least.

There were some lovely pictures of Leonidas and me in the village but my favourite was one he'd given me last year, an old one of him as a child up in the village of Platanos, in the Taygetos mountains where his family had come from and where by co-incidence our search for Kieran had led us. In the picture, Leonidas was serving tables at a local *yiorti* celebration, looking so handsome even at a young age. And innocent. It was touching.

And finally, the small wooden icon of St Dimitrios, the dark-haired saint riding his russet-coloured horse. It was ironic, the way I had come across the image by chance, as he would be the character who would play such a crucial but unexpected role in solving our family mystery – and a saint who hadn't rolled out all his miracles yet.

What enticing and uncertain images would I add to these in future months and years, if I was still here?

As if he'd read my mind, Zeffy came crashing into the room, a blur of thick fur, a faint aroma of *kokoretsi* and chlorine. He leapt onto the end of my bed. "What about me?" his chestnut eyes seemed to say. "What could I do to get my mug on the chest of drawers?" A picture would be required, I thought, but until then I would forever have a vision in my mind of Zeffy diving into the pool with the 'sausage' in his mouth, swimming in crazy circles, cocking a snook at the anti-dog league, mad aunts, minxy dentists and fickle doctors.

The next morning, Angus brought me coffee and found Zeffy sleeping under the top sheet, his head on the pillow beside me. How and when he'd arrived there, I had no recollection. I wish I could have said the same for the lunch the previous day, but there would be no chance of forgetting it, or the unexpected infamies it was about to spawn.

19

Grime and punishment

"Bronte, I had to call and find out what's happening with you and Leonidas since the Phaedra woman turned up. My God! I was floored by that. Talk about making a dramatic entrance, stage left, darling!"

It was Eve at nine in the morning the following Tuesday. I was having breakfast with Angus on the balcony off the kitchen. He raised an eyebrow at me. "Eve", I mouthed softly. He did an exaggerated eye roll, even though I suspect he found her quite entertaining.

"Leo and I are cooling things for a bit."

"Oh! That's a shame, but I quite understand. But I have to tell you I didn't see much evidence after you left that things were hotting up again with those two. He spent his time fussing over the guests. Such a lovely man. I never saw him talking to Phaedra or the batty aunt. But I didn't stay till the bitter end. Angelos invited me to have coffee at that nice Kefi Beach Bar at Santova. He left his car at Myrto's farm and I drove down. It was rather nice. He's such a gorgeous guy, isn't he? So like Leonidas. Much less serious though. And such good company. I wish I were a few dozen years younger, I can tell you. I left him at the beach. He wanted to swim but I came back home. He asked me out to dinner some time. What do you think?"

What did I think? Jesus! A friend of mine going on a date with Leonidas's nephew, half her age? Leonidas would kill me, unless Thekla throttled me first. This would not be good. And I wondered how it must have looked to some of the

191

Greeks at the lunch, them leaving together. Gums would already be bumping around the village.

"I don't know," I said in a tinny voice full of apprehension. "No reason why not, I suppose. If you think you can handle it."

"What do you mean?"

"Well you know, don't get too serious …"

"Don't fall in love you mean." She laughed theatrically. "One little dinner. How can that hurt?"

Oh it could, I thought, but I decided not to say anything else. It wasn't my problem – today. I had my own issues to mull over. My mental health shelf stackers were working overtime.

When I hung up, Angus grilled me over the call. I told him about Eve and Angelos. He tipped his head back and roared with laughter, nearly overturning the chair.

"Oh, another clusterfuck!" he said, rubbing his hands together. "I never thought life in this village would end up like a Christmas pantomime."

"Calm down, you'll do yourself some damage." I watched him eating his breakfast, spreading a great slick of butter over his toast. I could almost feel his lipid levels rising like a Jellystone Park geyser.

Later in the week I was in the Zefiros, checking emails. Leonidas had organised wifi in Villa Anemos but it was sometimes unreliable, and I liked going to the *kafeneio* to escape the confines of the house, to have some time to myself, though that was rare in a Greek village. Elpida, as usual, sat down for a while at my table for a gossip. She had a twinkle in her eye.

"So, Bronte. How did you like your Sunday lunch at Leonidas's house?"

"Lovely, thank you. How was yours?"

"Oh, same as always. Too much food, too much bla, bla, bla!"

She had her elbow on the table, her chin leaning on her knuckles. She bent in a bit closer to me. "So, I hear that Phaedra, she turns up at lunch. *Po, po, po!*" She windmilled her arm at me.

I didn't answer straight off. I was no longer shocked at her candour. And I wasn't surprised at the speed with which one of the villagers at the lunch had foghorned this bit of gossip all over Marathousa.

"Yes, she was there."

"Don't you worry, my girl. Leonidas, he is smart. He never did follow her to England as they planned – remember? Now he's with you. End of the story," she said, smacking the flat of her hands together with vibrant finality.

When I said nothing, she continued, "And I hear that it is Thekla who brings Phaedra. *Panayia mou!*" She crossed herself three times. Yep, it was *that* bad! "You know, when I first heard that Thekla is coming back to the village I feel it can't be good. I know her. Gets bored, wants to stir things around, like poking a stick in the *sfika* nest. Hornets, Bronte. *Poli kako.* Very bad …."

While I found her conversation entertaining as always, I was distracted after a while by the sight of two men on the road talking, their heads close together. One had a cigarette and was blowing smoke out of the side of his mouth. It was the creep, Dionysos, with another man, bald and shifty-looking, whom I thought was an expat I'd seen in the Zefiros before.

I interrupted Elpida's monologue. "Elpida, who's that man down there talking to Dionysos, the guy I keep seeing on the road?"

She squinted towards the pair. "He's a *xenos*, British man, Derek, lives down the hill," she said, waving towards a low-lying valley within the vast stretch of olive orchards, north of the village. "I don't like that one, Bronte," she added, with a vibrant grimace.

"Does Dionysos speak good English?"

"I don't think so. But Derek speaks Greek. Not good like your *babas*, Angus. But okay."

"Are they friends?"

"Seems to be."

When I got home, I told Angus about the incident.

"Are you sure the expat was Derek?"

"That's what Elpida said."

Angus frowned. "Don't you remember we were in the Kali Parea one night and a table of expats were sitting outside? He was in the group with the cackling coat hanger, remember?"

An image leapt into my mind: a thin woman with a disproportionately loud and annoying laugh. "I do, but why would Derek be friends with the creep?"

"Derek's a bit of a numpty, ex-army, likes guns. Likes to hunt with other expats, but mostly Greeks. Likes wild boar and shooting thrushes – disgusting business – to make those appalling pickled delicacies called *tsikles*. Derek's one of those expats who says he loathes Britain but spends all his time reading news reports about Britain on the internet or watching the BBC on satellite TV. The fact he might hang about with Dionysos doesn't surprise me. Derek's very right-wing, so he would hang about with supporters of the EPE party like Dionysos. Give guys like Derek a big body swerve. They don't do anyone any good."

I felt uneasy when I went to bed that night. Zeffy came bursting into the room after me, carrying a lamb bone in his mouth.

"Get out. That's disgusting!" I said. The lamb bone was obviously from his cache of Sunday lunch offerings he'd hidden somewhere in the house. He ran out of the bedroom and I decided to put his dog bed just outside the door for the night and shut it in case he tried to bring in more food. He had to learn the bedroom wasn't for stashing treats. I could hear him moaning outside but tried to ignore him. It was my fault because increasingly I let him sleep on the end of my bed. It was a bad habit now but I found it comforting. Zeffy and I had bonded well. I liked the fact we were, in our different ways, both *xenoi*, outsiders, genial misfits, if you like.

I slept badly. Somewhere close to dawn Zeffy started up a low growl outside the door, which exploded into a barking session. I got up and went into the sitting room, where he was dancing about the front door. I try to quieten him down before he woke up the neighbourhood. The front windows were shuttered but with slats that could be angled different ways. I peered outside. There was a glimmer of pearly light behind the mountains. Nothing moving on the road, or anywhere for that matter. There was no other noise, apart from a few dogs on chains barking back. A donkey brayed, probably Myrto's.

I went back to bed and Zeffy followed, jumping onto the bed. I let him be. I felt uneasy, thinking about Dionysos, wondering if he would ever come to the house with mischief in mind. But why would he do that? When I got up, I let Zeffy out through the back door into the garden, as I often did before his first walk of the day.

"Did you hear Zeffy barking in the night?" I asked Angus, sitting at the dining table. He shook his head. He must have slept more soundly than I had.

After breakfast I got a call from Leonidas. He sounded irritable.

"Bronte, I know you do not want to talk to me at the moment but something a little disturbing has been brought to my attention. I don't like to get involved in village gossip if I can help it and I have six patients outside waiting to see me right now. But this is something I don't want to ignore. I hear that your friend Eve has become very friendly with my nephew Angelos. They've been seen together down at the beach. Is it what I think it is?"

"They're just friends. They were chatting at the lunch on Sunday. Nothing wrong with that."

"Yes, *agapi mou*, but a woman like Eve … she doesn't just have friendships with men."

"I don't see why not," I snapped, just to annoy him. But this was what I'd been afraid of. Eve and Angelos, and I knew what he meant. The Eve I'd seen lately – not the one who was guarded and a bit flaky but the relaxed, sexy Eve – gave the impression of a woman who would go to bed with a man and then have him for her next meal. Hell, even floss with him afterwards!

"Angelos is a young man trying to find his way in the world. He's intelligent and very handsome. I don't think Eve has his career in her mind."

I laughed, a nervous girly giggle. God, but I wasn't in the mood for this now.

"Don't worry, Leo. It's a harmless friendship. She's going back to London soon."

"Good. Forgive me, but rural Greece is not Mykonos. Perhaps you can persuade your friend to move her attentions elsewhere while she's here."

I stared at the phone after he'd hung up, wondering if I'd just woken up in a parallel world where Marathousa had just collided with a Jane Austen novel. I felt like Elizabeth Bennet being chastised by a pompous Mr Darcy.

It was quiet in the house now. Angus was in the shower. I went outside. Zeffy was nowhere to be seen among the fruit and olive trees and the oleander bushes that grew right to the boundaries, which were marked out by a sturdy wire fence. I called but he didn't come. I noticed the side gate was open, which was unusual. We always shut it at night.

Zeffy wasn't in the front garden either, so I returned to the back, calling him as I went, walking right to the end of the garden this time, where there were a few rows of grapevines, the descendants of what Leonidas's grandfather had tried to grow in the past, but which weren't thriving, especially under Angus's spasmodic care. I had an instinct that something very bad had happened, something I'd expected for a while now.

20

The reckoning

I finally found Zeffy under an olive tree near the bottom fence, being sick, a pile of foul-looking vomit on the ground, streaked with blood.

I thought of what he might have eaten. The lamb he'd hidden? But it wasn't that old, not for a dog who'd lived rough and eaten out of bins.

"What's wrong, Zeffy?" I rubbed one of his ears. He lifted his head a bit off the ground and gave me a desolate look, whimpering. I was afraid for him.

I raced back inside for Angus. He was just out of the shower.

"Quickly, come with me. Zeffy doesn't look well."

We rushed back to Zeffy and found him still retching onto the ground. Then I noticed blood oozing from his nose.

"Bronte, you know what. I think Zeffy's been poisoned. Someone's dropped something nasty into the garden, probably rat poison, that's the usual stuff. Animals bleed to death if they eat this stuff."

"Someone's been here early this morning. Zeffy was barking a lot."

"Look, Bronte, the farmers here all keep syringes with some antidote formula inside. They all know how to inject. Myrto may have it. Go see her and tell her what's happened. I'll stay with Zeffy."

I ran to Myrto's farm. She was watering some of the olive trees near her house. Angelos was there also. They both looked startled when they saw my panicked face.

"What is it, Bronte?" said Myrto.

"Zeffy. We think he's been poisoned. He looks very sick. He's vomited a bit. There's blood. Angus said you might have an antidote."

She gave me a despairing look. "I used to keep these things on the farm but not now." She looked at Angelos.

"I know some farmers who might keep it but I think it's best to call the vet. Do you use Dr Mavrofidi down on the coast?" he said.

I nodded.

"I will call him. I have his number on my mobile." He dialled and after a while started talking rapid Greek.

"He says we must bring the dog straight down. You go back to the garden and I will park my truck in front of your house, okay?"

When I got back to the house, I found Angus in the same spot, leaning over Zeffy. The dog was panting and whining lightly. What a disaster to have saved him from a life of misery on the streets only to suffer this.

"Angelos is going to drive me down to the vet."

"Do you want me to come with you?"

"No, it's fine. You stay here and I'll see you soon. I'll call if there's a problem."

Myrto had arrived now, out of breath, and stared down at the dog.

"Who do you think does this terrible thing?" she asked.

"Don't know but we think it was some creep who's been hanging about the village," said Angus.

"Not the *malakas* on a scooter who pushes Bronte on the road?"

"We don't know. Could be."

She crossed herself. "Let's hope he gets a bad fate now; hit by a big truck, or struck with lightning," she said, dramatically. Then she put her hand up, as if palm-slapping

199

the air, muttering something under her breath. It looked almost scary, like some kind of Greek curse.

We heard the sound of Angelos's truck at the front gate and moments later he ran towards us. He picked Zeffy up gently and carried him to the truck, where he'd spread out old olive sacks. He placed him there delicately.

"Come with me, Bronte. We must be quick."

Angelos roared past the village, down the coast road, screeching around the hairpin bends with their small shrines to other souls lost in dodgy driving manoeuvres. But today I didn't care. I hadn't even bothered with my seat belt. Angelos parked on the road in front of the vet's surgery and carried Zeffy inside. It wasn't a busy day and Dr Blacksnake was waiting for us, dressed in his white medical coat. Angelos lay the dog on the examination table.

"I remember this dog now. You got him as a stray, yes?" said Dr Blacksnake.

"I wanted to give him to the dog rescue group but then I decided to keep him. He's very sweet."

"Well, now you see how some people here have no regard for dogs," said the vet, as he started to examine Zeffy." *Or no regard for their owners either*, I thought, which was doubly chilling.

"I see too many of these poisonings, you know, but it's lucky you got him here straight away. I am fairly sure that your dog has been given a rat poison in some meat. He has the symptoms. It causes internal bleeding and if not caught in time obviously the animal will bleed to death. I am confident I can reverse this. I am going to do something to induce vomiting and give him some injections and tests, so perhaps it's better if you both wait outside. I will call you."

There was one other person in the waiting room, a man with a tiny fluffed-up dog. It sat on the man's knee like a ball of wool with eyes. The man stared lovingly at it, as if it were a baby. It was good to see there were Greeks who did value dogs as pets, even in the crisis.

When the vet came back out, he told us he wanted to keep Zeffy overnight for observation.

"I think he will be fine. You did the right thing to bring him straight here. But you may see him before you go."

I went into the examination room on my own. Zeffy was lying on the table, tired but less critical. He raised his head slowly off the table and licked my hand.

"Poor wee guy. But don't worry, I'll make the evil bastard pay," I said softly as I turned and left with a heavy heart. I knew absolutely that Dionysos was behind it.

"Let's go for a coffee. I think we need one. There's a nice place across the road," said Angelos as we left the surgery.

The café was right on the beach with a view towards Kalamata. It was a glorious spot, the sea was calm and glassy and several people were swimming. I was glad of the distraction. We sat at a table under the trees and Angelos ordered two cappuccinos.

"Thank you so much, Angelos, for helping with Zeffy. I appreciate it. It's been a terrible morning."

"Do you know who might have done this, Bronte?"

I shook my head. Maybe Myrto had already told him but I didn't want to throw accusations around in case, like Elpida or Myrto, he tried to do something about it and put himself in danger.

The coffees arrived, with two tall glasses of water and small biscuits. We didn't talk much at first. Angelos seemed a bit thoughtful. It struck me once more how much he resembled Leo, a younger version, with similar dark hair and eyes. I could see how Leo would have looked some 15 years earlier. Devastatingly handsome. At 42, Leo still looked remarkable, yet there was also a certain gravitas in his face, from the seriousness of his profession, no doubt. It was attractive in its own way, whereas Angelos had the carefree freshness of youth. I understood why Eve had so easily taken to him.

"Did you enjoy the lunch last Sunday?" I asked.

His eyes widened with interest. "Very much, even Zeffy's performance in the pool. Though I'm afraid Leo was not so entertained by it," he said with a subtle eyeroll, and I guessed that Dr Darcy had probably already ticked him off about Eve. "But Leo does a nice Easter lunch. He's a great host. In fact, my uncle is a wonderful man. I really esteem him very much. But I do hope the appearance of Phaedra at lunch has not caused a problem between you. That would be a great shame. I know the story and you must forgive my uncle this lapse of good sense, not telling you about Phaedra. He has had much on his mind lately with the crisis. Many people are suffering here, as you know very well. I give you an example if I may. A few weeks ago, Leo told me, one of his older patients had killed himself because he could not pay his tax bill. Jumped off the top of his apartment building. Can you imagine? Now the government is getting tougher on tax debts, and people can end up in jail. It brings family shame and some people would rather be dead that be shamed over debts."

"I didn't know any of this. How awful!"

"But keep this between us. My uncle would not want me to tell you. He doesn't like to shock people or make them unhappy. I tell you so you can see what pressures he has right now."

"Thank you," I said, wondering if this was the story Leo had not wanted to share with me the night we were at the coastal restaurant. I felt heavy with guilt but I reasoned that if he confided in me more about his life it would make things so much easier.

"What do you think about my friend Eve?" I asked him in a bid to change the subject but also keen to gauge his opinion. He fidgeted with the spoon on his saucer before answering.

"Oh, she's wonderful, isn't she? Now I must try to read some of her books."

Don't bother. They're not her books, I thought, acerbically.

"Can I just say something to you while we're being so candid with each other?"

"Sure," he said, spooning the froth from the cappuccino into his mouth.

"Leo is worried about you having a friendship with Eve."

He laughed, with a touch of dread in his dark eyes. "Yes, he mentioned that to me. He has nothing to worry about. Eve and I had a drink on Easter Sunday and then dinner one night in a beach taverna. It's very innocent."

Already they'd had dinner! That was news. So, not so innocent.

"And she's nearly 20 years older than me, although she doesn't look it."

She lied about her age!

"Yes, she looks great. So … will you see her again, do you think?" I said, trying to affect wistful interest only.

He beetled his eyebrows together. "I'm sure we will sometime. She goes back to London soon, I think."

"I'm sorry, I shouldn't have asked. It's really none of my business."

It wasn't, but here I was, turning into Thekla.

"Don't worry, Bronte. I see you're just trying to look after my good reputation," he said, with a sardonic smile. "Eve is a good person. She's good company, interesting. We don't have too many people like her coming to the village. Apart from you, of course."

He was quite the diplomat when he wanted to be. But why did I feel he wasn't being completely honest. A family failing?

21

Beastly solutions

A few days later I opened the front door to find Leonidas holding a bunch of roses. "Sorry for what you have endured recently with Zeffy. And for everything else," he said, with a contrite smile. The 'else' could only be Phaedra.

I ushered him inside, flattered at least by his gesture. Zeffy rushed towards him, putting his paws up on his knees, which he'd never done before.

"He senses you're a doctor and he wants to keep on your good side now," I said.

Leonidas ruffled Zeffy's head lightly and brushed a light smudge of dust from the front of his trousers.

"The dog looks healthy now."

"He's made a great recovery in just a few days, but he's not eating much yet."

"His system is still recovering. He will be fine."

I had called Leonidas on the day of the poisoning to let him know. He wanted to drive over that evening to see me but I didn't want to waste his time over a matter that was less serious than some of the issues he'd had to face lately with his patients. And things were still a bit cool between us.

When I picked up Zeffy the day after the poisoning, the vet told me the blood test confirmed rat poison but the quick treatment had saved him from any lasting effects. He told me not to leave him alone in the garden and to try to find out who had done this. He was a fierce campaigner for animal rights and said the culprit should be reported before he did it again. He was also surprised Zeffy had survived so long as a street dog without succumbing to a poisoning earlier. That thought had often occurred to me too.

I took Leonidas onto the balcony and brought out some cool drinks. Angus wasn't home. He was in Kalamata having one of his usual meet-ups with old drinking buddies, which he convinced me, as usual, was partly to do with research for his book, as Greeks of a certain age still had stories about the Battle of Kalamata, even if they weren't involved directly. And an ouzo or two to aid the memory.

"I have spoken again to my detective friend, Nikos. He was pleased to hear Eve had returned safely. Just as well, Bronte, because I don't believe the investigation into her disappearance had gone very far," he said with a shrug. "But this time, I told him about Zeffy. I've told him about this man Dionysos, too, and where he comes from. He knew who I was talking about. He's known as someone who hangs about with troublemakers from the EPE party and shows up sometimes at demonstrations in Kalamata. But this man is cunning and he knows how far to push things before he breaks the law, like so many of these people. But one day he may go too far – and that's what I am afraid of."

"If he poisoned Zeffy, he's already gone too far, in my eyes."

"But we have no actual proof, that's the problem. We must be vigilant. I will also ask some people in Marathousa to keep a watch out for him and to challenge him when he next comes to the village. If he puts a foot out of place, I will call Nikos. He will send a constable out here. So be very careful. Don't walk to the village any more while he's still about."

He took my hand and squeezed it. "And can we please forget about Phaedra's visit now that she's gone back to England."

Our chairs were side by side. He leaned towards me and pulled me close, giving me a lingering kiss. I felt great longing for him, but in the end I gently pulled away. Despite the flowers and the sympathetic words, I was still smarting with resentment. Phaedra may have been far away in Brighton, but old lovers can cast a long shadow.

"I realise she's gone, but I'm still perplexed over why you kept everything so secret. That's all." As well as why Phaedra needed to talk out her sudden dislike of life abroad with Leonidas, of all people. Why now? When next?

He sat quietly a moment, playing with a gold signet ring on his pinkie finger, his brows furrowing, with confusion perhaps.

"We have discussed all this. But I understand if you are still angry with me, Bronte. I am still so sorry about the lunch, about Phaedra just turning up like that. It spoilt your day, I fear."

"Thekla," was all I said. He nodded and fiddled more with the ring. Oh yes, he knew her malevolent intentions.

"And you looked so beautiful. That dress!" he said, trying to move the conversation on, but failing.

We fell silent for a while, then he asked, "So how can I make it up to you?" His smile had a flicker of pleading about it, as much as someone like Leonidas ever could plead. But it nudged at my conscience. How long could I keep this righteous huff going, especially when I recalled what Angelos had told me about the pressures his uncle had been under?

"I will be back again on Saturday. Let's have dinner out. Our favourite taverna. Let us be a little more carefree, yes?" he said, looking up from under the errant curl swinging down over his brow.

"Yes, if you like," I told him, but I fizzed inside once more. Had I not been carefree before Phaedra turned up? Had things not been close to perfect?

I got up and went inside, taking his roses to the kitchen sink and putting them in a vase. I sensed him behind me,

206

watching my slightly rushed movements. He leaned against a kitchen bench, thoughtful, his arms crossed over his chest. Then he flicked his car keys, as if they were worry beads, and after a few more seconds of awkward silence he said he had to return to Kalamata to see a patient. He squeezed my shoulder by way of goodbye and left. I felt mildly relieved when he went, just for the freedom of not having to think any more about the Phaedra situation, and yet wondering how to put it all behind me because the problem was, as a journalist, I always had an instinct for when I wasn't getting the whole story. And I had that feeling now. What was it about Phaedra that Leonidas couldn't tell me?

Angus was in good humour when he returned from his Kalamata jaunt, which cheered me up enormously. He looked slightly tipsy. I was in the kitchen, taking a dish of moussaka, which had taken hours to prepare, out of the oven. A bottle of red wine I'd just opened sat on the kitchen counter.

Angus sniffed the air appreciatively and helped himself to some wine.

"You're supposed to let red wine breathe a bit, Angus."

He gave me an impatient look. "Bronte, it'll start hyperventilating if it breathes any longer."

I laughed, as I always did, at his mad outpourings.

He was quiet a moment, though, quaffing his wine with relish. Then he put the glass down and rubbed his hands together.

"Well, I think I've worked out a cunning little plan to get rid of Thekla."

"Really? Tell me then." Best news I'd heard all day.

"So, it's like this. In Kalamata I met up with my village friend Panayiotis. He does work for Thekla in her garden.

He can't stand the old bat but she pays okay and on time. So, he was in the garden the other day, trying to fix her dry-stone wall, which is crumbling in places. He told me that while he was working on it Thekla came out and asked him if he'd seen scorpions in the wall. 'Not yet but there *will* be scorpions, there always is in these old walls, and plenty of them, especially with me rebuilding them,' he told her, to wind her up a bit. She told him to poleaxe any he found, and spray between the rocks to destroy any nests, that kind of thing. Panayiotis said she's terrified of scorpions." Angus chortled.

I interrupted him. "Myrto told me she's got a scorpion phobia." I told him the story about Thekla and the olive harvest and how she went crazy when a scorpion fell from a tree onto her head. Angus laughed merrily.

"We're on the right track then. So, here's the plan. Panayiotis has another Greek friend, whose house he's helping to renovate, and it's got plenty of scorpions – in the garden, and the house, big beige ones – so Panayiotis is going to transfer a few across to Thekla's place. She'll go doolally. Maybe it'll persuade her to go back to Athens."

"You don't want to kill her though, surely."

"She won't die, even if she got bitten. In Greece it's usually no worse than a wasp sting, but with her, the fear is all up here," he said, tapping his head.

"How will this friend catch the live scorpions?"

"That's it, you see, they won't be alive. Panayiotis will kill the ones he finds and he'll bring them over to Thekla's house concealed in a box or something and kind of plant them in the walls and pretend he's killed them there. And he'll bring Thekla out and show her. Dead scorpions everywhere!" Angus was cackling now.

"Is this what you sit and dream up with your friends in Kalamata? How to frighten old Greek women?"

"You're not going soft on her now?"

"Not at all," I muttered, a vision in my head of Thekla slinking into the Sunday lunch with Phaedra still fresh in my mind.

"Okay then. I'll give Panayiotis the signal to start gathering the little blighters. Yes?"

I found the idea amusing, and troubling at the same time.

"Okay, go for it! Dead scorpions, how bad could that be? But don't kill her, for God's sake. She doesn't deserve that. She's not the psychopath Rose West."

Not yet. But for me, the main problem with Thekla was that she confirmed what I already knew about Leonidas's family, that on the mother's side, whose forbears came from the Deep Mani, there had been a devious family member implicated in some of the worst betrayals of allied soldiers who escaped down the Mani after the Battle of Kalamata, when the Germans put a bounty on their heads. It showed there was bad blood in his family – and Thekla was up there with the worst of them.

"And don't give her a heart attack either," I added. "Leonidas won't thank me for that and just when things are beginning to thaw – kind of," I said, glancing at the red roses on the table.

"So, you've made up. Good, good," he said, skulling a lot more red wine.

"I don't know if you can call it that – yet. It's me really, still festering about that damned lunch. It'll pass but there's another problem brewing as well. He's not well pleased that Eve has been seen out and about with Angelos. My fault because I brought her to the lunch."

"More than out and about, Bronte. I saw the way Eve looked at him that Sunday lunch. *Po, po, po!*" he said, in the Greek manner, waving his arm around. "If lust had legs, hers were doing the London Marathon."

I laughed, wishing I'd seen that for myself, but I'd been too busy chasing Zeffy around the garden and arguing with Leonidas upstairs.

"So, I take it you're not going back to Scotland?" he asked.

"I don't think I ever said I was. It was your suggestion. I don't know if I could now anyway. I've burnt all my bridges."

"Great. They were probably old shoogly bridges anyway. Better off burning!"

Why wasn't Angus this crazy and diverting when I was young? It would have made life more interesting in reserved Stirling, where we lived. There were so many times, living with Angus in Greece, that I doubted I really knew him properly when I was growing up. He was so different now to the way he'd once been as a teacher and family man. Occasionally he seemed like a stranger, an entertaining one mostly, and sometimes he actually scared me with his reckless spin on life.

We had spent a fair bit of time together when I was young. In my teens Angus used to take me hill walking in Scotland, up the baldy hills he missed so much, and we'd had great times, hiking about in our waterproofs, sometimes having to stay over in bothies, old sheds set up to shelter ramblers in stormy weather. Maybe it was me who hadn't tried hard enough to see what constituted my own father and what an interesting character he always was. Now I was getting the measure of him. For him at least, Greece had been an epiphany, to use a Greek word, and had changed his life.

"I admire you for coming here and assimilating as well as you have, Angus. I know now how hard that must have been," I said.

"You know, what would help you is to learn the language properly. The council has started up free classes again and there's a teacher coming to the school down on the coast road a couple of times a week. I think if you could talk to Greeks more, really integrate, you'd be less overwhelmed by the culture."

"You're probably right. I'll think about it. But if a really top gig *were* to come up in Scotland in journalism, I suppose it might be hard not to consider it, shoogly bridges or not."

"You're kidding, right?"

"Yeah, of course," I said, winking at him.

22

Elpida goes large

On Sunday morning, Leonidas decided he wanted to make the church service in Marathousa by 9am for the last hour and for me to go with him. He'd never taken me to the ordinary Sunday service before, unless I particularly asked to go, thinking that perhaps I would find it too tedious, as other foreigners often did. However, occasionally I liked to go to church, as it was a rare chance to see Greeks in their own private world, engaging in rituals that were timeless, unchanged in over 500 years.

I guessed it was another gesture designed to seal our warm reconciliation of the previous night. We'd gone out to dinner as he'd planned, talked a lot, drank a bit and retired early to Villa Ambelia to finally forget the Easter fiasco, which would simply have to be filed under 'things I didn't understand about Greek life and Greek men – but would one day'.

When he parked the car near the *plateia*, the sound of the chanting in the church of the Anastasi was fanning out over the whole village through the loudspeaker pinned to the front wall. I liked to think it was the cheeky Orthodox way of getting sleepy heads out of their beds on Sunday morning.

In church, Leonidas sat on the right, in the men's section, where I was surprised to see Angus, already seated. Angus was generally not an early riser on Sunday but then I realised this was not just an ordinary service but a memorial service as well for a villager who had died 40 days previously. There was a table set before the *iconostasis* with vases of flowers and a black and white photo of a severe-looking old man. I sat on the left with the other women.

After all these months, and the week of Easter services, I was no closer to grasping what went on in the church but I enjoyed the theatricality of it, the chanting, the incense. There was something here to engage all the senses at once. Several times I glanced over at Leonidas. He looked solemn and it was hard to imagine that an hour earlier we had been rolling about in his bed.

My mind was sobered by a glance at Thekla, sitting on one of the high-backed wooden chairs along the wall beside some of the other village matrons. She caught my look and gave me an unblinking stare. I wondered what infamy she was plotting against me now. Could it rival a slew of scorpions? The thought of it made me smile to the point where it threatened to become a chortle, the nervous expression of having to be serious in church when the mind is jumpy.

Leonidas glanced over and caught my moment of levity, giving me a curious look, then a wink. I looked away and fixed my mind on the young priest, someone new, with a neat black knot of hair above the nape of his neck. He was striding with agile steps in and out of the sanctuary at regular intervals, meaning there was much standing up and sitting down by the congregation. It was making me sleepy, until Myrto arrived with Angelos. She sat beside me and squeezed my arm, giving me a broad smile. I liked Myrto a lot. She was considered slightly eccentric by the other Greeks, only because of her decision to farm alone and her years spent in Australia. That had given her a certain wisdom and broadness of vision that perhaps the others lacked.

Angelos sat next to Leonidas and together they looked like handsome brothers. At least Angelos hadn't brought Eve. Unconsciously, I turned and looked behind me just to make sure she wasn't dawdling in, over-dressed in a glamorous retro outfit. But she was nowhere to be seen.

After the service we trooped to the *kafeneio* for coffee, as was often the custom, particularly after a memorial service. The family of the deceased and friends congregated around several tables in the shade of the tall plane tree. Leonidas, Thekla, Myrto, Angelos, Angus and I sat at two tables further towards the edge of the *plateia*.

Elpida had briefly visited the church to light a candle and kiss the icons by the door. She was still wearing a black dress and a gold cross around her neck. She looked elegant in her own way: her hair more brushed and a tiny smear of lipstick. Today there was no time for her usual chat. Coffee was ordered but before she left our table, we saw a few men walk in off the road and head for a table further back in the *plateia*.

I froze when I saw that one of the two Greek men was Dionysos the creep. The third man seemed to be Derek the expat. I bent over the table towards Angus and identified Dionysos. Now Angus knew what he looked like. I then whispered the same in Leonidas's ear.

"Really?" he said, turning his head to see for himself.

We watched the men sitting down, talking loudly, cockily. Dionysos looked pointedly in our direction and tried to stare me out. I felt Leonidas bristle. Elpida left us and walked quickly towards the newcomers. She flew into a loud tirade in Greek, which caused everyone to stop what they were doing and listen. The group of men tried to ignore her, so she started shouting and pointing to the road. Perhaps for the benefit of the other few expats present, or for ours, I don't know, she ended the tirade in English: "You can leave my *kafeneio* now, we don't serve fascists in this village. Go!"

Elpida's outburst earned a few gasps from the other church party but there were a few mutterings of approval, it seemed, when the interlopers got up. With surly looks, the men slouched slowly back towards the road. When they were nearly level with us, Leonidas got up. He looked angry and I feared for what was going to happen. Angus shot me a warning look. Thekla was tutting.

Leonidas approached Dionysos and had a sharp exchange with him, which was dignified but left no-one in doubt he was not impressed with the man or his band of brethren.

The expat Derek looked scruffy in old jeans and dirty T-shirt. "This is ridiculous," he said loudly, looking towards our table, and Angus in particular, as if appealing for someone to back him up.

"Don't look at me, Derek. I don't like fascists either," Angus said loudly.

As they left, Dionysos strafed us all with a toxic stare, me especially. I was glad the men had been challenged. Now these people were exposed, but a knob of anxiety sat in my stomach.

Leonidas returned to the table and sat down. Angus patted him on the back. "Thank you, Leo."

"What did you say to Dionysos?" I asked him.

"I told him the village doesn't welcome supporters of far-right parties, and not to come back. And that I don't welcome him harassing you, or anyone else in the village. If this continues, I told him the police will become involved. I doubt Dionysos took much notice though. These people have no shame. And worst of all, there seems to be an Englishman involved with them. I don't know what he hopes to gain from that and from antagonising people in the village."

"Most of the expats here don't like Derek much either. I'll be keeping an eye on him, don't worry," said Angus.

Elpida brought our coffees, and glasses of ouzo, on the house. But it was we who owed her much more for firing a salvo at the sinister trio. I wondered then who the other Greek was. Someone else from Glika Nera?

"I won't have these people in my *kafeneio*. I will tell everyone in the village to throw them out of their shops, and have nothing to do with them," she said.

"Bravo, Elpida," said Angus.

We stayed a while, and the ouzo was particularly welcome after the heated exchange. I noticed that Angelos was quiet and Leonidas too was looking thoughtful. It wouldn't be long until I found out why. Thekla and Myrto got up to spend time with some of their friends at the other tables, while Angus wandered over to a group of men inside, watching the TV, to have a few more drinks, I didn't doubt.

Leonidas, Angelos and I strolled back to Leo's car parked along the road. Leonidas and Angelos were talking all the way but as we reached Leo's four-wheel drive, the chat became heated. Then they seemed to be arguing. I heard the word 'Eve' several times, blipped out like Morse code, and Angelos stormed off towards his parked truck to drive back to the farm compound.

Leonidas drove home in silence. So, a tranquil morning at church then. I thanked him though for confronting Dionysos.

"I had to do that, *agapi mou*. I won't have Dionysos threaten you again, or your dog." Then he said nothing more until we were back at the villa.

"Are you going to tell me what all that was about with Angelos?"

He took off his jacket and put it neatly over a chair and sat down on the sofa, running a hand firmly through his hair.

"I am sorry you had to see that argument. I let my temper get the better of me. The problem is, Bronte, that I hear from some villagers – who, let us be honest, like to gossip – that my nephew is still seeing that woman Eve. They don't try to hide it. So I challenged him about it and it turns out they are becoming more serious. They are lovers now, I think. This will not help his life at all."

Oh, Eve! What was she doing?

"Leo, it's just a phase he's going through. I don't think they've actually …. not yet."

"Oh, and you can know that?" he said, with an arch look.

"I speak to her a lot now. She's never said anything like that. She has to go back to London soon, anyway. Just be patient."

He looked exasperated and tugged on his bottom lip with his teeth. "I know you must be thinking, what is this to me? I'm not his father but I promised my brother Mihalis that I would help Angelos, and you know how he was drifting before, because of the crisis. Buying some of Myrto's land and giving Angelos the task of running a small olive oil operation with Myrto was supposed to give him something to do, and to learn. It won't be forever. One day, he'll get a real job. He's a smart boy, but this …. this thing with your friend is not going to help him, especially with people talking about it."

"Who is talking?" I asked, as Thekla popped unbidden into my mind.

"It doesn't matter who told me – a few villagers who know our family well – but in the end everyone in the village will know. The trees have ears, as I tell you often," he said, with a wry smile. "Can you talk to your *friend*," he said emphasising 'friend', reminding me that this was my fault. I winced. "She might listen to you. I can't get Angelos to be sensible. He's infatuated with her and wants me to mind my own business."

"Does his father know about it?"

"No, not yet, I'm sure. But he will go mad if he does. Mihalis has his own troubles in the crisis. He's an accountant but with all the new taxes that are levied and the fact everyone must file a proper tax return now, his work has become more complicated. You know – Greece and bureaucracy. My brother is working day and night. He's very stressed. He doesn't need this too."

I admired Leo's concern for his family, but in the great scheme of things I couldn't see Angelos's love affair as a major drama.

"Leo, your nephew is having a moment of madness, that's all. Didn't you when you were young?" I said, trying to smooth it all down with some feminine logic.

I couldn't imagine that Leonidas, with his good looks and his prospects, would have escaped the attention of some dangerous women in his youth. He shrugged my comment away and went to the kitchen to make coffee, or maybe just to calm his mood down. In the months I'd known him I'd never seen him as angry as he'd been that day. I felt sympathy for the issue he'd raised, yet I was also exasperated. We'd just gone from being more or less reconciled over the weekend to being thorny with each other again.

I followed him into the kitchen, where he was leaning against the cupboards, staring out the window. He looked miserable and I felt sorry for him, thinking about what Angelos had told me: about Leo's patient who'd committed suicide. These weren't the best of times, clearly.

I squeezed his hand. "Thanks anyway for what you said to Dionysos in the *kafeneio*. I appreciate it."

"In the end it probably won't make a lot of difference. These people don't care what anyone thinks. In fact, it might make him more vindictive. But we have to stand united in the village against these thugs. They are trying to win support all over Greece. I fear we will head back to the 60s and 70s and the era of the junta."

I'd heard Angus mention this fact, no doubt something that his café cronies in Kalamata mused over constantly, ramping up political gloom between them. However, I didn't think it was something that Leonidas would fear.

"About Eve, Leo. Don't worry. She is behaving like a giddy teenager. She'll snap out of it. But I will talk to her."

"Good. Thank you, Bronte. I have too many other things to worry about these days." He didn't have to say more, I saw the anguish in his lovely dark eyes.

"I do understand. And everything will be fine, I promise," I said, stroking his cheek.

He kissed me sweetly on the forehead, like you might a misguided child, then he went to the bedroom to change out of his Sunday clothes.

23
Girls allowed

"**D**arling, I think I'm in love!" trilled Eve. *Shit, shit, shit, no!* "Really? Let me guess. You and Angelos are now *shagging*!" I replied. Why beat around the bush now. So much for my hollow 'promise' to Leonidas that all would be well.

"I'm afraid we are," she said boldly, leaning back on her white sofa, ruffling her blonde hair. "A few times now." Was this the prim, flaky woman I first interviewed a few weeks ago, who was in a funk over a writing blockage? Or even the glamorous woman who came to the Easter lunch, looking fetching in fuchsia? And oh so understanding about living the Greek life. Thank God I'd clinched the Markham interview before she lost brain cells to coitus.

That morning Eve had called me on her mobile, asking me to come to her villa for a chat. I had hoped she was going to tell me she'd decided to cool the affair with young Angelos and be sensible, but here she was telling me it had climaxed. I almost felt she'd summoned me to gloat over the circumstance, the way a cat drops dead birds on your doormat so you can see what a clever predator he is.

Being in 'love', or lust at least, suited her though. She was glowing: her skin was lightly sunkissed as the days became more hot and summery. Her eyes were glossy and bright.

"Tell me it's just a holiday romance, Eve. You know, a kind of Mrs Robinson interlude with beaches and Feta. That it does not contain love!"

"Bronte, I'm in thrall at the moment. It's been so unexpected. He is such a *fabulous* guy in *every* way," she said theatrically, and I knew where her mind was going. I felt sick. Leonidas would be furious. Oh hell! He'd strangle me.

"Yes, but the age difference. It can't last, Eve."

She looked mildly shocked. "Well, we're not talking about marriage, my dear. I'm just living in the moment. Isn't that what Greeks do?"

"Your moments are somewhat longer than the Greek ones, I think."

She laughed, briefly.

"I hope you'll be discreet," I said. "Leonidas knows about the two of you, and other people have commented. You know how it is here. Nothing's private."

"Oh, for God's sake! How people do over-react."

"The thing is, Eve, back home it wouldn't matter a fig how much you were shagging, but this is a rural village in an area that other Greeks describe as 'wild'. A place of historic retributions; Maniot towers, remember? You can't break wind here without everyone commenting. Deal with it!"

"Don't get fractious, Bronte. It doesn't become you."

So, I had a Jane Austen moment, to rival Leo's Mr Darcy. I had to stifle the urge to slap the back of her hand like an impatient dowager, just to bring her to her senses. As if that would even work!

"If you get more serious, there will be hell to pay. Leonidas helped Angelos to get a small business operation going with Myrto since he lost his job in the crisis. I don't know if he's told you about all that."

"Yes, he did, poor lamb. He's so smart and *so* good-looking. I don't know why he wanted to come back to village life. I've told him to go to London. Plenty of young Greeks are getting work there now, and in other places: Germany, Sweden. I could probably help him to land some work."

Good God, it was getting worse! Angelos going overseas now, ripped clean away from his family. Everyone he knew would be lining up to throttle me. Where were the smelling salts?

"Eve, can I be frank with you? Greeks ..."

She cut me off. "Oh, don't lecture me now. I'm a grown woman and Angelos is no child."

I ploughed on nevertheless. "Greeks still have strong views about people having relationships with foreigners, especially in rural Greece. But the age gap between you is the thing. And Leonidas is nettled with me over this – just when we were getting over the Phaedra episode. Your love trysts have put me in a difficult situation. And really, you don't know what you're getting into here."

She gave me a wide-eyed stare. "If I can digress slightly, I can't believe you are the same woman, who at the Easter lunch said something about the culture here being challenging and 'how can you love the country as much as you love the man?' In fact, you have your head around the whole thing. Well done you! You understand the cultural narrative exactly – apparently."

"I try," I said, sarcastically. "And can I remind you in turn you also said at that lunch you've never had the urge to get serious with someone whose culture was still a mystery to you – remember?"

She shrugged. "Look, the culture thing isn't such a big deal – for me. Lust is much more fun," she said with a lascivious smile. "It's been a while since I said that. And you know the best thing? For the first time in ages I'm not thinking about books and writing all the damned time. I'm not feeling stressed-out."

"Why not just take a few tranquilisers. That would be less trouble."

She gave me an arch look. "That was mean, Bronte."

"Maybe, but when your affair comes to an end, you'll still have to face your other problems, won't you?"

She gave me a black look and fiddled with her hair, gathering it up into a ponytail, dropping it again and shaking it out over her shoulders.

"Look, Eve. I'm just asking you to be sensible."

"I don't care for sensible, or what people around here think," she said with a defiant lift of her chin. "I will see Angelos for now, and I know he feels the same."

I began to seethe with anger. Maybe I'd been blind-sided by Eve, with her charm, her generosity, if not her gift for deception and plundering the writing prowess of a good friend. But now I was disappointed with the fact that she had turned out to be so incredibly selfish and wilful. I was growing tired of her, and I only had one card left to play.

"Okay, you don't care about others, but I *do*. And don't forget I'm the only person in the world who knows your story – about the books, that is."

Her mouth sagged in shock.

"You wouldn't say anything, Bronte. You promised."

"I wouldn't *want* to, believe me. I'm not that kind of person, and as a journalist I respect what's strictly off the record, always have. But this is a peculiar situation I find myself in. And you are pushing a lot of envelopes."

She pursed her lips in annoyance. I thought she'd ask me to leave, but she fiddled with her hair again.

"So, you're giving me an ultimatum. If I don't stop seeing Angelos, you'll grass on me?"

"Something like that," I said, trying to look like I really meant it because in my mind it could only ever be a last resort. It was a threat only that I could never carry out with a good conscience. Clearly she was losing all sense of reality. What had started weeks ago as a series of eccentric endeavours – disappearing, holing up in a Maniot tower, falling for someone young enough to be her son – had become something more troubling.

"You wouldn't squeal on me, Bronte. I know you. I know you're not that vindictive."

"Watch me," I said, like some well-practised minx.

Her nostrils flared and I knew she had no idea if I was serious or not. I could almost see the struggle going on inside her. After a few tense moments she appeared calmer; a pitying look in her eyes.

"The thing is, Bronte, I don't know if I can stop seeing him. Not right now. But I will talk to him. I will try to sort it out, okay? Don't do anything rash."

I sighed. That would mean another meeting with Angelos, another dinner, another session of love-making and more opportunities for someone else in the village to see them together, for things to get worse. For Leonidas to go ballistic.

"Forgive me saying this, but you're one of those people lucky enough to have a holiday villa. You come here and do what you want, mess up and then you leave again. But the rest of us will live with the consequences. Not you."

She got up from the sofa briskly. "Okay, I think you've made your point. I said I'd sort it." She walked to the door and held it open for me.

"I trusted you, Bronte."

"And I you," I said. "But you've shifted all the goal-posts."

I turned and walked quickly to the car and drove fast up the hill, my heart pounding with irritation. I don't think I'd even scratched the surface of who Eve really was. That's when I started thinking about Douglas Markham. It had always intrigued me that she'd agreed so readily to do the interview for The Daily Messenger, and was so candid. With so much at stake with her reputation as a best-selling author and the ghost-writing secret, I wondered why she wanted to draw attention to herself. No-one could doubt that Markham was a sleazy sex pest, but the truth was, I felt convinced that Eve had been no angel either. She was just as self-regarding and probably a terrible coquette in her acting years, cultivating a man who had always had a certain reputation, drawing out the worst in him perhaps, playing up to the cameras, revelling in the attention. I was sure she must have cheated on Markham as well. Perhaps when they split, it was he who'd made a lucky escape, rather than her. And she knew that only too well. Perhaps she wanted to denigrate him before he ever got in first. I'd have loved to get his side of the story.

But about one thing she appeared to be right: I did have a better understanding of Greek village life than I'd imagined. I may not have spoken the language much, but I was beginning to see what was in the Greek heart and what the complex lines of navigation were between friends and family. It didn't always make me feel comfortable, but now I think I recognised it.

24

A chasm appears

When I wrote my Greek column the following week, I decided on a more serious approach this time to the economic crisis, as there had been fierce riots in Athens due to another round of punishing austerity measures forced on the country by the EU in return for another tranche of bailout money.

I wanted to write about the way these measures were impacting on ordinary Greeks, especially in rural southern Greece, and their inability to pay taxes and deal with slumping wages. I thought it was apt to mention the growing influence of the far right because that particular week there had been violent attacks in Athens on migrants and in Kalamata a demonstration about austerity. A few members and supporters of the EPE had turned up wearing black T-shirts and chanting their slogans – no doubt Dionysos may have been amongst them. Angry scuffles had broken out between them and groups of left-wing students. There was little support for EPE in Kalamata among most of its residents, but enough to keep their antics bubbling along.

I ended the column with an outsider's perception that the crisis had tapped into a darker side of the Greek psyche beneath the sea-and-sun veneer. I left it at that, even though I had personally experienced it. And it wasn't over yet.

As June progressed with heatwaves and temperatures around 40 degrees, I found myself busier than I'd expected with freelance work. I no longer spent time wondering whether I'd done the right thing the previous year, walking away from my full-time job on The Alba at 37, at a point in my career when I could have taken it much further but in the end took redundancy. What I was doing here seemed as relevant, perhaps more so, with a slew of features as interesting and varied as anything I'd done as a staffer.

In the summer, I worked in the early morning and later went down to the sea, often with Angus, and Zeffy as well, to one of the hidden coves set along this stretch of coastline. We usually had lunch in the village of Paleohora, at a small taverna with tables by the water's edge, waiting for a breeze to pick up before returning home for a siesta. It was a month I would always think of with certain fondness and nostalgia for its wound-down ambience when anything that took too much physical effort was never worth doing. It was a time for reflection as much as anything.

"Greece suits you," Angus would often say as we passed an hour or two over lunch. And I was beginning to agree. Other things may not always have gone to plan but I began to feel healthier and happier than at any time in my life. I even managed a respectable suntan.

I heard nothing from Eve and neither did I call her, though I had no reason to think she hadn't gone back to London as planned. Angelos continued his work with Myrto and I heard no adverse reports from that quarter. If the affair was still alive it must have continued in great secrecy. All of which puzzled me, mildly, as well as the fact that Leonidas didn't mention it either, but he had other things to occupy his thoughts.

Angus had finally banished his malaise with writing and had completed over a third of his book, which he showed me. It was surprisingly good. He had nosed it off with the background story of my grandfather Kieran, arriving in Greece with the Royal Army Service Corps and later going missing. By the end, the book would reveal how we unravelled the mystery of Kieran's disappearance and how and where he died. It would be a tribute to Angus's father as much as anything.

One Friday afternoon, it was cooler than it had been previously. With my work up to date, I decided to drive into Marathousa for a walk around the village with Zeffy. I parked near the *kafeneio*, intending to stop for a coffee on the way back. We strolled past it and I saw Elpida standing by its front door. She waved as we passed. We took the stone steps at the back of the *plateia* that led to the narrow Palios Dromos, the Old Road, which ascended towards a high plateau above the village. Situated here was the small chapel of Saint Konstantina with its wooden bench at the front with a stunning view of the gulf. It was a place that Leonidas and I often walked to and I would always associate the chapel with us.

I sat for a moment to catch my breath. Zeffy hunched up beside me, being strangely needy, nudging my shoulder with his head. I kissed his ruffled head and smelt honey cake. I had an urge, however, to walk further. From here the rural path split: one way led up to the church of Ayios Nektarios, from which you had a clear view of many of the Taygetos peaks. The other way led south to the Rindomo Gorge, a deep rocky gash that started as a narrow slit in the mountains and cut a wide swathe thereafter to the sea at Santova. There were other rough tracks from the main road below up to this plateau of fields and orchards that could take vehicles, but generally this was a quiet and remote part of the village where I'd walked before. I set off towards the gorge, but not intending to go all the way, as the tracks along the top were rough and slightly perilous.

In the fields that spread out to the edge of the gorge there were just a few stone houses, mostly shuttered as they belonged to Athenians and expats who hadn't returned yet for the summer. A donkey was grazing near a copse of olive trees, tethered to one of them. When I rounded a bend in the track, there he was – Dionysos. I stared at him, uncomprehending.

"Ridiculous," I heard myself say out loud. How had such a perfect morning once again begun to spool away from me in seconds – and all because of him?

He was alone, standing beside an olive tree, smoking. His blue scooter was parked nearby. When he saw me, he stubbed out his cigarette. Zeffy started to bark, straining at his lead. He hadn't forgotten what Dionysos had first done to him. I reached into my pocket for my phone and tried to speed-dial Angus. But there was no reception up here. I turned to retrace my steps, ready to bolt across the fields back to the chapel. I had no desire to be up on this lonely hillside with the creep, and for the first time I regretted my over-confident decision to walk here alone. As I started back, I heard him running up behind me.

"Stop!" he shouted. I turned.

He looked the same as always: greasy hair, dark menacing eyes. He was wearing the kind of grubby padded gilet that hunters favoured, with a dozen pockets for stuffing God knows what into. Zeffy barked again. Dionysos eyed up the dog and smirked. It was then I knew absolutely that he was the one who'd left the poison.

"I'm going back to the village, don't follow me or I'll set the dog on you," I said, firmly.

Dionysos just laughed, showing a poor set of teeth.

"You set dog to me and I shoot him with this," he said, pulling a small handgun from one of his pockets. I recoiled in fear. I knew Dionysos was belligerent but I never thought he'd go this far. It crossed my mind that his presence here wasn't a coincidence, that he must have seen me from somewhere in the village, ascending the road to the small chapel, and doubled back to take one of the other farm tracks from the main road, which would be quick on the scooter.

"You come this way," he said, tipping his head in the direction of the Rindomo Gorge.

"No, I will not. You can shoot me first," I said, stupidly trying to call his bluff and walking quickly towards the small chapel again, hoping that somebody would be around.

"Stop, or I shoot dog."

I stopped and turned again.

"Why should I go with you?"

"Because I say," he snarled in his pigeon English, pointing the gun at Zeffy. I couldn't risk it.

Now I had no choice – but what would I be walking into? My heart was throbbing with fear. I thought of making a run for it, letting Zeffy go, hoping he would run and hide somewhere safe. But knowing Zeffy, he would go for the creep, and then what?

Dionysos seemed to sense my thoughts. He waved the gun in the direction of the track that led to the gorge. "Keep walking straight. And you give to me your *kinito*, mobile."

I hesitated. "Now!" he shouted, pointing his gun at me.

Terrified, I handed over my mobile and turned towards the gorge. While I walked, I anxiously plotted an escape, but nothing felt possible. I'd had many adventures and mishaps as a journalist and had come across shady, violent characters, but I'd never been kidnapped at gunpoint. I could only imagine what he had in mind for me at the end of the track. When he'd finished with me, he'd push me, and Zeffy, over the edge of the gorge. I'd recently written about the dark side of Greek life, but now I was in the midst of it.

I tramped along the path with Dionysos behind me. I thought of nothing but the gun pointing towards my back. But would he use it? I had a sense that Dionysos was just evil bluster but I couldn't take the chance. Zeffy turned every now and then to growl, or bark, pulling on the lead. I had a struggle to calm him. I knew he was seething inside, wanted to have his day with Dionysos, but I didn't want to lose the dog. Not like this.

It didn't take long to reach the edge of the gorge, where the land was overgrown with gorse and there were outcrops of rock. Below was the pebbly riverbed that was often in spate after the spring thaw but was now dried-out, given over to snakes, wild boar and other animals that Dionysos probably liked to hunt. Hunting was surely what he did best.

Dionysos stepped in front of me. "This way, you follow me," he said, taking a narrow stony path covered in places with scree. It cut down the top section of the gorge. Once I started to follow him, the drop seemed less sheer than it did from above but it was perilous enough. It was a difficult descent and I was sweating with panic, Zeffy trotting beside me on a tense lead, his urge to have a go at Dionysos undiminished. But he was a smart creature and I knew he was just waiting for the right moment. Dionysos kept a safe distance in front of us, however, glancing back at us now and then.

As we descended, I eyed up loose rocks, wondering if I could lob one at his head. But what if I missed? My legs were beginning to tremble from the effort and the fear of it all, but my mind was constantly turning over every possibility for escape. Finally, we arrived at a wide ledge in front of the mouth of a cave, which was concealed from above. The mouth was vast, triangular in shape, narrow at the top. The cave at the back was dark and uninviting.

"Sit in there with dog," he snapped, shaking his gun towards the front of the cave. Before he followed me, he reached in his pocket, took out my mobile and pitched it into the gorge below, where it made a tinny clattering sound.

I sat down with my back against the cave wall, with Zeffy at my side. I could sense he was still bubbling with rage, but he kept vigil beside me, his eyes flickering towards me every now and then. Dionysos sat on the opposite side and took out his mobile. It must have been possible here to get a signal. Pity my phone had gone.

Dionysos had a shouty conversation with someone in Greek that seemed to go on and on. Then he snapped the phone shut.

"We wait now, for a friend."

"What friend?"

He sneered at me. "Not your business."

God help me: this was going to be gang rape now. My mind was fizzing with anxiety. I should have made a run for it when I had the chance. This was a place where no-one would see or hear me. I'd probably rather take a risk and just jump off the edge of the ravine. It was closer here to the bottom anyway. Zeffy started whining.

"Shut him or he gets this," he said, jabbing the air with the gun.

I looked properly at the gun and thought it looked more like some old kind of World War Two handgun that probably didn't work, but I couldn't be sure.

"Why are you doing this? What have you got against me?"

"You are the enemy of Greek people," he said, in an echo of the EPE party slogans Angus and I had seen on the posters in Glika Nera.

"No, I'm not. I love Greek people." *Engage him in chatter,* I thought. *Keep his mind occupied.*

"You are enemy!"

"You mean of Ellines Patriotes Enomeni? You're a follower, aren't you? You come from Glika Nera. You know you have already been reported to the police."

"Police useless." Then he continued in a long Greek rant. "I saw you in Glika Nera, with your *malakas* father."

I ignored the insult.

"Why am I the enemy? I'm just a foreigner living here."

"You are one who ..." he stuttered around with his English. "You ... *grafeis,*" he said making a scribbling sign with his hand, and it wasn't hard to understand *grafeis* meant write. "You … *grafeis* … things for the English. I see it."

"See what, my work? How is that?"

"*Skase mori!* Shut it up, you bitch!" he said, making the insult sound even worse than it was in his mangled English.

"Don't speak to me like that," I fumed, uselessly.

He laughed, a greasy cold laugh.

"You tell me how you've seen my work."

"Friend Derek, he English. He knows. You *grafeis* … bad things."

I didn't know what was more appalling, his English or that the expat Derek was involved in this. Was it possible that Derek had got hold of some of my columns, from a Scottish contact perhaps, particularly the recent one about the rise of the far right, and had shared them with his Greek pals? From what Angus had told me, Derek was a traitor who seemed to hate his own compatriots, who'd been only too happy to escape from them and who apparently now preferred the company of creeps like Dionysos.

"Is that why I'm here? As a punishment?"

He got up, pointing the gun at me. He looked agitated. "You don't come here and be enemy of Greek people!"

Zeffy was on his feet as well and barking loudly. I couldn't stop him this time. He looked like he might want to rip the creep's throat out and I probably wouldn't have stopped him. Dionysos pointed the gun at him. I felt a rush of blood to my head, and cringed against the wall of the cave. Zeffy first, me next. Was this possible? I felt an acid rush of liquid filling my mouth. I thought I might vomit but spat instead on the dirt floor.

Dionysos had his finger on the trigger but nothing followed. No shot. I screamed. The creep cackled. It was meant to frighten us, but the next time it might be for real. Or perhaps the gun wasn't really loaded. I didn't want to push it. I pulled Zeffy back but he was on his back legs now, snarling. He felt suddenly powerful, wound-up, and he lunged towards Dionysos, pulling the lead right out of my hand.

Zeffy, in a lightning move, lunged and clamped his teeth around Dionysos's leg below the knee. The guy didn't have time to think and, in shock perhaps, dropped the gun. As he bent and scrabbled for it near his feet, Zeffy held on tight, shaking his head over the attacker's leg. I got up quickly and estimated whether I could lunge for the gun and manage to pick it up. What then? But he was too quick for me. He kicked hard with his other leg against Zeffy's side. The dog squealed and released his grip a moment. Dionysos bent down and recovered the gun, but with a trembling hand.

"*Gamoto!* Fuck it!" he shouted, his face wincing in pain.

"Let me get the dog's lead," I said. As I bent down for it, to pull Zeffy away, he did something I didn't expect. He bolted out of the cave, dragging the lead behind him. I could hear him paws scattering stones as he ascended the path.

"Dog coward, leaves you now … too bad," he scoffed.

Without Zeffy, I felt completely stranded but, in my heart, I was sure he'd somehow summon help. I hoped that was the case.

Dionysos sank down again against the wall opposite and waved the gun at me. "You sit."

He pulled up the leg of his jeans. "*Gamoto*," he said again, his face snarly. The bite looked deep and was bleeding a lot.

"Your *malakas* dog, I sorry I not shoot," he said, waving the gun.

While Dionysos throbbed away with indignation, I tried to figure out again if I could bolt out of the cave before he aimed the gun. I would wait until he was distracted or he put the gun down. But he was watching me carefully, his greasy hair hanging over his face. His mobile rang. There was an angry exchange again. The friend? I got the sense Dionysos was berating him, probably for his delay in fronting up, wherever he was. The creep pinged the phone off.

"We wait," he said with a snarl.

We sat in silence for about half an hour. It seemed an eternity. When he reached over to check his leg again, I slowly inched a bit towards the mouth of the cave. I was sitting against the wall with my hands slightly behind me. To my right, I felt the outline of a small rock and clasped it in my hand. At least if he came for me, I'd launch it. I leaned my head against the rough wall of the cave and wondered if this was the place Angus had once told me about.

During some punitive raids in the Mani by the Ottoman Turks in the 18th century, a group of villagers, mostly women and children, had been sheltering from the sun in a cave after visiting a nearby spring water outlet. A group of Turks had come to the edge of the gorge and discovered their presence, probably when a baby cried. They clambered down a track and lobbed sulphur 'bombs' through the mouth of the cave, killing almost all the group. The story had become historic legend in the village. I could well believe it had happened here.

There was a pernicious feel about this place, especially at the back of the cave, where it was dark and fetid. It was then I remembered, like the twist of a knife in the guts, that a cave had figured in Kieran's tragic story after the Battle of Kalamata. Was his fate to be my fate as well? History repeating itself all over again in another part of the Mani?

I was starting to feel faint and very thirsty but I had no water with me. Dionysos looked even worse and I noticed he had a large patch of red blooming on the leg of his jeans. He surely couldn't run at all now. Zeffy had done a good job. I gripped my rock and waited, trying to ramp up my courage to spring to my feet and flee. But then I heard a faint noise coming from the top of the dirt track, of stones being dislodged. My heart sank. Creep number two? In moments, he'd be here and then all was lost. The noise grew louder, a frenzied tramping, scree flying.

Then I heard Zeffy barking, people shouting. Zeffy appeared first and rushed over to me, licking my face. I got to my feet, feeling faint again, but this time with relief. Two men were right behind the dog and I was overjoyed to see one was wearing a police uniform. The other was Adonis, the church elder who'd been at the Sunday lunch. The police officer had his gun drawn and rushed at Dionysos, shouting in Greek. Dionysos dropped his gun on the cave floor. The officer manhandled him into a standing position and cuffed his hands behind his back. He picked up the gun and checked it. No bullets apparently and it probably wouldn't have worked, even if it had been loaded. My intuition had been right: it was an old piece of junk. The officer prodded Dionysos towards the path. More scree tumbled down towards the mouth of the cave from the path.

Leonidas came quickly into view, carrying his medical bag. I rushed towards him and hugged him.

"Are you all right, Bronte?"

"I am now," I said in a thin, tired voice.

"Are you sure, my love?"

I nodded.

Adonis came over and tapped me gently on the shoulder and pointed to Zeffy.

"*Kalos skilos, poli mangas*," he said, and I remembered what it meant from the Sunday lunch, as far as I could recall anything at that moment. Zeffy was a good dog and a plucky character. I agreed. I even managed a smile.

"*Efharisto*. Thanks for helping, Adonis," I said, feeling teary.

"You welcome," he said, rushing out of the cave to follow the others, leaving me and Leonidas alone with Zeffy.

"Leo, I'm so happy to see you. I thought that bastard was going to kill us both, Zeffy and me." I threw my arms around his neck again and cried tears of relief. He rubbed my back

234

like a consoling parent and it felt like the safest place in the world to be.

"You're okay now, Bronte. But you're in shock." He pulled out a small bottle of water from his medical bag.

"I brought a few other things with me in case you were injured. I'm happy I don't need them, but are you okay to walk back to the village?"

"Yes, I'll be fine once I get away from this horrible place."

I gulped the water as Leonidas took Zeffy by his lead and we climbed slowly up the path to the lip of the gorge, where we stopped for a breather. From there we could see the commotion of Dionysos being led over the field in handcuffs with the policeman and Adonis. They were followed by some other village men, whom Leonidas said had come as back-up and who had waited at the top of the gorge. They were talking loudly and chivvying Dionysos along. He had his head down, limping. In a few moments they were out of sight.

Zeffy sat patiently beside us, his tongue hanging out. He was panting. I streamed water from the bottle into one of my cupped hands for him and he drank eagerly.

"Zeffy saved my life today – for the second time with that bastard Dionysos," I said, venting my anger. Leonidas smiled.

"It was fortunate that Zeffy went straight back to the village and made sure he got everyone's attention. He's a very smart dog. Elpida saw him first, running about the *plateia*, barking. She remembered seeing you both earlier and raised the alarm. And Dionysos won't be troubling you any more, Bronte. Or his friend. Some man from the same village of Glika Nera, I think. The police caught him trying to escape by car from the village. I don't know any more details yet. God knows what they had in mind. I can't bear to think of it. But we must get back to the village. You will need to give a statement to the police."

When we arrived in the *plateia* there seemed to be a lot of villagers milling around. They were talking loudly and excitedly about the kidnapping, as if nothing so dramatic had happened here for years. I was surprised to see that even Myrto was there, having heard the news somehow. She'd come straight from her farm compound, riding Zeus, dressed in her work clothes and wellies. She rushed over and gripped me by the arms.

"I am so mad I didn't find that man for you and shoot him with my rifle, like the mad kangaroo he is," she said.

Next it was Elpida's turn to fly towards me and hug me in big strong arms.

"Oh, Bronte! When the dog came back on its own with the strap dragged behind, I knew something is not right and I call people on their mobiles: Leonidas, your *babas*. Thanks be to God they found you in time." She crossed herself several times.

"Thank you, Elpida. You had great instincts all along. You knew Dionysos was up to no good."

"Yes, stomach was twitching but I didn't act quickly enough. Still, could have been worser," she said, mangling her English in all the excitement.

I saw Angus getting out of his car and walking towards the *plateia*. His face looked grey. I don't think I'd seen him look so sickly since he'd been on the verge of a heart attack the previous year. Leonidas instructed him to sit down and asked Elpida to bring a glass of water. He wouldn't sit before he'd given me a good hug and rubbed my back.

"Are you okay, pet?" he said, pushing me back a little so he could see for himself how I was.

"Yes, I'm fine now. I'm more worried about you."

He sat at one of the *kafeneio* tables and sipped his water. "I'm okay now but the ticker got in a flap when I finally got home and played a message on voicemail from Elpida. If I'd driven up on the coast road instead of the Mani road, I'd have seen all the commotion and would have stopped."

He rubbed his hand over his forehead. "I blame myself for not making it clearer, not to go roaming about the village alone with that guy on the loose. When I came here 10 years ago, I wouldn't have dreamt of telling anyone to be careful out on a Greek hillside. Things are different now," he said, suddenly out of breath.

"Are you having chest pains, Angus?" asked Leonidas, with medical authority.

"No, no, don't worry. I'll be fine."

"No more talking," said Leonidas, patting him gently on the shoulder.

After my police interview, in which Angus added a comment of his own about the suspects and Derek's possible collusion with Dionysos, Leonidas drove us back to Villa Ambelia and offered to pick up Angus's car later. He didn't think Angus was in a fit state to drive it after his shock and told him to take it easy for the rest of the day.

25

Under every stone, a scorpion

"I only wish there had been a way to get the police to arrest Dionysos sooner, but he was cunning. He hadn't broken any laws yet," said Leonidas as we sat in the living room of Villa Ambelia early in the evening with Angus, now recovered from his shock. Zeffy was sitting in front of us on a colourful dog rug.

Leonidas had agreed that as Zeffy had become the hero of the day, he should be allowed to stay where he liked. As a reward, Zeffy was given a large dinner of cooked chicken.

"I shouldn't have gone up the path in the direction of the Rindomo Gorge. That was stupid. But I didn't think for a minute Dionysos would ever go up there. Perhaps he was stalking me a lot more than I realised," I said.

"Looks like it," said Angus.

"How were you to know what you were up against? We Greeks have been through a lot of upheavals in our history but the crisis has brought new challenges we have not had for a very long time and we're not equipped to deal with them," said Leonidas.

I was keen to know how the posse of rescuers had come about and Leonidas filled me in on the missing parts of the story. He had left the surgery early that day and decided to go straight to Villa Ambelia, but found I wasn't there or in Villa Anemos. He was about to drive into Marathousa when Elpida rang his mobile. Elpida had always been like the unofficial mayor of Marathousa. She had a pinboard inside the *kafeneio* with dozens of local numbers on it, practically the whole village, including Angus's number. When she called, there was no answer. When she rang Leonidas, she told him she was worried because she remembered seeing me and Zeffy walking through the village earlier and then, much later, I hadn't returned but the dog bounded onto the *plateia*, dragging his lead. Elpida thought something bad must have happened.

Before Leonidas drove to the village, he called my mobile, with no success. My phone was lying at the bottom of the ravine. He also called Kalamata police station and, name-dropping his detective friend, summoned a patrol car to Marathousa immediately. Luckily for me, there was one not far away on the southern outskirts of Kalamata.

When Leonidas got to the village *plateia*, the place was in a flap, Zeffy fizzing with anxiety. Villagers were gathered into a group, talking excitedly, with Elpida at the helm.

"The dog was incredible," Leonidas told me. "He kept barking to keep our attention and sometimes running towards the back stairs of the *plateia* and back again, as if to make us follow him."

When the police car arrived, one young officer said he would go with Leonidas to wherever the dog led them. Adonis offered to take charge of Zeffy. The other policeman would stay in the village in case I happened to return. A few other men were to follow on as back-up. Miltiades from the taverna wanted to join in but didn't think he was fit enough to keep up. He could dance, he said, but hillwalking was something else. Leonidas was to take his medical bag in case I'd had an accident, or worst of all, fallen into the ravine. No-one at that point was thinking of a kidnap, or a sinister incident with Dionysos because none of the villagers recalled seeing him, yet he must have been lurking somewhere out of sight. He could then have gone by scooter up one of the narrow farm tracks that led off the main road to the fields above. Or else it was just an unfortunate co-incidence that he was up there.

So the rescuers set off, with Zeffy leading the way. When Zeffy got to the edge of the ravine and led the group down the narrow path, they feared the worst. Leonidas said he was afraid I had gone over the edge and was lying in the ravine. Adonis had been hopeful that I was sheltering for whatever reason in the infamous cave all the villagers knew about, though few ever made the tricky journey down to it these days. What they found at the cave took them all by surprise. No-one expected to see Dionysos there with a gun.

Later I discovered that the friend of Dionysos had driven into the village but when he saw the patrol car he tried to bolt. Some of the villagers tipped off the waiting police officer and he went in hot pursuit down the coast road and managed to run him off the road into an olive grove. The friend was brought back to the village and interviewed. Several witnesses later identified him as a troublemaker from the same village as Dionysos.

After I gave my statement, the two thugs were taken to Kalamata police station, where Dionysos was charged with abduction and the other man with lesser offences. With the statements from Angus and me, and several other locals, Derek was also to be interviewed, as the trio were thought to be involved in a slew of other misdemeanours.

"I always knew Derek was a bad seed," said Angus. "He knew what that pair were cooking up and was probably goading them."

Angus was even more convinced of that fact when I revealed Dionysos had implied that Derek had showed him copies of my columns, particularly the one where I'd mentioned the far right and the EPE.

"Well, I can see exactly now what transpired. I never could understand why Dionysos had picked on you," said Angus. "It worried me that it could be a sexual thing. That he might corner you one day – evil bloody numpty. But now I see what was going on. It was Derek who was feeding Dionysos a lot of hateful rhetoric about your newspaper articles. Derek, as I've said, is always looking at UK news online but he must have had friends in Scotland sending him newspaper clippings related to Greece, or scanning in items. Derek would have translated the columns for Dionysos and wound him up. So that's how you were painted as the enemy of Greece – according to their cracked polemics. We probably won't be seeing Derek for a while."

Leonidas looked slightly confused.

"Angus, I can see how sick people like Dionysos will follow the mad beliefs of the far right, believing foreigners and migrants are enemies, but I cannot understand Derek, when he is a foreigner himself, how he could support these people."

"Derek was obviously a twisted individual when he was living in the UK, and very right-wing, and he's just continued his beliefs here. He probably doesn't see himself as a foreigner here."

"Then he is delusional, I am afraid," said Leonidas, shaking his head. "And dangerous."

"People don't change just because they've moved to sunny Greece, Leo. If I may quote your great poet Konstantinos Kavafis in The City: 'As here in this small strip you spoilt your life, the whole earth felt your squanderings'."

"Well said, my friend," said Leonidas, impressed with Angus's scholarly bearing. "Some people seem to bring all their old prejudices with them to their new life in Greece."

And he was right.

In the following days, Leonidas and I talked a lot about my kidnapping ordeal, and agreed that things would be better, and safer perhaps, if we spent more time together at Villa

Ambelia, at least another evening in the week. Moving to Kalamata was not an option for me. Despite everything, I liked village life, and I needed to keep an eye on Angus. But in my heart, I wondered if we'd just be scuppered by the geography again, and our timetables.

We rarely ever mentioned Phaedra and sought to put the whole thing behind us, but one day he innocently dropped her name into a conversation. He noticed that I flinched.

"All right, Bronte, I see you still don't believe that Phaedra won't suddenly appear again in Kalamata. You still don't have complete trust, do you?" he said, tipping his head to the side, trying to get the measure of my mood. After everything that had happened, and the fact Leonidas and I were again as close as we could be, Phaedra remained like a phantom between us.

"All right then," he said, in slight exasperation. "I will tell you something about Phaedra that I promised not to tell anyone. But now I see I must."

We were sitting on the balcony of his villa, sipping wine. It had been a hot day but an Ionian wind was now playing with the gulf, teasing the water into rows of white crests. An owl was hooting in the nearby olive groves. Too nice an evening to hear an awkward confession about Phaedra perhaps. But he had all my attention.

"Go on," I said, keenly.

"Phaedra met me in Kalamata the day Angus took his picture. As I told you at the Easter lunch, she said she had a personal problem to discuss with someone she trusted. The truth is she doesn't want to come back to Greece, as you imagined, and she doesn't want me back either," he said with a wry smile. "She has met someone in England, no Greek but an Englishman, and she says she loves him." He stopped a moment to gauge my reaction. I deadpanned it but I hadn't seen that coming. Busy old Tooth Fairy then, not just content to mine molars.

"Phaedra is worried her family won't approve. Her father is very strict, very traditional. She is afraid when he finds out he will be angry. They are very close, and he always wanted her to marry a Greek from this region."

"Like you," I interjected.

"That had been the plan *once*, yes," he said, with a flicker of impatience in his eyes. "But, can I say, she didn't want me to tell anyone about this new relationship, not even you. She is very conflicted."

I shrugged, a good Greek one, a gold-medal one: arms out, shoulders to ears.

"I don't get it, Leo. She's living in England. Her choice. It's inevitable an attractive woman like Phaedra would meet a local rather than a Greek."

"Okay, it's easy to see it that way, but she is worried that she will offend her family."

Offend her family? Dear Lord! I wondered then that if most of Leonidas's family, and not just Thekla, knew about us, they too might be greatly offended if we became more serious. I had never met any of them. I don't believe I'd even come close. Angus had once assured me that perhaps Leonidas didn't want to do that too soon, that he wouldn't want to scare me away, especially if the rest of his family were anything like Thekla. But now Leo's explanation had opened up a fresh seam of doubts for me.

"So, what's Phaedra going to do?" I asked.

"If she really loves this man she will have to go against her family and marry him."

"Is that what you told her?"

"Yes."

"Good for her then, if she does," I said, wondering what kind of woman needs the advice of her former partner about who to fall in love with. She couldn't figure all that out without Leonidas?

"Thanks for telling me this – finally. I just wish you'd told me the truth before. It would have made things easier, don't you think?"

"Yes, perhaps, but a promise is a promise."

"But can't you agree it all looked secretive, suspicious. It looked like she wanted to come back to Greece, to her old life."

"No, Bronte, it was your assumption only, and that she wanted to restart the relationship. I tried to sway you from that idea but I remember well you were very stubborn and walked out of the villa, saying you wanted a break."

"I did assume that was Phaedra's aim, it's true, but it was in the absence of the whole truth. In the end, surely it's always easier to be completely honest," I said, a bit too primly.

"But I thought you would trust me. Trust that Phaedra and I meeting up was not something that affected you, or us. But I misjudged things, I admit."

Perhaps the lack of transparency had been a little bit of Greek machismo surfacing, I thought. A man not feeling he's required to properly explain his actions. The woman having to blindly trust him. But I was glad to know my own instincts had been right. I always sensed there was a lot more to the Phaedra business than I'd been told.

I think I would have been mad not to see that Leonidas and I faced a few storms ahead, no matter how much we loved each other. This business with Phaedra was just another cultural thing I didn't seem to understand; the peculiar hold that family members and former lovers can have over Greeks when it seems illogical or clannish to outsiders. I also didn't understand this extreme loyalty of the Greeks that to me seemed corrosive when you were not in on the whole issue. More worryingly, had Leonidas not trusted *me* with this top-secret Phaedra information? But in the end, I had to let it go, or there was no future here for us.

"You look worried, Bronte."

"No, I'm just thinking."

"So that's what thinking looks like," he said, impishly, trying to ease the tension. "Look, *apapi mou*, sometimes I admit I am so absorbed in my own work and what's going on in Greece that I forget how you must feel confused about the way we do things here."

"I am, *agapi mou*," I said, in mock seriousness. *About time he flagged that up*, I thought. Then I changed the subject, though it was no less thorny.

"Have you heard anything from Angelos about the affair with Eve? She hasn't called for a while."

I had expected her to contact me after she heard about the Dionysos business. Everyone in the village knew and Angelos would have told her, surely.

Leonidas blew air out between his shapely lips. "Don't let us talk about them. I will get *mad*! I have heard they have been seeing each other somewhere outside of the village. You know, I think she takes him sometimes to Vathia. She rents a tower there, is that right?"

"Yes, that's where Angus and I found her after she went missing." That little minx! The love tower – how appropriate. I had seriously hoped Eve was winding things down. Would I have to issue another threat?

To use one of Angus's favourite folky sayings: Might as well dig a well beside a river.

On Saturday morning a week later, as we finished breakfast, Leonidas took a call on his personal mobile. He had a short conversation in Greek, in which I definitely heard the word *skorpios*, scorpion, several times. I was alert. He hung up.

"I hope you don't mind, Bronte, but Thekla is coming over to the house right now. She says she's been bitten by a scorpion in her garden, so I better see to her. She has a thing about scorpions." He smiled thinly.

I hadn't seen Thekla for a while and I had forgotten to ask Angus how the scorpion plan had been going, the one he hatched with a Greek friend to hide a slew of the critters around Thekla's dry stone walls. Obviously, it had worked – but the scorpions were supposed to have been dead!

When Thekla arrived, Leonidas ushered her into his library on the ground floor, where he sometimes saw patients. When he finished, Thekla came out looking pale and lemon-lipped, her big hair more limp than I'd ever seen it. Her arm was a bit swollen and she had a large plaster over the bite. Leonidas offered her coffee. She pulled a face and plodded off back to her villa.

"Where was the scorpion?" I asked, feigning surprise.

"In one of her garden walls. Apparently, there's been a plague of them."

I was ashamed to admit I felt no remorse for Thekla. I was just keen to talk to Angus about the scorpion attack but had to wait until later when he came back from another jaunt to Kalamata. In any case, I was preoccupied with the evening that lay ahead. Leonidas was taking me out for a romantic sunset dinner at the Irini taverna, our favourite place on the coast, as a way to cheer me up after the recent drama with Dionysos and also to finally make amends, I thought, for the Phaedra business.

It was late in the afternoon when I slipped back to Villa Anemos and found Angus in a jovial mood, sitting as usual on the back balcony, drinking beer.

"I saw Thekla today. She had a nip from one of those pesky scorpions."

"Yes, I heard about it," he said, his eyes lighting up with mirth. "It was nothing really."

"But you were supposed to use dead scorpions!"

He laughed wildly, enjoying Thekla's misfortune, and I admit it was blackly amusing.

"My friend used the dead scorpions. After he sprinkled them around, he showed Thekla what he'd 'found'. She went doolally, of course, saying he had to hunt them all down and kill them, spray the wall, bring in the Greek National Guard, that kind of thing. But anyway, one of them mustn't have been dead, or else he didn't banjo it hard enough. And as it happens, I was in the *kafeneio* this morning before I went to Kalamata and in walked Thekla with a plaster over her bite. She couldn't wait to tell Elpida the whole story, very loudly. The place was hoaching, mostly with old guys, playing their backgammon and drinking ouzo. She had a right old moan about life in the village and why she thinks it's not such a good plan to live here now when she has a lovely apartment in Athens: no scorpions, no power cuts, no water cuts, no foreigners."

He paused to gauge my reaction. I tried to be sensible but, in the end, I punched the air with my fist.

"Then she said, 'And in Athens there are no crazy men with guns kidnapping women. This village isn't safe for us any more'. One of the old boys piped up and said, 'Don't worry, Kiria Thekla, no-one will bother to abduct you now'. A few other guys had a right old laugh over that, but Thekla didn't see the joke, naturally."

"I can well imagine," I said, appreciating this rural tableau. "So, is that it? She's really leaving?"

"Let's hope so anyway, or else we'll have to organise another scorpion infestation."

I felt relieved. While Thekla seemed like a harmless old crone on the surface I knew she didn't have my best interests at heart, after the Phaedra incident. It was a piece of mischief. But I couldn't help but smile, wondering what she'd say if she knew the Tooth Fairy was in love with an English *xenos*. Brilliant!

26

Saints march in

We were supposed to be heading off well before sunset to the Irini taverna to watch the sun sliding down in spectacular fashion behind the opposite peninsula. But before we drove to the coast, Leonidas said he had a whim to satisfy first and wanted to park the car by the *plateia* and walk up the back of the village to the small chapel of Saint Konstantina to light a candle. Ordinarily I'd have loved the spontaneity of this and the fact he said he also wanted to give thanks for me surviving my kidnapping ordeal, even if, ironically, it had happened not far from the chapel. I felt overdressed for a village hike. I'd decided to wear again the lovely dress Eve had given me and high heels. Leo was smartly dressed in a white shirt and black trousers, carrying a small backpack.

"What's the backpack for?" I asked, as I wobbled my way up the steep path at the back of the village onto the track leading to the chapel. It would be a miracle if I didn't fall and twist an ankle, which is why at all times a woman should only walk on the wild side accompanied by a doctor.

"You'll see," he said.

As we trudged up the path, a Greek woman dressed in black came hurrying towards us with a cheery "*Kalispera*", good evening. Leo exchanged a few words with her and then she was gone in the direction of the village.

"You should have warned me to wear some sensible walking shoes, Leo," I said, as we neared the top.

"Sorry, *apapi mou*, I forgot. Nearly there, but I assure you it will be worth it. Look at the sunset already."

The sun was slipping down behind the hills on the Messinian peninsula. No matter that we'd probably miss watching the sunset now from our taverna table. But it was spectacular enough already, the sky a riot of purple and pink behind the long grey landmass.

The chapel was ablaze with candlelight when we reached it, a golden glow beaming from each of its small windows. Leonidas pushed open the door and ushered me inside. I briefly shielded my eyes with one hand; it was as if the chapel was on fire. Many dozens of candles stood tall in the sandboxes and on shelves in front of icons. And the flowers! There were dozens of fresh flowers around the church in tall glass vases.

"How beautiful, Leo. Is this a special saint's day today?" I asked him.

"Every day is a saint's day somewhere in Greece, but not for Saint Konstantina, not today," he said, smiling.

"Is there a service of some sort then?"

"Something else. You'll see."

I felt excited by the prospect of 'something else'. The biggest icon was dedicated to Saint Konstantina, in front of which candles burned, but there were many other icons as well – a celestial line-up of saints, their golden halos also reflecting the candlelight. All my senses were assaulted: the rich primary colours, the aroma of flowers, and incense, its pungent smoke wafting from small silver burners perched on window sills. It was ravishing.

"I've never seen anything like this."

"I know," said Leonidas with a grin. He put down his backpack and walked around the chapel beside me as I admired everything.

"Who did all this?"

"The village women come up here and do these things for special days."

So it *was* a special day. Leonidas was being particularly secretive.

"We must be the first here then," I said, thinking we should sit down and wait for the other villagers.

He turned and stopped me, putting his hands on my shoulders. "All in good time, *agapi mou*," he said, kissing me softly on the lips. I felt that errant curl of his tickle my forehead. It filled me with a tremor of delight.

"First, I must say something, Bronte, that we must have no more doubts between us, no more bickering over other people, okay?"

I nodded. "Of course."

"There will only be trust and happiness from now on, yes?" I knew he was referring to our last conversation about the 'Phaedra problem'.

"Is that why you brought me here, my love, to tell me that?"

"Yes, and no. Come and look at this," he said, propelling me towards one of the nearby icons with a gold sandbox in front filled with lighted candles that seemed to burn especially bright. It was an icon of the popular saint, Ayios Dimitrios, who'd had such a starring role in our search for Kieran the previous year. I recognised the icon because I had a smaller one on my chest of drawers in Villa Anemos. The image of this crusader saint with the boyish face, riding his sorrel-coloured horse, was burned into my consciousness now. I was confused, however, as to why this saint seemed relevant today.

This particular icon, like that of St Konstantina, had a thin silver chain across the front of it, on which were hung small metal tokens that I knew were called *tamata*, votive offerings that represented the wishes of those worshippers who came to plead for some miracle or other. The *tamata* had carved images of small babies, hearts, legs or arms, both touching and bizarre. They would be left there in the hope of an intercession by the saint for a good outcome for an illness or some problem or other.

"Are we here to make a wish for something?"

"In a way, yes," he said enigmatically, gazing at the *tamata* on the icon of St Dimitrios. I smiled. Was this his idea of filling in time until the church 'event' began? But I dutifully scanned them all again.

"Look at this. Someone has tied a ring to the collection, an expensive one, by the look of it. How extravagant! Is it in the hope of a romantic union?" I said, my eyes fixed on the diamond ring that scintillated in the candlelight, sending off shards of colour around the chapel. Leonidas said nothing but daintily untied it from the chain so I could see it better. It dangled on a silver ribbon. He held it out in front of me, his eyes black and glossy in the candlelight.

"Take it," he teased me.

And then it dawned on me, even before he untied the ribbon and put the ring slowly on my finger. Standing in a bowl of light, under the shrewd gaze of a few dozen benevolent saints, he asked me to marry him. I gasped, delighted at the unexpected romance and inventiveness of Leo's proposal.

"Well, since you've gone to all this trouble, it would be ungracious not to say yes," I said, laughing.

"That's wonderful, Bronte. *S'agapo poli,* I love you very much, and I hope you've always known that."

I nodded, a little tear twitching at the corner of my eye. "Yes, I have and I love *you*, more than I can say."

We hugged and kissed in front of St Dimitrios. I had never expected that if a proposal came from Leonidas it would be as fantastical as this. What an unfathomable man he was sometimes.

"Now for the champagne. That's why I carried the backpack," he said with a wink, retrieving the bag and walking towards the chapel door. "Let's sit outside. I don't know how the saints might take to us drinking in the chapel."

We sat close together on the wooden bench outside and drank chilled champagne from two crystal glasses and watched the sun disappear from sight. Everything about the evening had been so beautifully orchestrated. Perfect! Including the fact we were sitting now on this same bench where we'd sat the previous year and had a long conversation about our love for each other and the logic of me staying in Greece, even though there seemed to be obstacles in the way. It had been Leonidas who'd had faith in overcoming them, as well as all my recent doubts and fears that love would never be enough to close the gap in our cultural differences. His good sense and genial nature always carried the day. That's what I loved about him the most. And he was right. It was all a matter of trust.

With the chapel at our backs and the gulf spread out before us, it seemed like the most perfect place in the world to seal our fate. We sat there a long time, not saying much, just enjoying those precious moments.

Later, at dinner, we talked of many things to do with the past and our future life. Finally, I was to meet the rest of his family in Kalamata, who were going to be told of our engagement. I didn't know whether to be delighted or terrified. At least Thekla might have ridden back to Athens on her broomstick by then. That would be a small blessing. And there was the small matter of his nine-year-old son Adonis in Athens, whom I was also to meet finally when he came to spend part of his summer holidays in Marathousa. There was so much I was still to learn about Leonidas and the world around him.

"I can't finish this evening without asking you the most important thing of all," I said. He tipped his head slightly, a wrinkle of curiosity between his brows. "How did you manage to organise that scene in the chapel, in secret?"

He laughed keenly. "I did get help from Stavroula, the woman you saw rushing down the path. She's the keyholder and looks after the chapel for the local *papas*. She organised everything: the flowers, candles, and put the ring on the icon. She was also the sentry up there until she saw us approaching and made sure that no-one else went inside. She was sworn to secrecy. I didn't want the surprise to be spoilt."

I scoffed at him a little. "But nothing's ever a secret in a Greek rural village, right?"

"When it comes to death and marriage. There are rules, Bronte," he said, with a wink.

Slowly and predictably, however, the villagers discovered our news and it was the talk of Marathousa. First the *xeni* gets kidnapped, then she's saved by her one-time homeless dog, and then she gets engaged. *Po, po, po!*

When I told Angus, he was pleased but philosophically so. He gave the diamond engagement ring a paternalistic nod of approval.

"I'm pleased Leo finally popped the question, pet. I was beginning to wonder and I'd have been scunnered after the Phaedra business if things had just slid along in first gear," he said, with a mock grizzle in his voice.

There was still much chatter about the village over the abduction and it sometimes spilled into heated debate in the *kafeneio* between a few of the older men with different views on politics, though I doubted any of them supported a party like EPE. Most of the villagers were glad to see that Dionysos and his cronies would be dealt with, just as the EPE were beginning to see there was rising opposition to their violent, racist tactics.

One day when I was at the *kafeneio* checking emails, Elpida came and sat with me. We talked for a while about the kidnapping and once more she was remorseful that although she sensed the danger, she hadn't been able to act on it quicker.

"Don't worry, Elpida," I said, "you are too busy being mayor and police constable as well as running a business. What more could you do?"

She shrugged. "But all has come good in the end. So, we all a bit happy these days, Bronte. Not everything in crisis in Greece, eh? Especially for you and Leonidas," she said, impishly, rubbing me affectionately on the back.

Zeffy always came with me to the *kafeneio* now and he was still very much remarked upon. He was declared a hero and even offered a glass of Mythos beer now and then by one of the village men, which Zeffy would drink with great relish, much to everyone's amusement. He even made it into a feature story in the local paper after Dionysos was charged with his offence. The dog who saved the foreigner in the Rindomo Gorge. There was a photo of Zeffy and a picture of the gorge and the *plateia*, with Elpida standing proudly at the doorway of her *kafeneio*. Elpida had pinned the page proudly to her board inside the *kafeneio*. It would in its way become part of Marathousa legend in years to come.

It was during these happier days that I got some news via email that I was keen to share with Angus. I found him one day in Villa Anemos, working away at his laptop. He turned and looked at me as I came into his study with a mug of coffee for him. He had a face like a sunken soufflé.

"Ah, that's not a happy face. How's that book going?" asked him.

He rubbed his hand over his eyes. "More than halfway through now and it's going well. More for you to read." He handed me a small pile of typed paper. I was slowly working my way through his book, offering a few suggestions, doing a bit of editing.

"It's all fine. I've told you that. But how's the rest of it taking shape?"

"If I'd known what a long, hard task writing was I might not have started," he grizzled, not for the first time in the past few months.

I squeezed his arm. "Well, you probably need some extra motivation. And I know just the person who'll do it," I said.

"Who's that?"

"Polly, of course."

His face brightened.

"I got an email from her today and she says she's finally coming back to Kalamata. I think she's grown tired of the good life in Australia and she's yearning for a bit of chaos and crisis."

"Aye, as if!" he said, with a wry smile.

Despite his affection for Polly, I marvelled that I had become a kind of go-between, sending and receiving emails from Australia because Angus didn't like spending time on the internet unless it was for research. It was one of the curious things about my father that I was also learning. Or was it more the case that he was slightly niggled with her for disappearing to Australia and that was his way of showing it?

"She'll be back in a couple of weeks. She's missed us, but you especially, I think."

Angus smiled and tapped away at the keyboard – something nonsensical.

"Did she say that?"

"Not in so many words, but a woman knows these things. Therefore, I think you should send her an email very soon."

"Aye, you're right, Bronte. I should."

I was secretly thrilled by the news of Polly's return. With her warm personality, she had been a positive influence on both of us. Perhaps this time, despite the age gap of some 12 years between Polly and Angus, their relationship might have a better outcome. Less conventional than many perhaps but satisfying all the same. If Polly had been here in the past few months, I knew she would have prodded Angus on with his book. She would have known what to do about the prodigal Phaedra and the thorny and embittered Thekla, who had kept herself strangely scarce in the days following my abduction.

There had still been no congratulations from her either about my engagement to Leonidas, which was, I imagined, not a normal occurrence in Greek society. But I did hear that she would be returning to Athens at the end of August. She would never come back to live permanently in Marathousa, she said. I punched the air and thought that my life as Kiria Bronte Papachristou would be much less troublesome with her far away.

27
Eve's creation

"I suppose you knew I'd legged it back to London," Eve trilled down the phone. "I wasn't sure. I did hear a rumour that you'd been holed up in your tower in June with, on occasion, a certain young man," I replied.

"No comment."

It was now July and I hadn't seen her for weeks, nor had Leonidas mentioned any sightings of Eve and Angelos together at their favourite haunts along the coast. She never contacted me, and Angelos appeared to have turned up most days for his work at Myrto's farm. I assumed the affair was fizzling out.

I had called her one day from my new mobile, after the dramatic loss of my first one in the kidnapping. I expected she might be in London but was surprised when she told me she was back in the Mani.

"Call by and see me, if you like. Well ..." she broke off for a moment. I could hear the tinkling of ice in a glass as if she were drinking something cool and strong. "I was rather angry with you when you made that threat to expose me over the book, but I'm over that now. So, let's be friends again, shall we?"

"Sure, let's, but I have to say, Eve, I can't see you if you're still seeing Angelos, even now and then. It might sound prim to you, but Leo will be angry. He just adores Angelos."

"And he thinks I will pollute his nephew's lovely mind?" she said, peevishly.

I sighed down the phone.

"Calm yourself, Bronte. I've got so much to tell you. Why not come to my house tomorrow afternoon. By the way, I've heard about your kidnap. Appalling business. Obviously, you've got a lot to tell me, too."

"Why not come to Villa Ambelia? My new home."

It was the first time I'd ever said those words. It was Leo's wish that I should move properly into the house, now we were engaged, and it would be our main house, with him spending a bit more time there. Angus would have Villa Anemos all to himself.

The following day, I was busy setting up a study for myself out of one of the smaller bedrooms, with a table by the window for a desk and a view down towards the gulf. Eve arrived in the afternoon with a chilled bottle of white wine and a large plastic bag.

"More dresses, Bronte. The other one suits you so much I wanted to give you a few more in the same style. A thank-you gift from me," she said, kissing me on the cheek.

"That's very kind. But a thank-you for what?" I asked, as I took the bag and glanced quickly inside at two neatly folded dresses in sumptuous colours.

"Well, firstly, for making me see sense over my dalliance with Angelos, which is over, and has been for a few weeks," she said.

"Good," I said, hugely relieved. "What's the other thing you're thanking me for?"

"I'll tell you in a minute. First, I did hear that you were engaged. Many congratulations," she said, pulling my hand towards her and checking the ring, like a pushy mother. "Well done you! Leo's quite a catch. In fact, he's gorgeous. I wish I'd met him first." She winked.

If I hadn't known her better, I would say it was a cheeky gesture, nothing more. When I'd first met Eve, I hadn't marked her out as a siren on the rocks, but now I knew differently, though she carried it off with panache.

We sat on two matching sofas, facing each other. I poured two glasses of wine. She looked thinner but more relaxed. She stared around at the room, giving nods of approval.

"So, you really aren't seeing Angelos any more?" I asked.

"No. And not because you threatened me, which I didn't appreciate," she said, with a pout. "The thing is I could fall madly in love with that man. He's wonderful, but I admit he's too young and I'm not ready to be garrotted by his family as a cradle-snatcher. The old Thekla woman, for a start, would probably stick a knife through my head. She looks capable." I nodded keenly at that. "As for Angelos, well, we had our fun and now it's over. Easier to end it sooner than later. I'm not being vain but I do believe he liked me a lot, too," she said, with a pensive look.

I had no doubt he liked her. Eve was a very sexy woman. But I was relieved to hear all this. We drank more wine and I filled her in on all the village news.

"Honestly, Bronte – you being kidnapped by some fascist thug. When I hear something like that, I just know I couldn't live here full-time. To be honest, I could *not* marry a Greek. I'm much too opinionated and bad-ass for that! And I admit too, I've not behaved very well of late in any respect."

"That's all true," I said, with a sardonic grin. "But what's the other thing you wanted to thank me for?"

"It's about the book. For a start, I'm grateful for you listening to the whole saga. You can't imagine how depressed I felt about it when I came here in the spring. I had a real go at it in Vathia, but I didn't get one sensible word out. I wrote quite a few overdue letters to friends, as I recall." She sniggered lightly.

"How has it all panned out then?"

She settled herself back on the cushions with a cat-like grin. "You'll be surprised. While I was in London, I sorted through Grace's apartment which, as I've told you, she left to me. In accordance with her will I gave most of her personal items to her niece Imogen. The computer and its contents were left to me, as well as the contents of her desk.

"I went through the computer documents again and didn't find the rest of the book. But when I was sorting through her desk, where she kept diaries and notebooks, I came across a key taped to the back of one of the desk drawers. It was well hidden and I might easily have missed it. It was a small squat thing and looked to me like some kind of safe key. So, I hunted about, looking for a hidden safe. I eventually found a low wall cupboard behind a small chest of drawers in a spare bedroom. There it was, the hidden safe inside the cupboard attached to the floorboards. The key fitted. Grace never mentioned it, but then why would she. And she didn't expect to die suddenly either.

"There wasn't much inside the safe: paperwork relating to the property, some family photographs, letters and some small storage discs, nothing very valuable, but there was also a cardboard box file in which I found a sheaf of handwritten pages, which included ... the last chapters of my latest book!"

She paused for effect. I gasped.

"I know. It's amazing, isn't it? God, my hands were trembling with relief when I took out the pages and read them – all I needed to finish the book."

"Wow! Did she always write a first draft in longhand like that?" I asked.

"No, not at all, but it seems she'd decided to write the final chapters while on holiday in Scotland. At the end of the chapters she'd signed them 'Anstruther, March 2013' and then stored them in the safe, I suppose, until she could transfer the work onto her computer document. But she died before that happened.

"But let me explain properly. You see, Grace had been feeling slightly off-colour at the end of February. Possibly the prelude to her heart attack, I don't know. She said she wanted to have a break in Scotland. I didn't think it very peculiar because every year she went there, to the Fife coast, where she'd spent time as a child. Grace's parents were Scottish. She was very sentimental about the place and always rented the same small cottage for a week or two. She wasn't one for holidaying abroad. The cottage was simple, with a view to the sea. There was no phone line or internet there, a bit like my Mani tower, and she only took a very basic kind of mobile phone with her. Grace liked the freedom of being without modern technology, and I absolutely agree with her on that score.

"I wasn't worried about her going to Scotland but I certainly didn't ask or expect her to carry on with the book, even though we were close to a copy deadline back then. But Scotland must have inspired her to write and she penned the last chapters."

While Eve was telling me this, I realised finally why the style of writing in Eve's books seemed slightly old-fashioned to me, despite a slew of raunchy characters. It was because they reflected Grace's own conservative style.

"Perhaps Grace had some presentment of her own death and wanted to finish the book for you while she was away," I offered.

"Possibly. And it's the kind of unselfish thing Grace would do," Eve said, with a pensive look. "Anyway, I was away when she returned to London. She called me but didn't say anything about the book. Perhaps it was to be a surprise. She would have wanted to transfer the work to her computer document first and in the meantime stored the final chapters away without telling me. She rarely wrote longhand. She worked on the computer and kept copies on storage discs in her desk and duplicates in the safe, which I discovered after she died. She had backed up the latest book, apart from those last chapters."

We were silent a moment and all I could think of was how impeccably careful and kind Grace had been. But her one oversight was not mentioning the safe – for whatever reason. And Eve might not have discovered the key taped secretly inside the drawer for months and months, if ever!

"So now you can finish your book," I said.

Eve's expression became wistful. "Well, it's not quite mine, is it? But I can write up the last part of it, and hand it over to the publisher, finally. And that's the end of my writing career."

I drank my wine. We were silent for a while, lost in our own thoughts. I wondered how such a capable woman as Eve could ever have embroiled herself in this long deception. It seemed shabby and yet once you knew all the facts you realised how cunning a plan it had been. It gave purpose and a healthy income to two very different, independent women. What did it matter in the end, and who did it hurt? No-one really, not even the readers, who were at least oblivious, and entertained. But I could see why she would never want the deception to become known.

"I expect your publisher won't be thrilled when you tell him you're not penning any more bestsellers."

"Oh, we have a shaky relationship, as I've told you. I'll just tell him the creative spring has dried up and I need a long break. I was due to sign another contract for future books, but that won't go ahead."

"What about all your fans? They'll be gutted."

She shrugged majestically. "I'll tell everyone the same story – a break from writing and that I may go back to acting for a while."

"Are you?"

"Well, that's my final bit of news. I've been offered a role in a historical TV drama set in Sussex after the Second World War. I play the sexy, flighty wife of an ex-army officer, living in an aristocratic pile. Sounds like me, doesn't it?"

"The sexy and flighty bits are spot-on," I said, sarcastically.

She laughed. "Anyway, it's a great role. And you'll never guess how I caught the eye of the casting director, hmm?" she said, flicking up her well-shaped eyebrows. "It was because of the article you wrote about Douglas Markham. As you know, The Daily Messenger added loads of pictures to the article, including me in early TV roles, and it jogged the casting director's memory when he happened to read the piece. So, I'm very grateful for all that.

"The years I spent 'writing'," she added, winking, "were rather fun and lucrative, but they took me away from having the kind of profile you need as an actress. Even if you're selling millions of books, you're not in the public eye much. You're just seen as a batty woman who scribbles romances and gets mentioned in review pages now and then. Your article reminded people I'd been a bit more glam once."

"That's all fabulous news, Eve. Everything has dovetailed nicely." I could see now how easy it was to ditch the toy boy when there were glitzier things to focus on.

"So here's to you, Bronte. And if you ever need any contacts in the film and TV world for freelance features, I can get them for you. It's the least I can do."

I had to hand it to Eve: she was born lucky. To have pulled off her literary deception for so long, and to have sailed onward to new, vibrant escapades, was remarkable. I didn't doubt she'd been depressed when I first met her – over the loss of her good friend Grace – but as for the rest of it? People describe depression as the 'black dog', something that tails you and pulls you down. But for the entertaining and essentially self-regarding Eve Peregrine, her depression would have been akin to being smothered by a clutch of well-coiffed, yapping toy poodles.

28

Thekla's confession

Thekla was standing on the doorstep. For once, she wasn't holding a plastic bag. No last foray then through the wild plantings of Villa Ambelia before she left for Athens. Her hair seemed freshly done, reaching its typically dizzy heights – a personal peculiarity I would never forget. She was wearing a black tailored dress and smart shoes, as if she'd just been to church, which is how she nearly always looked.

"I've heard the news about you and Leonidas. I am disappointed to be the last person to be told, it seems," she huffed, looking past me into the house.

"Sorry. Would you like to come inside?"

"No," she said, sharply.

Good, I thought.

"Are you busy?" She looked me up and down, at my shorts and T-shirt, my battered sandals.

"Not at the moment."

"I thought you might like to come to my house. I have something to say to you there."

"You can say it here. Leonidas is in Kalamata."

"It's better at my house. Come over in 10 minutes. I won't keep you very long."

"Okay, whatever you wish," I said, with a heavy heart, wondering what the 'something' was and why it had to be done at her house. Was it easier to bury a body over there among the scorpions? Would it be a lecture on marrying into *her* family? I had a lecture of my own, if one were required.

She turned and walked away with a backwards wave of her hand. I shut the door. It was tempting not to go. But I finished what I was doing on my laptop and changed into a fresh pair of trousers and blouse and brushed my hair. My stomach felt queasy. *Get it over with*, I said to myself, *and then I'm shot of the old crone for good*. I wanted to take Zeffy with me, for moral support, but Thekla would have had a strop. I gave his cockatoo crest a little tweak.

"If I'm not back in half an hour, fetch the cavalry. You know the drill now," I said. The dog gazed at me with his lovely big eyes. I didn't doubt now he would.

I ambled down the road towards her house and wondered why Thekla had to drag me out on a day of searing August heat, even so late in the afternoon. The gulf in the distance was glistening flat, 'like oil', as the Greeks say. The orchards were tinder dry but some fig trees bordering the road were hanging partially over it, their fat ripe fruits heavy on the boughs. Within days, everyone passing would have had their fill of these special figs the villagers told me were grown in the previous century from produce brought from the port city of Smyrna, in modern-day Turkey, after the 1922 Greco-Turkish war. For the descendants of Smyrna refugees, the unique strawberry jam goodness of these figs was prized not least because they were a succulent link back to their rich but beleaguered heritage.

I ate quite a few figs on my way to Thekla's to sweeten my visit, but I felt a bit queasy when I arrived at her sturdy house, with its faux Mani tower and solid wooden door. I had a curious desire to see just how she lived. I rapped at the brass knocker, shaped like a hand, and waited. She ushered me inside. It was cool, airy and elegantly furnished with folksy Greek pieces but also some expensive modern additions like a three-seater embroidered sofa. It reminded me that although Thekla acted like a villager a lot of the time she must have been quite wealthy from her previous business venture. I guessed her Athens apartment would be stylish and comfortable.

She led me to the sofa and wandered off to the kitchen to fix some cold drinks. She put them on the coffee table then retrieved something from a heavy sideboard, sitting in a chair opposite me.

"This is an engagement present for you," she said unsmiling. She placed a small gift-wrapped package on to the table. I was surprised, confused. I had heard that engagement presents weren't the usual thing with Greeks. Perhaps this was a personal wedding gift because she hadn't planned to be at the event.

I fumbled nervously with the wrapping and came to a velvet box. Inside was a necklace. There were alternating amber-like stones and quartz with the inclusion of several intricately carved gold beads. It was surprisingly beautiful and looked expensive.

Her hands were clasped tightly on her knees. "This belonged to my mother and since I have no daughters I have decided to give it to you. I see you are set on marrying my nephew, so ..." It was said in a begrudging fashion, devoid of warmth.

"The orange stones are carnelian. It has been in my family a long time. It's something very Greek and traditional. So now it is yours. *Kaloriziki*, as we say. May it bring you joy in the wearing of it," she said, with a twitch of a smile, but very fleeting, like rain settling on a hot pavement.

I was shocked at this unexpected offering.

"It's very beautiful, Thekla. Thank you. Are you sure you want to part with it?"

"Of course. Would I give it to you if I wasn't?" she said brushing keenly at her knees, as if removing imaginary crumbs.

266

"Perhaps I will wear it for my wedding," I said, even though the arrangements were still sketchy. "You will come, of course," I said, out of politeness.

"Of course, my husband and I will come. Why would we not? Leonidas is very dear to us."

"That's great," I said, flatly. I couldn't do warmth with Thekla. Not yet. I placed the necklace back in the box. I drank my lemonade. It fizzed as it hit my stomach, like a bout of heartburn. *Strange woman*, I thought. At least we'd part for now with no bad feelings.

"Are you well after your recent scorpion bite?" I asked her.

"Yes, thank you. And I have no desire to repeat the experience."

"You'll be pleased then to go back to Athens."

She brushed at the phantom crumbs again. "I won't miss the scorpions, no. But … I … as the time grows close to leaving the village, I begin to remember the things about Athens I did not like: the riots in Syntagma Square, the migrants, the summer heat." Good God, would she be happy anywhere?

We sat in silence. I glanced at an old-fashioned clock on her sideboard. It ticked loudly, like the beating of an anxious heart. I wondered how soon I could leave without causing offence. She noticed my eyes on the clock.

"Bronte, can I say … I know we have not been friends. I am a difficult old woman in your eyes perhaps. You were angry I brought Phaedra to the lunch, yes?"

I nodded. "I didn't understand why you did that, Thekla. It caused a lot of discomfort for everyone." There, I'd said it.

She pursed her lips. "I apologise then. You see, I have always liked Phaedra. I admire her and her family. I thought she was a good match for Leonidas. In some ways I still think it." Her dark eyes looked brazen, with no sense of apology. I glanced at the clock again.

"Perhaps I saw her as a daughter, the one I never had. That was a mistake. I admit I have made mistakes and I am sure you will never forgive me for them. But now I will tell you something I never usually speak of. We Greeks do not like to talk of the dead. We struggle with that. We are superstitious, sentimental. Everyone knows I do not talk about my son, Philippos. He was my only child. He died in a car accident when he was 21. He was so handsome, clever. I thought he would make a wonderful life for himself. Everything on his side. Then the accident. I could not forget it. My husband and I worked hard at our business, day and night, but without Philippos there was no joy there. I poured my hopes and dreams into the rest of my family, but nothing has replaced my son," she said, with a single tear coursing down one cheek, which she dabbed at with a white handkerchief.

This story had come like a small punch in the guts. Why hadn't Leonidas told me this? Another secret. Why hadn't he told me lots of things? Why hadn't the local gossips? Why had I been led to think that Thekla was a she-devil when in fact what I saw now was a broken, embittered woman who had lost the best thing in her life?

"I'm so sorry, Thekla. I wish I'd known before."

She shrugged. "I don't talk about it. Everyone knows that. I only tell you of this because it's better you know and I don't want to bring Leonidas any pain. He is special to me. In a small way he reminds me a lot of Philippos, in his character at least. I hope you will look after him and make him happy."

"Of course I will," I said, dismayed she thought I might not.

We sat in painful silence again. She squeezed the fingers of each hand in turn, nervously. She looked tormented and it pricked my conscience. I had no control over what I said next, as if my mind had lost its edit button.

"Why don't you stay in the village, Thekla? Why go back to Athens when you don't have to and you don't really like it there? You love Marathousa really."

It was out. I could never take it back. What was I thinking?

Her gaze was cool and unflinching. "Do you think so? Well … I don't like the scorpions or the rural demons who seem to have crept in during the crisis, like the monster who took you to the *farangi*, the gorge."

"Well, aren't there creeps in Athens too?"

"Yes, more than we can bear."

"You haven't given yourself enough time to adjust to living here full-time."

Something flickered in her eyes. It looked like hope, as if I'd just thrown her a kind of lifeline.

"I will consider it. Perhaps," she said in a wistful voice.

I walked home, clutching my present, my head reeling. Thekla's story partly explained her contrary behaviour. But what was I doing, encouraging her to stay? Had she worked some kind of spell on me? I wondered too what kind of gritty stuff Greek women were made of that they could live their lives and repress something as life-changing as the loss of a beloved son. Leo told me once that Greek women were like the Parthenon. They weathered a bit but they could withstand almost anything. Yet I didn't think that applied to Thekla. She may have been granite on the outside, with big hair, but now I saw the pitiful inner core. She was a damaged soul who would probably never heal.

29
The magic of Marathousa

On the following Friday, when Leonidas was back in Villa Ambelia, I brought out the necklace to show him.

"Thekla gave you this?" he said, his big dark eyes full of amazement. "I knew she had this. It's been in the family for years, but to give it to you now is a big honour, Bronte. Deep down I think she must like you a lot."

"You didn't tell me about her son – about him dying."

"She told you that as well? *Po, po, po!*" he said, shaking his head.

I gave him a quick report of everything Thekla had said.

"All right, I should have told you. I thought about it when I guessed you were having problems with her, but she was right when she said we Greeks have strong ideas when it comes to death. Thekla told us years ago never to speak of Philippos. Ever. To let him be. So no-one does. Some people in the village won't even be able to remember she had a son, but every year she goes quietly to a graveyard in Kalamata on the anniversary of his death. He died in the city. She wanted him to be buried there. I always thought she never came back to this region so much because it reminded her of her son. In fact, I was surprised when she said she would move here more or less permanently. But perhaps she is finally making peace with his death – just when she wants to go back to Athens," he said, looking puzzled.

"Ah, but it seems she's no longer sure about leaving the village and ... I told her she should stay. Now I know the truth, I feel bad that we didn't get on." I felt even worse that I'd helped wind Angus up to the scorpion attack.

"That was kind of you to accept Thekla, despite her faults. And now you know why she sometimes acts as she does, you'll never have a problem with her again. She might prove to be one of your greatest allies."

"Leo, if you knew why Thekla behaved so oddly at times, why didn't you explain everything to me in the beginning? It would have made things easier, just like the Phaedra business."

He shook his head. "Ach, Bronte! Greek ways – even we don't understand them sometimes. There are rituals, customs, things that aren't easy to explain. You'll see. It will all make sense in time, I promise, *agapi mou.*"

I laughed. "Well, no need perhaps to worry about what I know and don't know about Greek ways. I'm about to be immersed big time anyway."

He gave me a quizzical look. "You mean with our marriage?"

I stroked his cheek lightly. "Yes that, but more importantly … I'm going to have a baby."

His eyes widened with surprise, and then he looked a bit annoyed.

"You don't like my news?" I said, feeling panicky.

He shook his head. "Of course, I like it. I am thrilled, my love, but I am angry at that creep Dionysos. To think he put you through that ordeal that day and you were probably pregnant then, yes?"

"No, not pregnant then. It's only been six weeks or so in the making," I said, tapping my stomach.

He smiled vibrantly and sat close to me on the sofa, taking my hands in his. "And are you feeling well? There are no problems?"

"No, I'm very well."

"I will send you to the best gynaecologist in Kalamata. D
not worry."

He reached for his mobile, flicking through names an
numbers already.

"I'm not worried, Leo. And you don't have to do tha
now," I said, pulling the phone out of his hands. "Chill!"

And so he did. They say that women glow when they'r
pregnant but Leonidas seemed to glow by proxy. In fact,
don't think I'd ever seen him look more handsome. His eye
glistened with joy and that lustrous black curl that I love
was falling over one eyebrow. I felt it caress my forehea
when he gave me a long, lingering kiss.

"Oh, Bronte, I am so happy for us. This past year in Greec
has been the worst, but this …," he said, rubbing his hand lightl
over my stomach, "is a gift. And I think we owe this to St Dimitrio
as well. I think it was the night of our engagement, yes?"

I calculated back and thought he was probably right. An
it had a wonderful symmetry to it, since this saint had bee
so fundamental in Kieran's story in a curious way and i
bringing Leo and me together, and also in healing m
once-difficult relationship with Angus.

"Was it the engagement ring, do you think, tied up wit
the *tamata* on his icon? Is this the answer to an unspoke
prayer?" I asked him, looking down at my still-flat stomach

Leonidas considered the point, then offered a slightl
lascivious smile.

"Perhaps, *agapi mou*, but I think it was what happene
later, after the dinner, in Villa Ambelia," he said, winking.

"Possibly a surer kind of magic, don't you think, *agap
mou*," I said, copying the assured way he always said 'my love

We both laughed merrily. I didn't think it was possible t
feel any happier than I did at that moment. I felt I shoul
do the *ftou, ftou, ftou* pretend spit that Greeks often emplo
to ward off any passing troll, but thought better of it.

Angus was speechless when I told him the news later. Not a circumstance I'd seen often with my father. And then he hugged me and became teary.

"Och, look at me, I'll be greetin like a bairn soon," he said. Crying like a baby was also something I hadn't seen Angus do too much. But he was thrilled. First the engagement he wasn't sure would eventuate – now this. He took my hand and his hazel eyes had a lovely softness to them and I knew what he was thinking, that apart from the joy over the pregnancy, something else had blossomed. Out of the thorny relationship we'd had the previous year that seemed hard to heal we now had a relationship that was precious to us both.

I knew I would enjoy the next couple of hectic months helping to arrange our wedding and it was agreed it would have to be in early October. I decided to keep the pregnancy a secret for a while yet, before the whole village knew about it. Some might suspect, of course, almost by osmosis. Like Elpida, the Oracle of Marathousa.

The next time I was in the *kafeneio*, she sat beside me and we chatted about the wedding and other village gossip. When it came to the news of Thekla staying on, it only inspired the Greek no-comment thing: eyebrows flicking upwards, the holding out her arms, and even a tut. After we dispensed with gossip, she leaned over the table, dropping her voice.

"Bronte. My stomach is twitching, and now this time I am feeling that so is yours." Then she laughed heartily. "I have the strange feeling you are going to have a baby. Correct?"

I was stunned but said nothing. She gave me a knowing smile. "You have that look, Bronte. Calm, like a mother cat, and secretive. I see it many times. You are looking … what is the word ..?"

"Radiant?" I offered with a smile.

"Yes, I think so. And now you tell me."

I shook my head. "No, Elpida. I've just caught some sun on my face, that's all. Nothing else I'm aware of, unless you know something I don't."

She gave me an ironic look. Damn it but her instincts, as always, were good! She knew I was lying but I couldn't tell her the truth. If I did the whole of the Peloponnese would know it within days. There would be time enough for the big revelation.

It was now September. I had been in Greece a year and it had been a time of challenges, leavened with humour at least, and incomparable love. However, I well remembered that at the Easter lunch, I had posed a question to Eve Peregrine: "Can you learn to love the country and the culture as much as the man?" Many times in that year, I'd felt that conundrum acutely. I'd had many doubts about what I was doing in Greece. Despite my deep love for Leonidas, the greatest love of my life, I had secretly shed tears over how I would ever fit into this ravishingly interesting but alien world that I still knew so little about, whose people and culture bewitched and frustrated me by turns. I had often doubted my sanity in giving up my life in Scotland, my career and family, to chart this new life in a country in one of the darkest periods of its history. Now I was on the threshold of marriage and motherhood. It had been a short and startling trajectory.

One day, Angus and I decided to go to the Marathousa cemetery with flowers to pay our respects to Kieran, and find some closure over past events, for both of us.

The graveyard was a small, walled enclosure overhung with trees. It scarcely had room for another grave. But last year the villagers had given us one of the few remaining plots to bury Kieran's remains, which we had finally uncovered in a hidden location after a difficult search. In their eyes, he had been a hero, fighting with the allies, and many scores of local Greeks as well, to try to save southern Greece from the German occupation, even though the allied effort failed in the end.

Kieran had a simple marble tomb with the headstone engraved: Kieran McKnight, 1941, filellinas, 'Friend of Greece'.

We placed the flowers on the grave and Angus and I stood side by side, my arm looped through his. I knew that Angus had been strangely emotional since I'd told him about my pregnancy. Although he had two grandchildren in Scotland from Shona, I sensed that this one might have a special place in his heart. At the graveside, I saw him brush away a tear with his hand.

"I can't tell you what I'm thinking, Bronte. There's just so much ..." he trailed off and lapsed into silence.

"You know what *I'm* thinking," I said, eager to flesh out this moment. "I can't get it out of my mind how Kieran's tragic fate in this region of Greece 70-odd years ago will indirectly result – God willing – in his own great-grandchild being born in the same location, not that far from where he died. If Kieran could possibly be looking down on us right now, he would surely feel his war service in Greece had been worth all the suffering."

"Aye, Bronte, you're right," Angus said. "That's an incredible thought but I think it's all because of you that everything turned out the way it has. You came here last year when I summoned you and had the patience with an old man's whim to finally solve this war mystery. On my own, I'd never have done it."

He turned and looked at me, his eyes swimming with tears. I gave him a long hug. I couldn't have loved my father more than I did at that moment, and the symmetry of what we'd achieved was perfect.

A thread had now been drawn between my family's past and its present, and had connected Scotland with Greece and a time of war and suffering to a place of inspiration and new life. The past year had changed my life like no other, but when it came to my love for Greece itself, just how great was it now? Let's just say that at the end of a tumultuous 2013, with an economic and social upheaval still impossible to predict, my love might teeter from time to time, and on into the future. But it would never need a major bailout. It would hold!

Epilogue

In October 2013, Leonidas Papachristou and I were married in the Church of the Anastasi, in Marathousa's square, at a service attended by all our closest village friends and family, including Leo's parents Grigoris and Eleni, and Thekla and her husband Kostas. (Thekla slowly adapted to village life and even enrolled in a scorpion-desensitisation programme, without much success). Adonis, the elder of the church, had a special role at the wedding: to guard Zeffy, just outside the church. With Zeffy still a village hero, it would have been a crime not to invite him. He was smartly groomed and wore a white satin bow around his neck. He was the first dog in the village to have been officially invited to a wedding, though walking down the aisle wasn't an option. Times are changing – but not *that* much!

Eve was also there, accompanied by a suave, middle-aged man she described as the Athenian owner of a certain Mani tower. There was a story there that I would have to tease out of her one day. My mother Marcella had flown in from Scotland with her second husband, a little overwhelmed by his immersion into Greek life, and finding that Angus was not quite the man who'd once left Scotland. She said he was like a modern-day Odysseus with his 10-year wanderings. But unlike Odysseus he never did go home again. He simply became Greek.

Phaedra was demonstrably not there! Navigating dark and dreary root canals no doubt, or cementing her relationship with the new contentious love of her life. *Po, po, po!*

In the following months, now that Polly had swapped Bondi for the Big Fat Greek Crisis, and was once more a motivating influence in Angus's life, he finally finished his book and was taken on by a Scottish agent. Eve's book, set in Scotland, was due out the following spring, a dubious romance titled *The Glen of Sorrow*, which seemed appropriate given the saga that preceded publication.

After weeks of mulling over Eve's book drama, I wasn't sure any more if Eve had got it completely right about saintly and pernickety Grace. Or if Grace had somehow engineered a final slip-up, with her secretive behaviour over a certain key. It was an outrageous idea, cruel perhaps, but in her final days, when she may have sensed her own demise, did Grace want to set her prodigy a delicious challenge? Or worse, catapult Eve into a literary scandal, for reasons I would never know. I have my own suspicions but my lips, as the Greeks would say, are 'zippered'. But in my mind, you see, this strange case will never be closed.

THE END

Acknowledgements

Thanks to the many friends in Kalamata and the Mani who inspired me to write both the prequel to this novel, *A Saint For The Summer*, and this one. Grateful thanks to the distinguished Kalamatan historian and writer Nikos I. Zervis (who sadly passed away in 2019 in his eighties) for generously agreeing to meet on several occasions to talk about the Battle of Kalamata, 1941. This battle was a narrative thread running through the prequel and to a minor extent was touched on in this sequel. Nikos was one of the few Greek writers to shine a light on this dark era of Greek war history.

Many thanks to acclaimed author Peter Kerr for his unstinting support and wise counsel in literary matters.

Thanks also to Athenian poet and teacher Margarita Nikolopoulou for her advice on Greek subjects, including language. Any errors are mine alone.

Grateful thanks to my husband Jim for his enthusiasm and encouragement of all my projects and his excellent editorial guidance and formatting of this edition through www.ebooklover.co.uk.

I am indebted to artist Tony Hannaford for yet another vibrant cover illustration.

Thanks also to Joanne Meris and Sheila Endersby for an early reading of this book and their kind comments. Finally, I'm grateful to a certain Athenian historian for some Greek political pointers.

Cornwall, England
February 2020

The prequel and the Peloponnese series

If you enjoyed this novel, you may also like the prequel, *A Saint For The Summer*, and Marjory's four Greek travel memoirs (The Peloponnese series), starting with *Things Can Only Get Feta*, which charts her four years living in the southern Peloponnese during the economic crisis. The sequels are *Homer's Where The Heart Is*, *A Scorpion In The Lemon Tree* and *A Donkey On The Catwalk*.

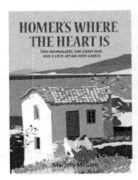

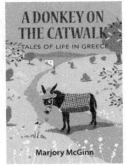

Praise for Marjory McGinn

A Saint For The Summer:

"I absolutely love this book. The writing is spectacular. In my opinion, this is the author's finest work." **Linda Fagioli Katsiotas, author of The Nifi**

"This story has humour, tragedy, mystery, history tradition religion and even a little romance. A compelling book." **Effie Kammenou, author of the Gift trilogy**

"Marjory McGinn is a skilful writer adept at creating characters that feel like your friends. This story will renew your faith in mankind. You are reminded that all relationships can heal, that we are all connected somehow." **Windy City Greek magazine, Chicago**

"I couldn't put this book down. The author has made the challenging transition from non-fiction to fiction. It cleverly combines elements of fact with gifted storyteller – a rare combination of skills." **Peter Kerr, best-selling author of the Mallorcan series of novels**

Why readers love A Saint For The Summer:

"McGinn has hit a home run! I couldn't put this book down."

"An excellent book. I was hooked from the first page."

"When I read this author's books, I walk the journeys, and with this book, I am Bronte."

"I loved the characters and found it all so moving."

"A brilliant read … there is closure, reconciliation and the hope of new life."

"Marjory is a wonderful author, very funny and entertaining."

Things Can Only Get Feta:

"Delightful – Gerald Durrell meets Bill Bryson." **Goodreads reviewer.**

"A book to relax into, written with wonderment, admiration and wit." **Anne Zouroudi, author of the Greek Detective series.**

"This book might become a future reference source about life in 'unspoilt' Greece." **Stella Pierides, author and poet.**

"I loved the characters, including Wallace, the colour and life, and the enthusiasm that drives the narrative. It was most enjoyable." **Mark Douglas-Home, author of the Sea Detective novels.**

Homer's Where The Heart Is:

"Marjory takes us on an odyssey with mind, heart and great skill." **Pamela Jane Rogers, author of Greekscapes.**

"A fascinating and heart-warming memoir." **Valerie Poore, author of Watery Ways.**

"A book to make your heart sing." **Amazon customer.**

"Marjory is a great storyteller." **Amazon customer.**

A Scorpion In The Lemon Tree:

"This book is rare within the travel genre. It cleverly combines a travel narrative with enlightened observations about Greece." **Peter Kerr, best-selling author of Snowball Oranges.**

"Her empathy with Greece and refusal to lapse into sentimentality makes this a witty and poignant book." **Richard Clark, author of the Greek Notebook series.**

"I could read this series forever." **Amazon reviewer.**

A Donkey On The Catwalk:

"There are tales to make you laugh and some that will touch your heart. Brilliant stuff." **Reader review, UK.**

"Marjory has captivated me with her story-telling. I love the way she can turn a few words and phrases into a sentence of magical joy." **Reader review, US.**

"Well written, informative and entertaining; I cannot recommend this book highly enough." **Sandy's Book Talk, Australia.**

Did you enjoy this book?

I love to hear from readers and feedback is always appreciated. You can contact me through my website info@bigfatgreekodyssey.com or through my books page on Facebook www.facebook.com/MarjoryMcGinnAuthor.

If you liked this book please consider writing a small review on Amazon. Thank you.

Printed in Great Britain
by Amazon

31552400R00159